Nancy Mencol

Jeremiah 33:3

Someday

Nancy Merical

ISBN 0-7414-1896-7

Published by:

PUBLISHING.COM

519 West Lancaster Avenue
Haverford, PA 19041-1413
Info@buybooksontheweb.com
www.buybooksontheweb.com
Toll-free (877) BUY BOOK
Local Phone (610) 520-2500
Fax (610) 519-0261

Printed in the United States of America

Printed on Recycled Paper

Published March 2004

DEDICATION

I dedicate this book first to Jesus, my closest confidante, who listens to all my complaints, lightens my burdens, lifts me over seemingly unconquerable chasms of discouragement, carries me up hills I find too steep to climb, and leads me through valleys too dark for me to make my way alone.

I dedicate this book next to my second closest confidante, my husband, Jack, whose sacrificial love reminds me of Jesus' love. Without his constant encouragement, my inferiority and shyness would long ago have eclipsed my desire to become a published author. In the forty-eight years since we've known each other, Jack and I have traveled sometimes-rocky roads, sometimes smooth, but his unfailing support always cushions the ride.

Like windshield wipers swiping away rain, his solace during tearful disappointments helps clear my insight, and, like headlights illuminating the future, his vision for me brightens dark times and gives me direction. I love you, Jack, and always will. I know you love me. You have proven it by fulfilling the scripture: "Husbands, love your wives, even as Christ also loved the church, and gave himself for it."

--Ephesians 5:25 KJV

SOMEDAY
Prologue

On a frigid February night in 1946, at the age of five, I waited with my mother, Louise Miller, and two older siblings, Frank and Eleanor, for a bus that never arrived. Our destination a train station in Charleston, West Virginia, we were to welcome our father, Frank, Senior, home from the war. During our fruitless wait, Mom wrapped me in the flaps of her warm coat, protecting me from the freezing weather. When the bus failed to arrive, we endured a long, bitterly cold walk to a neighbor's house to call a taxi.

My story begins with this experience, carved indelibly on my mind, but the plot and characters are entirely fiction, intermittently woven with facts supplied by my own personal experiences and insights gained from hours spent with my elderly mother, a proficient story teller.

The fictitious characters are composites of people I have known throughout my life, as all writers' characters must be, for we write what we know. If you think you recognize yourself in this book, rest assured you are not there, at least not in entirety. I may have borrowed a trait or two from you.

I will admit Mary's older brother, Billy, inherited his kindness toward his little sister, and his industry, from my brother, Frank, Junior, known to me as "Bub," and Jewel inherited her compassion and industry from my older sister, Eleanor, known to me as "Doodie." Many of Mary's memories are my own, but her faith and integrity far exceed mine. Perhaps I created Mary with attributes I always desired, but could never attain.

I derived my theme from a true story, which I swallowed with a grain of salt when I first heard it, until a stranger affirmed it. At the age of sixteen, Mom accepted Christ, kneeling at an old altar in Davis Chapel Church on Chandler's Drive, on the outskirts of Charleston. Attending the same service, Dad declared a halo shone around my mother's head after her experience. Twenty-two at the time, he told his friend, "That's the woman I'm going to marry."

Years later, Mom and Dad sat together as man and wife in Sugar Creek Community Mission on Falcon Drive, a short distance north of Chandler's Drive. A visitor stood and recited an unbelievable story, but one that affirmed the one I had been told.

"I attended a revival at Davis Chapel forty years ago," this stranger testified. "One night, when a young woman raised from the altar after accepting Christ, I saw a halo shining around her head of black hair. I've never forgotten the glory of that night."

And I've never forgotten the story. You will find it incorporated in my book, along with another story that also takes a stretch of the imagination to believe. "When I got up from the altar," my mother told me, "I looked up to see the church roof open up. You know," she explained, "like one of those animal cracker boxes we used to buy you kids? I saw Jesus in the clouds, leading a flock of sheep. A little lamb snuggled in his arms. I knew that lamb was me."

I must admit, for those of you who knew my mother well, her halo often slipped. Severe trials and chronic physical and emotional illnesses plagued Mom throughout her eighty-one years of life. Although her frequent lack of emotional control frustrated me, I don't doubt her earlier experience with God. I'll leave the consequences of her later actions up to Him, for He knew Mom better than any of us. I knew her well enough to know that, in spite of her failings, she was a compassionate, sacrificial woman.

Chapter 1

Daddy's Home!

Mary Creel was so cold! Shivering from the frigid February wind blowing around her skinny legs, she snuggled deeper into the lining of her mother's coat, wishing she were small like she once was. Then Mama could pick her up and hold her close, protecting her from the penetrating wind, but at five, she was too lanky. Lindy Creel did the next best thing. Opening the flaps of the worn coat, she let her daughter in, folding its satiny fullness around Mary's thin body, like a mother hen snuggling a chick under her wing.

But the cold wind still whistled around Mary's exposed legs. Her feet felt frozen in her cheap shoes, too frozen for her to run like Billy and Jewel, who raced in wide circles around Mama, playing a game of their own invention. Frosty vapors from their warm breath blew sheer, silvery balloons on the piercing winter air. Ice skimming shallow puddles crackled like thin blown glass under their feet.

Mary wished she had warm boots and mittens, like her older brother and sister, but with money so scarce, until she had to attend school every day as they did, her thin shoes would have to do.

The cozy heat from her mother's body slowed the chattering of Mary's teeth. Clamping her jaws tight, she stiffened her small frame, attempting to control spasms running from head to toe. If Mama knew how cold she really was, she might head back home before the bus came that would carry them to the train station to meet Daddy.

"Don't look like that bus is comin' tonight," Lindy said with a sigh.

Mary's heart jumped. Daddy had written in his last letter for them to meet him at the train station in the big city. It was February, 1946. World War Two had ended in September, 1945, just as an immense warship carried Bud Creel overseas to join the fight. Mary's daddy was coming home, after nearly a year in the United States Navy.

1

When Lindy had received the letter, she opened it with a big smile on her face, then flopped back in the old oak rocker and cried. Mary thought something awful had happened to her father. She had overheard talk of soldiers and sailors killed or crippled in the war. She was relieved when Mama wiped her tears away and called her children close, hugging all three at one time to her breast.

"Daddy's comin' home!" she cried, brown eyes shining. They had all jumped up and down, clapping their hands and laughing while more tears slid down their mother's cheeks.

Tears welled up now in Mary's eyes at the thought of heading back home and missing her daddy. Billy and Jewel's enthusiastic game had stopped abruptly when Mama spoke, leaving them standing in dejection. Mary's anxious face peeked out at her siblings from her mother's coat-front. Static electricity from the satin lining clutched at her hair, fuzzing the neat braids into disorder.

A breathless minute passed, the only sound the gurgling of Rushing Creek, tumbling under the bridge and curving alongside the one lane road toward Kanawha River, where the waters divided Charleston, capital city of West Virginia, into North and South.

"Kids," Lindy's voice broke the expectant silence, "do you think we could walk down to Mrs. Crooney's house? I could borrow her phone to call a cab."

Shivers vibrating up and down Mary's spine picked up momentum. Mrs. Crooney was the nearest neighbor affluent enough to afford the luxury of a phone, but she lived at least a mile down the dark and dreadful road of Rushing Creek, where more monster shadows lurked along the way.

Darkness settling around tree limbs cast scary apparitions over the narrow dirt road, like skeletal fingers reaching out to creep up Mary's legs. The nearby bridge loomed a black and frightening bulk in the approaching night's gloom.

Lindy Creel often soothed her daughter's bedtime fears with the admonition that darkness was only a warm blanket God spread over the sleeping light, but this thought did little to relieve Mary's fears tonight. A spastic shudder passed through her thin frame, lightly tapping up her backbone and circling her neck, choking off her breath with icy fingers of dread.

But tonight Mary decided to be brave. Thoughts of riding in a taxi for the first time to meet her daddy gave her courage. Taking a deep breath, she crept from the warmth of her mother's coat, forcing painfully frozen feet to take one step after another.

Mary's round, frightened eyes, dark as the night, strained to make out ominous shapes and shadows in the surrounding blackness. The eerie hoot of an owl floated across the deepening sky, followed by the sudden mournful baying of a dog. Mary started, gripping Mama's hand a little tighter for comfort. She had lost all feeling in her feet by the time they reached Mrs. Crooney's house.

"Lights are out," Lindy said with a discouraged sigh. "Guess she's gone to bed. I hate to wake her, but I don't know what else to do." But only silence inside the darkened house answered her persistent knock. Another long sigh escaped Lindy's lips. Unbuttoning her coat, she stooped and picked Mary up, wrapping her close against her own thin bosom. Shivering and whimpering, Mary snuggled against her mother's slight breasts, sliding her little frozen hands into the warm, damp pockets of her underarms

Picking her way carefully down the steps, Lindy stood for a moment in indecision at the end of the walk. Looking up and down the deserted road, she hoisted her heavy burden higher on her shoulder. Turning toward Cranshaw's Grocery, she staggered a little beneath her daughter's weight.

Several yards from the store, Lindy paused. Rushing Creek dissected the narrow road, shallow waters rippling over a gravel bed beneath a crystallized blanket of ice. In spring, torrential rains brought the creek flooding from its banks, halting sparse traffic until muddy water ebbed to make safe passing. But this February night, with the creek not much more than a trickle, the covering muffled the sound of the water's timeless journey. Lindy carried Mary safely across, ice crackling ominously beneath their combined weight. Billy and Jewel skated gleefully behind.

Suddenly Jewel screamed. The ice beneath her feet had shattered into splinters. Tumbling backwards into frigid waters, she threw her hands behind her to break her fall. Shrill barking from startled dogs across the way choked off Billy's delighted giggles. Darting to his mother, he clutched her arm, pressing close against her side. His high, trembling wail aroused sleeping dogs to eerie howling.

"Shush, Billy!" Lindy scolded. Setting Mary down, she hurried back to rescue Jewel. Billy stumbled after his mother, hanging on to her coattail, head swiveling, keeping watch on his flank. Fear immobilizing her feet, Mary stood rigidly where her mother had left her.

Tears tumbled down Jewel's frozen cheeks, but she proved more frightened than wet, chilled waters beneath the fragmented sheet of ice dampening only her gloves and the seat of her heavy snowsuit.

"Hurry, kids," Lindy instructed. "We've got to get Jewel in where it's warm!" She grabbed Mary by the hand, nearly dragging her to their destination. Billy kept his death grip on Lindy's coattail, eyes stretched wide, searching the darkness, short legs pumping a fast cadence to keep up.

Chapter 2

The Cranshaw's

Cranshaw's Grocery loomed dark and vacant, but bright lights blazed from an overhead apartment. A radio blared out the lively tune, "The Lone Ranger Rides Again!"

"Now, behave yourselves, kids," Lindy warned. Setting Mary down at the bottom of the stairs, she stood for a minute, catching her breath and stretching strained muscles. Then, gently shoving Mary ahead, she climbed the sturdy wooden steps. Billy and Jewel followed in single file, fighting a stubborn battle over a handhold on the railing. Lindy turned, eyes conveying a serious but silent warning that ended the conflict.

At Lindy's hesitant knock, the radio's volume lowered. Heavy footsteps approached and the door opened a crack. An elderly, heavy-jowled face peeked through, registering surprise.

"Mrs. Creel!" Mr. Cranshaw exclaimed, concern drawing white eyebrows into a dip over a Roman nose. "What are you and them little'uns doing out at this time of night? Is something wrong?"

"We must'a missed the bus, Mr. Cranshaw," Lindy explained. "We was headin' to town to meet Bud. I thought maybe we could call a cab at Mrs. Crooney's, but she's not home or just didn't answer when I knocked, and Jewel's fell in the crick and needs drying off. Could you please call a cab for us and let her stand before your fire till it gets here?"

"Why, of course, Lindy! Of course!" Jovial Mr. Cranshaw swung the door wide, rubbing his hands in a brisk rhythm. "Come on in and warm yourselves, all of you. It's near zero out there. You must be about froze. Mrs. Cranshaw told me Bud would be home soon. I was sure glad to hear that, but probably not mor'n you and them young'uns."

Smiling down at the top of Billy's head, the elderly man gave it a soft pat, then tugged gently at one of Mary's disheveled braids. "Mrs. Crooney's gone for a few days to

5

visit her son," he explained. He turned toward the kitchen, bellowing, "Mrs. Cranshaw, we've got company!"

Still rubbing his hands together, he hurried to the gas heater. Turning the fuel higher, he motioned Jewel to come stand before cheerful flames licking the top of the stove.

The plump wife of the storekeeper rushed in from the kitchen, wiping squiggles of soapsuds on a ruffled white apron dotted with bright red strawberries.

"Why, Lindy Creel!" she exclaimed, blue eyes rounding in surprise. "What in the world brings you out on a night like this? Oh, I recall!" A smile on her pink lips stretched wide. "Bud's train comes in tonight, don't it?" A frown crinkled her brow. "Of all nights! Colder'n a farmwife's hand on a cow's teat in the middle of January. Land sakes, childern!" she cried. "You all must be near froze. Get over here to the stove and warm up with Jewel."

A neat clutter of crocheted doilies, bric-a-brac, and framed photographs crowded the diminutive living room. Colorful rugs scattered over worn linoleum displayed remnants of Mr. and Mrs. Cranshaw's discarded clothing, braided in rainbow strips.

Pulling on a heavy pair of worn brogans, Mr. Cranshaw grabbed a cluster of keys from a hook on the wall. "I'll call a cab from the store phone," he said, disappearing with a blast of frigid air out the door. Metal taps on his shoes clattered a brisk rhythm down the wooden stairs.

Lindy slipped off Jewel's sodden gloves, hanging them on a shelf above the heater. "I'll hurry and fix you sumthin' hot to warm your innards," Mrs. Cranshaw offered. Before Lindy could protest, she bustled back into the kitchen, rattling cups and saucers. An enticing aroma of hot cocoa soon floated through the air.

Mary's mouth watered in anticipation. Enveloped in a big overstuffed chair before the cozy gas heater, she grimaced, her toes and fingers aching with thawing.

With a blast of menacing air, Mr. Cranshaw burst back through the door. Rushing to stand over Jewel, he extended his hands over her head to share the heat. "Land sakes!" he exclaimed, blowing at chilled fingers, "It's cold out there! Cab's on the way though." He smiled at Lindy, hooking thumbs through wide-striped, green suspenders stretched over an ample frame. "I told them to tell the cabbie to blow his horn when he got here, so you can wait in the warm. It ain't fit for man nor beast out there tonight. Terrible cold! Bus must'a froze up, do ya reckon?"

Without pausing for an answer, he asked, "Are you young'uns gettin' warm?" Blue eyes twinkling, his hands once again engaged in their game of friction. Billy and Jewel returned Mr. Cranshaw's smile, nodding bashfully, but Mary, intent on the storekeeper's hands, imagined smoke rolling between his fat fingers. She remembered Billy once saying that Indians could start fires by rubbing two sticks together.

"Mary's about froze up," Lindy answered for her youngest daughter. "Ain't got as suitable clothes as the other two and no meat on her bones to warm her. I carried her part of the way."

A spasm of coughing shook Lindy. She coughed a lot, even before Bud went away, but he hadn't seemed to notice. He loaded the old Model T in the summertime with tomatoes, cabbages, corn and other garden produce, heading for town at the break of day. Arriving home late at night, laughing and happy, with pockets full of change, he regaled his family with stories of customers on his route.

Sometimes he surprised Lindy with a string of silvery bass, caught in the stream running through his delivery route. His children loved to sit at his feet, fascinated by his stories, but it seemed Lindy never had time to join in the fun.

"There's supper to git," she'd say, stacking kindling in the hungry wood stove. After supper, there were dishes to be done and endless baskets of ironing and mending. Sometimes her children would wake at night, brittle snap of beans pulling them from sleep. Lying with heads propped on elbows, they watched Mama, humped over in a straight-backed chair, tireless fingers flying as she strung small mountains of beans or hulled piles of green pods. The ping

7

of peas clattering into an old aluminum dishpan at Lindy's feet soon lulled them back to sleep.

Lindy's work on the farm seemed endless. Bud's own work kept him busy in the summertime with hoeing and harvesting and delivering the results of his labor. But in the wintertime, with no produce to deliver and the creeks too frozen over to fish, he lightened Lindy's load somewhat.

With the canning done and the garden put to rest, endless washing, ironing and the satisfying of five hungry appetites kept her busy. The gaping fireplace ate up countless cords of firewood, stingily paying Lindy back for the feast, most of its heat escaping up the chimney.

Mrs. Cranshaw returned with the steaming chocolate. Fat marshmallows floated on sudsy foam in white mugs, like miniature sailboats on a frothy sea. "Land sakes, Lindy!" the concerned woman clucked, passing the welcome brew around. "You oughtn't to be out on such a night as this with a cold like that!"

"I'm all right," Lindy replied, pulling a flowered hanky from her coat pocket to wipe her nose. "A lot better than I used to be. Since Bud left and we rented the farm to Floyd and Corie, I ain't got as much work to pull me down."

"It sure was a blessin' for your brother and his wife to take over the farm, weren't it, Lindy?"

"Sure was," Lindy agreed. "For me and Corie both. She was just plumb tired of sharin' living quarters with Ma, and the farm was way too much for me to care for alone."

Lindy's younger brother, Floyd, had suggested renting out the farm shortly after they'd seen Bud off at the train station. "There's a little house with a tiny yard just down the road from here, waitin' to be filled," he explained. "I talked to the landlady, and the rent's cheap, less'n the rent I'll pay you for the farm. It's got a gas cookstove and gas heat. You wouldn't hafta chop wood or haul it in. And Corie says now's the time to go, before the cherries need pickin'."

Lindy moved into the little house with an almost audible sigh of relief, but not before harvesting the cherries. "If

Corie thinks she's gettin' my cherries, she's got another think comin'," she declared after her brother's pickup backfired down the hill. "I don't blame her none for wantin' a place of her own, after living with Ma all these years. Your Grandma Parsons is so set in her ways, she does git beneath the hide a little. Probably no treat for Ma neither, having that testy Corie under her feet all the time. Corie's welcome to the farm, but not to my cherries!"

Mary was glad Mama insisted on staying put until the cherries were in. She watched her mother, aided by Billy and Jewel, strip the fruit trees of their bountiful harvest. Lindy worked fast, plucking blood-red fruit from limbs burdened nearly to the ground. Hungry starlings and blue jays worked their way through the ripened orbs, leaving countless golden pits strewn beneath the trees. The race with the birds filled several baskets in record time. Mary sat by the baskets, stealing occasional tart treats until her stomach ached. Rusty squawks and shrieks of angry birds rent the air, scolding her for thievery.

Blowing to cool the hot chocolate, Lindy cleared her throat. "On the farm it weren't no wonder I couldn't shake my cold," she said. "The drafty old house and freezin' outhouse gave me no chance. I'm lots better now that we're in a warmer place with less work to do, but this cough hangs on like a bad habit. It just don't seem to want to quit."

The Creel's new little home nestled in a deep hollow behind the landlord's house. The one-room school just down the road proved a blessing, since Lindy had never learned to drive the rusty old Model T. Billy and Jewel, third and fifth graders, walked each day to the schoolhouse and back.

Lindy's move also saved her the arduous and time-consuming chore of hefting heavy, dripping buckets of water up the hill from the spring below the farmhouse. A pump now piped water into the house, heated by a big white cylinder occupying an entire corner of the tiny kitchen.

"Speakin' of bad habits," Mrs. Cranshaw remarked, chuckling, round form jiggling beneath her apron as she plopped down in a rocker, "did you hear about old Tom Hawkins gettin' religion?"

"Why, no!" Lindy's delight drew her up straight, setting off another spasm of coughing. The marshmallow in her cocoa, melting and spreading, reminded her of old Tom's sallow flesh. Tom Hawkins wasn't really an old man, but furrows of worry wrinkled his young brow, and constant imbibing reddened his bulbous nose. He was the last person in the world Lindy would have expected to admit his sins and turn to the Lord.

"When did this happen?" she asked, voice shrill with surprise. She sipped at the hot chocolate, cold hands encircling the cup's warmth, black eyes widened in inquisitive delight.

"Last Monday night, right here, downstairs in the store," Mr. Cranshaw interjected, glee shining from twinkling blue eyes. His hands started up again, rasping like fine sandpaper on blocks of wood.

"It was a miracle of the Lord," his wife interrupted in her eagerness to tell the story. "There was a green van went through here driven by that new pastor down at the Baptist meetin' house. He had a loudspeaker on top, and he was warning folks of the day of doom and how they'd best be gettin' ready."

The rocker picked up momentum. "Well, automobiles are scarce around here anyhow, and old Tom had never heard of such a thing as a loudspeaker. He was under the bridge yonder by Rushing Creek, passing time in his *usual* occupation. He must of been occupied for quite a while, because when that car passed over the bridge with its loudspeaker blaring, he thought it was the Lord speaking to him right down out of heaven, warning him of his wicked ways. He come stumbling zigzag up the bank and ran bawling into the store, right near sobered up by his fright, begging Sam here to pray with him."

10

Mr. Cranshaw grinned. "Why, shucks, I was right glad to oblige him. I'd never seen old Tom before when he wasn't drunker'n a skunk, but he hasn't had a drop to drink since. Come to Sunday meetin' with a big Bible tucked under his arm, sober as a sow contemplating her new brood. Stood up and told everyone how the Lord spoke special to him right down out of heaven."

Mrs. Cranshaw added in a more serious vein, "Poor old Mrs. Hawkins' patience had rubbed thin with Tom's shenanigans. She's near heaven now with her new man. He carries that Bible everywhere, warning people they'd best repent before the end comes."

Mr. Cranshaw whacked one knee in delight, wire-rimmed glasses slipping down his nose.

"God works in mysterious ways," Lindy murmured, shaking her head in wonder.

"God sure does work in mysterious ways." The storekeeper's smile faded. A look of concern curled his eyebrows into close association. Peering at his visitor over the brass rim of spectacles crooked sideways over his face, he asked, "Say, Lindy, do you have any plans of gettin' back in church? You know, God's been awful good to you, sparing your man from danger. And look at these delightful young'uns!" He gently tweaked Mary's slim nose and ruffled Billy's hair, then turned and patted Jewel's shining black tresses. "You owe the Lord sumthin, don't ya think?"

Mrs. Cranshaw sneaked a look at Lindy's impassive face. "Ain't had much time for meetin's after my marriage, Mr. Cranshaw," the woman spoke softly, "what with all the work to do on the farm and raisin' three kids alone while Bud was away. But I hope things'll be different with him home. I used to go to church pretty steady before I was married, you know. But Bud never had much truck with religion and wouldn't go with me."

"I know that, Lindy." Mr. Cranshaw's reply was gentle. "Well, we'll just keep praying that he'll find his way out of those dark fields of sin."

11

Dark fields of sin? Mary visualized her daddy lost in the dark of night in their huge cornfield on the farm, trying to find his way back to the little farmhouse. What did this grocery man mean by dark fields of sin? Was he talking about the war? Could Daddy be lost somewhere overseas and wouldn't be at the station to meet them?

The warmth that had come back to her body fled. A chill crept into her heart. She didn't want her daddy to be lost! He'd been gone so long now. She couldn't wait to get to the station to see if he was there.

As if Mary's thoughts caused the taxi to materialize, a horn blared. Lindy jumped up, handing her cup to Mrs. Cranshaw and collecting the others from her children.

"There's the cab. We sure appreciate your hospitality, Mr. and Mrs. Cranshaw. Hurry, Billy, Jewel!" She jerked damp gloves onto Jewel's hands. "C'mon, Mary. Your daddy's gonna be wondering if we're comin' or not!"

Mary's fears relaxed a little. Mama didn't seem to be worried about Daddy not being at the station. Before she could struggle out of the deep upholstery of the chair, Mr. Cranshaw scooped her up in strong arms and headed for the door. "I'll carry this little'un down for you, Mrs. Creel. Her feet must be paining sumthin' awful with their thawing."

Mary liked Mr. Cranshaw and his silvery-haired wife. They always sent home a big bag of candy with Mama when she got the government check in the mail and walked to the store to pay off her credit.

Lindy Creel was a stickler about owing no one any more than she could get by with, and that meant doing without a lot of things, like Mary's boots and mittens. She always remarked at the end of the month, when money was stretched tight, "Maybe someday our ship will come in."

Well, today it had. Maybe not money-wise, but the ship that had carried Bud Creel overseas, ominous journey interrupted by the war's end, had turned back, bringing him safely home, and that meant more than any amount of money to Lindy Creel and her three small children.

12

Chapter 3

The Station

Sitting between squirming Jewel and Billy, in the back seat of the warm taxicab, Mary scrunched her eyes tight, trying to call up a picture of her father. It had been so long since she'd seen him. The only image she could conjure was a vague one of him lying on the bed in their one room farmhouse, short legs crossed at the ankles, hands folded over his stomach.

Sleeping soundly, he drew in deep breaths of air, the rise and fall of his chest carrying his folded hands up and down in a steady rhythm. Compression inflated his face as fat as bullfrogs' ballooned throats in the pond below the farmhouse. When his cheeks could stretch no more, escaping air vibrated his lips in a comical putter. Mary, Billy, and Jewel giggled with hysteria, then sat with rounded eyes glued to their father's face, anticipating the next hilarious rattle. Their mother always wore a gentle smile, enjoying their antics, as she unfolded still another shirt from an endless basket of ironing.

The cab stopped. Three eager faces looked out the back window. A gargantuan black engine sat on the track before the station, puffing coal-smoke. Billows of gray mist, peppered with black ash, boiled into the air from a tall smokestack, layering everything in sight with fine grit.

Happy sailors and their families swarmed about, like buzzing flies at the screen-door in the summertime. Old and young, short and tall, fat and thin, the sailors all wore navy-blue suits trimmed in white with matching jaunty caps perched on their heads. Unashamedly crying, they took turns hugging tearful family members.

"Sugars!" Lindy complained. "How'm I ever to find your daddy among all these people?" She need not have worried. She had hardly climbed from the cab before being caught up and swept off her feet by a short, stocky sailor with hair as black and shining as West Virginia coal. The cab driver waited patiently, a pleased grin on his face, failing an effort to keep his eyes straight ahead. Bud Creel swung his wife in the air, then caught her in a close embrace. Mary blushed as her father kissed Mama smack on the mouth. She glanced around to see if anyone else saw, but no one seemed to notice. They were all busy hugging and kissing, too.

Bud finally let Lindy go. Stooping, he gathered all three of his children at one time into his arms. Tears streamed down his face. Billy and Jewel threw their arms around their father's neck, but Mary stiffened, a little afraid of this near stranger.

Bud plopped his sailor cap down over Billy's ears. Shoving out his chest, Billy beamed at his mother and the girls from beneath the oversized cap. Bud took some gum from his pocket, handing a piece to each of his children.

"Thanks, Daddy!" Billy and Jewel crowed, throwing their arms around their father's neck once more. Bud turned to Mary, standing quietly by with the stick of gum still clasped in her hand. "Well, Mary," he teased, "has the cat got your tongue? Or are you afraid of your old daddy? Ain't you got nothin' to say?"

Mary's face reddened. Her father tipped her chin so she could look into his eyes, the hue of blue skies after a cleansing spring rain. His black hair shimmered like crows' wings iridescent above the farm in summer's brilliant sunshine. His expectant smile revealed two rows of teeth, white as eggs cracked open for cornbread and cakes. "Daddy," Mary stammered, shy but earnest, "Will you take us to church Sunday morning?"

Bud's smile turned to a puzzled expression, then a frown. Mary's blush intensified. Her father turned without a reply, curtly directing the cab driver to take him and his family home.

Chapter 4

Back at the Farm

Now that Bud was home from the war, he had a hankering for the farm. Lindy would have preferred to stay on in her little home, where life was easier, but she meekly packed up meager belongings and obediently followed her husband. Her brother, Floyd, and his wife, Corie, helped pile their derelict furniture in his truck and Bud's, transporting it back to the farmhouse. Corie's sour expression added to the grand occasion.

Floyd was a big, jolly man, weighing over three hundred pounds. On frequent visits to the Creel's home, he always grabbed his nieces and nephews up in a big bear hug. Mary's slight form sank into his flesh with almost the same comfortable feeling as when she fell into Grandma Creel's deep featherbed on visiting nights. Being squeezed by Uncle Floyd felt almost like being hugged by a giant marshmallow, Mary thought.

But Aunt Corie was a different story. A thin, bony woman, she never hugged anyone. Mary was glad! If Aunt Corie did hug her, all those bones sticking out would probably prick her like cockleburs. Aunt Corie wore a dour expression and had what Mama called persnickety ways, though Mama declared that she had nothing to be persnickety about.

"Why, that woman acts like the whole world spins on her scrawny backbone and everything revolves around her!" Lindy snorted after one of her sister-in-law's trying visits.

Always barefoot, Corie had salt-and-pepper, flyaway hair, stringing from a scrawny bun tucked at the base of a skinny neck. She wore faded cotton skirts, wrinkled and unhemmed, fashioned from her husband's empty feedsacks. But the skirts, hanging nearly to her ankles, were always spotlessly clean.

The only thing Mary liked about her aunt was her scrumptious desserts, especially her applesauce torte. She'd

15

bake layer after layer of thin molasses cakes, alternating them with homemade applesauce until she had a big-sized stack. But no matter how high she made the stacks, Uncle Floyd always finished them off before bedtime, smacking his lips in lusty approval.

"Maybe," Lindy once remarked, "if Corie took a little more interest in her looks than she did her cooking, my brother might be a bit thinner."

Maybe, Mary thought. But I like Uncle Floyd just as he is. If he got skinny like Aunt Corie, he might get hateful, too, and not be so nice to know anymore.

Back on the farm, life took up a different rhythm. Billy and Jewel no longer walked to school. Bud danced a jig out to the truck each morning, singing at the top of his lungs, the old red rooster with its calico tail challenging his vocal endeavors. Mary liked to hear her daddy sing, but not so early in the mornings when she preferred to stay cuddled up in the big double bed, cozy and protected from frosty air sifting through cracks of the ancient farmhouse walls.

But no one could sleep with the strident complaint of the grumpy old rooster blending noisily with Bud's rousing songs. Mary crept, shivering, from her warm retreat to relieve herself in the icy-cold chamber behind the curtain. Washing her hands in the enameled washpan, she sat at the table, eating fried potatoes and chops with Billy and Jewel, until her father had cranked the truck's engine and carried them off to school.

With Bud home, Lindy's life took up a different rhythm, a rhythm of the old drudgery. She would stand three times a day, cheeks flushed and forehead beaded with sweat, over the old black cookstove, or for hours at a time over the ironing board, pressing stiffly starched little shirts and dresses. When Bud cut and chopped firewood and split kindling, she helped haul it in by the armloads.

In wintertime, those nearest the fireplace overheated while those with business in the other end of the drafty old farmhouse froze. Frail Grandma Parsons, on her visits to her daughter's home, could often be found standing with her back to the open flame, after reluctant visits to the chilly outhouse, pulling her skirts high over her wide hips to warm a cold posterior.

In early autumn, after Bud's return from the war, Mary sat with Grandma Parsons and Mama, watching them peel the crop of late apples from the orchard on the hill. Lindy had resisted her mother's offer of help, knowing her health was bad, but was met with the old woman's stubbornness.

"You cain't do all this by yourself, Lindy. I swear, Bud's a good man, and I don't want to fault him, but I will never understand why he insisted on bringin' you back to this dirt-poor farm. You're gettin' to be an old woman fast. You should have bucked him and stayed on down the road. You was gainin' weight and looking better before Bud came home from the war. Cain't he see how he's drivin' you into the ground?"

Lindy sat, not saying a word, deftly skimming the knife around one of the many apples. Mary watched the peel fall in long, curling strings, piling up on newspapers layered on the floor. Mama always said if she could peel an entire apple or turnip without the peel breaking, it would mean good luck. Somehow, no matter how carefully she peeled or how quietly Mary held her breath as she watched, the peel always broke.

One night, Bud awoke to the sound of his wife's dry cough. He had made a private spot for bathing in the one-room farmhouse by hanging an old sheet from a wire across a far corner. The soft glow of an oil lamp behind the curtain reflected Lindy's image through the worn sheet. Her long, thin legs hung over the edge of the tub.

Bud realized his wife was in tears. What made her so sad? It wasn't like her to cry. His heart twisted as he watched the thin slash of a shadow climb from the tub and dry off, then lift arms to pull a feedsack gown over its head.

Lindy's reflection looked as skinny as Corie, except more soft and curved. Wasn't she thinner than she used to be? Bud lay in the darkness, listening to the squeaking of bedsprings as his wife carefully climbed in beside him to avoid wakening him. He pretended sleep, but heard her deep sigh barely audible above the children's soft snoring.

It wasn't long after that until Lindy became really sick. She'd wake up in the mornings, pasty white, dragging herself out of bed to fire up the old cookstove. Just as she'd start the bacon frying in the big iron skillet, its delicious smell wafting through the room, she'd run for the outhouse, yelling for Jewel to watch the bacon and not let it burn.

Soon, Jewel could cook and clean almost like a grownup. Bud teased her by telling her she'd make some man a good wife, but she declared she'd never marry unless it was to someone from the city with a lot of money. Her terse reply curtailed her father's teasing, an odd expression wiping out his usual smile.

Mary and Jewel worried a lot about Mama. Billy hadn't an inkling of trouble, and their father didn't seem to think too much about their mother being so sick all the time, except he did help her out a lot more. The extra help must have been good for her, because she soon began to gain weight, and her trips to the outhouse slowed down a lot.

Lindy's appetite increased and her thin waistline soon began to bulge. "No wonder!" Jewel whispered to Mary. "Eating all those strange, fattening foods! If Mama doesn't watch out, she'll soon catch up with Uncle Floyd!"

Just when Mary and Jewel got over being scared and began thinking Mama would be okay, the doctor started coming around. He'd tell her she was doing fine and give her some syrup for her cough. She and Bud would be all smiles, eyes flashing secrets at one another. Jewel seemed to stop worrying, too, but Mary carried a dread in her heart and never forgot to mention Mama in her bedtime prayers.

Mary's odd request at the train station must have touched her father's heart. He began cranking up the old Model T on Sunday mornings, chauffeuring his family to church. But he never went in himself. In good weather, he'd drop everyone off, then fish until Sunday School was over.

Billy always begged to go with him, but Bud ignored his plea, sending him into church, where he sat with his lip hanging so low Lindy teased him about being careful not to trip over it. On bad days, Bud drove back home and listened to the radio until time to pick his family up.

Grandpop and Grandma Creel always attended Sunday School, saving space in their pew for their daughter-in-law and all the grandchildren. The Cranshaws occupied the pew in front of them with Mrs. Crooney, who always rode with her elderly neighbors, when her poor health allowed her to attend.

The storekeepers had been right about old Tom Hawkins. His face had lost its redness and beamed with an inner light. His wife had also lost her haggard appearance and seemed sweet and happy.

Mary and Billy's teacher, a kind, pretty young woman by the name of Miss Jenkins, had green eyes and hair the color of red oak leaves in the fall, matching the freckles on her face. Mary thought she looked like a sun-speckled peach – kind of creamy and pink. Miss Jenkins told them beautiful stories about Jesus being born and angels and shepherds coming to see him in a manger full of sweet-smelling hay. Mary always loved the smell of the fresh-mown hay her father harvested for the milk cow. She pictured Jesus snuggled in the warm hay with curious animals gathered all around.

Sitting in class, behind heavy curtains separating the children from the adults, her faded cotton dress clean and starched and her usually scuffed shoes shined by her father, Mary daydreamed. How wonderful it would have been to live in Bethlehem when Jesus was born, to hold him and touch his baby-fine hair! She wished she could have a baby as sweet as this one must have been for the Wise Men to travel so far to see him.

Sometimes, when Mary returned home on Sunday afternoons, she'd carry her doll to the barn loft and lay it, wrapped in a blanket, in the sweet-smelling hay, pretending it was Baby Jesus and she was his mother, the other Mary. She was glad she had been named Mary.

She liked her first name a lot more than her middle one. She'd been named after Grandma Creel. She loved Grandma Creel, but she hated the name Matilda! It suited her grandmother fine, being a grownup name, but it made Mary feel ancient and old-fashioned.

God must have looked into Mary's heart and saw her wish for a baby. Mama stayed in bed one morning, and Jewel shushed Mary and Billy when they awoke. She acted real important, with one finger pressed to pursed lips. Her mother's apron hung well below her knees. "Mama's not feelin' good," she said. "You two take this biscuit and jelly and go out on the porch. I'll bring you a glass of milk as soon as I get it poured."

"But where's Daddy?" Mary asked. Her little heart triphammered in fear. She loved Mama so much. She didn't want her to die. She whispered another prayer, hoping God wasn't so busy getting the day started that he wouldn't hear and could do something for Mama.

"Daddy went to get the doctor," Jewel answered. "Now go on. Do as I say or you'll get a thrashin' when he gets home." Jewel spoke in authoritative whispers, her brow corrugated like Aunt Corie's. Mary and Billy hurried outside to eat on the stoop. Mary fed her biscuit to the old rooster and hens pecking in the August heat. Worry had stolen her appetite away.

Soon her father came roaring back in the old Model T, the doctor tailing him in his little green sedan. Doc Hillman's long legs unfolded, like a wooden carpenter's rule, from the car. In one hand, he clutched the customary black bag. Mary was familiar with one thing in that black bag. She'd had the cold stethoscope warmed over the stove and held against her chest a few times when she'd come down with croup and could hardly sleep for coughing. She couldn't help but wonder what else old Doc Hillman carried in that big black bag.

"Hello, Mary! Good morning, Billy!" the doctor greeted. "Isn't it a fine morning?"

Mary, engrossed in her worry, hadn't noticed. Now she looked out on daisies in the far meadow, scattered like light snow over spring-green grass. Golden fingers of the pound-of-butter sun parted tree branches, peeking through at her and Billy.

Billy squinted at filmy clouds threaded across the windswept sky, like spun spider webs on a high blue ceiling. An old dead birch stood out against the green of the woods, silvery sheen more beautiful in the warming sunshine than all the living trees in their summer finery. The lifeless tree brought his mind back to his mother's illness. He swallowed his shyness and asked Doc Hillman if his mama was going to be all right.

"Why, child, she'll be fit as a fiddle in no time!" Doc knelt before the two serious children, smiling a crooked smile that made his gray mustache rise on one side like the high end of a teeter-totter. Scraggy eyebrows sheltered gentle gray eyes. "Now, kids, don't you worry," he soothed, patting Billy's arm in reassurance. "There's nothing wrong with your mama that a few hours won't cure. You and Mary run along and play. I'll see you later when I'm done in here." He patted Mary's head and hurried into the house.

Mary's heart lightened. She knew she could trust Doc Hillman to never tell a lie. Skipping to the old tire swing Daddy had attached to a limb of the huge oak, she yelled, "C'mon, Billy, push me! Push me real high!" The shade already felt good in the hot morning sun. It was going to be a good day after all.

Jewel joined Billy and Mary after she'd finished the breakfast dishes. They took turns in the swing, shoving each other higher and higher. Mary stretched out her toes, trying to touch the lowest tree limb. Her heart swelled with the love she felt for her brother and sister and her mama and daddy. She looked up into the expanse of blue sky. Gentle wind swept hair back from her forehead, cooling her perspiring face. Mary felt an awareness of something bigger than herself, bigger than the tall, tall oak – even bigger than the world itself. Mama would be fine, she knew.

Chapter 5

Baby Floyd

"Mary! Billy! Jewel!" Bud called from the opened screen door a few hours later. To the children, it seemed time had dragged on forever before the doctor came through the door and told them Mama was fine. He had talked to them for a minute before climbing into the car and careering away in a billow of fine dust.

"Hurry!" their father called. "Mama and I have a surprise for you!"

Jewel grabbed Mary's hand, yanking her up from her play in the dirt with Billy, running small cast iron cars and trucks over and around gnarled roots of the ancient oak.

"C'mon, Billy!" Jewel called with impatience, as if she knew something they didn't. Mary ran as fast as her legs would carry her, but Jewel tightened her grip on her hand, tugging her along. "Hurry, Mary!" Jewel could keep her secret no longer. "Mama's got a baby!"

A baby? A baby! Billy's cars forgotten, he raced for the house. Mary flew behind him, footsteps keeping rhythm with her rapid heartbeat. Mama had a baby? So that's what old Doc Hillman carried in that big black bag!

Bud held the screen door open, a wide grin splitting his handsome face. The three excited children scrambled up the steps and into the house, a few flies joining their race to get inside.

Bud's face beamed. "Come see your new brother!" Lindy sat propped up in the big double bed, looking tired but happy. Sweat plastered black strands of hair to her forehead. Her gown clung damply to a full bosom. Cradled in her arm, a tiny bundle lay wrapped in a flannel blanket. Mary stopped dead still, eyes wide and mouth rounded.

The baby looked just like pictures of Jesus in her Sunday School papers! Smiling, Mama looked serene and peaceful, just like Jesus' mother. Mary remembered her prayers. She knew for sure those prayers had been answered.

Jewel sat down in the cane-bottomed rocker by the bed. Bud gently placed the baby in her arms. Billy stood by the chair, tentatively touching one tiny little hand, awe brightening his dark eyes. Mary squeezed in beside him, earnestly studying the miniature face that looked to her as smooth as Mama's churned butter.

"You want to hold him, too, Mary?" her father asked. Mary nodded solemn assent, eyes wide and shining. She climbed in the rocker beside her sister. Bud placed the baby in her arms, helping support his head. Mary stared in wonder at the little tip of a tiny nose and miniature mouth. Black hair stood out around the baby's head like Billy's when he first woke up in the mornings, before Mama got after him with a hairbrush. Long black lashes lay on silky, cream-colored cheeks. Pursed rosebud lips sucked rhythmically.

"Well, Mary, what do you think?" her father asked softly, a note of pride in his voice. "Will he pass?" Lindy smiled at him from the bed.

"Daddy, can we name him Jesus?" Mary asked seriously, looking beseechingly up at her father. Bud frowned, but Lindy's smile grew.

"Dummy!" Billy cackled. "Cain't name him Jesus, can we, Daddy? Nobody can be Jesus but Jesus!"

Billy's derision caused Mary's cheeks to redden with humiliation. "Can, too, cain't we, Daddy?" She began to cry, tears splashing on the baby's soft head. The little arms flailed in fright and the tiny face puckered. Mary's usual calmness flared into anger. "I'm not a dummy, Billy! You're a dummy!" she yelled, cords in her neck distended.

"Am not!" Billy retorted. Sticking his tongue out at Mary, he yelled, "Dummy! Dummy!" Mary cried harder, wailing with the baby. Lindy looked distressed.

"Hush, Billy!" Bud sternly reprimanded. Taking the baby from Mary, he placed it back in Lindy's arms, where it once again settled into quiet sleep. A sullen Billy flung himself across the bed, burying his face in his arms. Bud picked Mary up, kissing her wet cheeks. "Jewel, get up and give me your chair," he asked. Rocking his baby daughter, he dried her tears with a gentle sweep of a callused hand.

"Jesus is a fine name, Mary," Bud said, "but, you see, Mama kind of had her heart set on naming this one after your Uncle Floyd. What do you think of that?"

The rocker thumped. Mary's sobs tapered into hiccups. Floyd! What a good name! She loved her Uncle Floyd. She bet he'd be proud to have her new brother named after him. "Oh, yes, Daddy!" she agreed. "That would be nice. 'Specially if the baby is as nice as Uncle Floyd."

Bud rocked, humming softly until Mary's eyelids drooped and she hiccuped in her sleep. Settling her in beside her mother, he loosened the ties of her dress. Kissing Lindy on the forehead, he took a petulant Billy by the hand. "Want to go fishin', son, and let these women get some rest?" he asked. "We could cool off in the shade of that willer down by the creek, even if it might be too hot to get a bite."

Billy's face brightened. Jumping from the bed, he raced off and soon returned with his fishing pole fashioned from a hickory limb.

"Jewel, you take real good care of Mama and your baby brother and sister," Bud instructed. "We'll be back soon. Maybe you can fry up some fresh bass and cornpones for supper. "

"Gonna have to step up our catchin'," he told an excited Billy. "Soon be another hungry boy sittin' at the table." He winked at Lindy and headed outside with his pacified son, catching the wooden screendoor before it could slam and wake his sleeping children.

Chapter 6

A Broken Heart

One day, soon after the baby's birth, Floyd and Corie came roaring up the hill in their old rattletrap truck that looked worse than Bud's. Corie came stomping into the house, with Floyd trailing behind her. He wasn't his usual jolly self (which he usually wasn't when his wife was in one of her moods).

Lindy sat on a low stool at the butter churn, immersed in thought. She looked up in surprise when her sister-in-law's feet came into view. Seemingly irritated that the woman would enter her door without so much as a knock, she ignored the bad manners for her brother's sake.

"Why, evenin', Corie!" she spoke pleasantly. She smiled a welcome at Floyd, who stopped just inside the screendoor, a few flies buzzing around his head. He came in with a hangdog look on his face. Standing over the baby's crib, he jammed his hands into pockets of patched overalls. Lindy knew that he was feeling lower than a cricket's knee. She wondered what her sister-in-law's quarrel was this time. Mary jumped up and ran to her uncle's side to show off her new baby brother.

"We come to fetch our share of the cherries," Corie stated flatly without a reply to Lindy's greeting or any show of interest in the baby.

Lindy looked puzzled. "What cherries are you talkin' about, Corie?"

"The ones out there in your cellar!" Corie retorted in exasperation, as if Lindy had stood out in the hot sun too long. "Floyd, let's git busy loadin' those cherries," she ordered, avoiding looking in her husband's direction, who made comical faces at the baby. "We ain't got all day to waste with foolishness."

Floyd's face froze and turned pasty white. Lindy's reddened to the hue of a pickled beet, but she ignored the slur. "Corie," she sputtered, "they ain't your cherries. I canned those cherries this year!"

"This year, maybe," an angry Corie hissed between clenched teeth, breathing hard and fast, "but I'm taking them in place of the ones you stold from us the year we moved in here. You ousted me outta my house, but you ain't gettin' by with stealin' my cherries! They were ours by rights."

"Now, Corie," Floyd interjected, but before he could say another word, his wife turned on him.

"Shut your mouth, Floyd! You're always sidin' with your sister, and I'm fed up with her always gettin' her way." Tears betrayed her. She gave the churn a vicious kick. Over it went, contents sloshing all over Lindy and the linoleum. Lindy jumped up, dripping with buttermilk, just as Bud came through the door.

Corie's fists started flailing. Floyd grabbed her around the waist. She gripped Lindy's bun, yanking her head back, pulling her hair from its pins. Thick, buttery milk oozing between Corie's toes sent her scooting. She pulled Lindy down by the grip in her hair. Floyd landed right on top of his puny wife. Whoosh! The wind shot from her lungs.

Mary stared in fright. Bud ran to save his wife from Corie's vicious fingernails. Skidding in buttermilk, he skated across the linoleum, eyes as wide as saucers and mouth as round as a dinner plate. *WHOOMPH*! He landed hard against the kitchen table, overturning it, sending empty milk jugs crashing and splintering to the floor.

Mary's shrill screams brought the pandemonium to a sudden halt. After a long moment of stunned silence, Floyd's belly began to rumble. A suppressed chuckle slowly erupted into loud, hysterical laughter. Mary stood watching, surprised at the sound. Her uncle's big overweight body quivered like Jell-O.

A grin tugged at Bud's lips, then spread into a full-fledged cackle. Lindy's musical laughter followed. Corie lay spraddle-legged and breathless in the thick buttermilk, her husband's huge body sprawled over her. Her reddened face screwed up in anger. Tears coursed down her cheeks. Bare feet slithering furiously over the buttery linoleum, she fought to free herself from Floyd's tremendous bulk.

Sliding over to Lindy, Bud carefully helped her to her feet. They leaned in each other's arms, weak with laughter. Floyd rolled off his struggling wife, but lay in the floor, face streaming with tears and belly jiggling with uncontrollable mirth. Lindy wondered if he laughed or cried.

By the time the mess had been cleaned up and the kitchen put to rights, Floyd's spasmodic giggles were almost under control, but at each new outburst, his wife fixed him with a baleful glare. Fury shone from her snapping eyes.

Lindy magnanimously offered her sister-in-law some of the cherries, but Corie flounced out the door, refusing the canned fruit or a washpan and clean dress. She sat in a huff in the hot truck, covered with drying buttermilk while Floyd murmured apologies and exclaimed over the baby that his wife had refused to hold or even acknowledge.

"Poor Corie!" Bud murmured after Floyd joined his wife and the truck had backfired its way through the dry creekbed.

"Poor Corie!" Lindy spat. "You mean poor Floyd! Mama and Daddy Parsons tried to warn him about that woman, but he was so lovestruck he could hear nuthin' but wedding bells."

"Ah, your brother'll be fine, Lindy," Bud said, slipping an arm around her waist. "He's big enough to take whatever that little spitfire can dish out. It's Corie you should be pityin'."

"And just why should I be feelin' sorry for her?" Lindy fumed, arms crossed over her bosom. "She had her mind so much on the cherries, she didn't even pay a lick of attention to baby Flo . . " Lindy stopped midsentence. She looked at Bud like she'd been thunderstruck. Dropping her head on his shoulder, she shook with sobs while Bud patted her solemnly on the back.

Mary couldn't figure out why in the world Mama was crying and why Aunt Corie refused to even look at their new baby. Everyone loved babies. Aunt Corie was the most hateful thing!

27

"Uncle Floyd is such a patient, loving man," her mother murmured. "Maybe someday some of his goodness'll rub off on Corie, and he'll have himself a good woman."

"If they both live long enough!" Bud added. They held on to each other, once again dissolving into gales of hilarious laughter.

Chapter 7

Good News Turned Bad

Mary sat patiently behind Grandma Creel's tall, colorful hollyhocks, waiting for Mama Duck to leave the nest for her daily ration of corn. The summer had proven hotter and drier than the one before. Grandma's black and white Border collie, Patches, sat by her side, long pink tongue dripping moisture. Spending her customary summer week with her grandparents, Mary visited the nest at the edge of the garden each day, hoping the babies would hatch before her father came for her on Saturday.

Noticing a sudden, slight movement among the eggs, Mary rushed to the house, the collie at her heels. "Hurry, Patches!" she urged. "I've got to tell Grandma!"

"That means it can't be long," Grandma Creel told her. "Those babies are outgrowin' their shells, feelin' all cramped and squeezed. They're beginnin' to fight their way out." She explained how the ducklings would peck at the inner surface of the shells with tiny beaks until they broke through. "It usually takes a while," she said, "so you just as well stay in here outta the sun for now. Your cheeks are awful red."

But Mary rushed back to her hiding place, crouching beneath the hollyhocks until the summer sun stood straight overhead, beating fiercely down on her. Patches finally gave up the vigil, crawling under the porch in the cool shade.

The prickly grass disintegrated beneath Mary's bare legs, too hot for comfort. Sweat soaked her cotton dress. The drone of honeybees pulling sweet nectar from towering hollyhocks made her drowsy.

"Ma-ar-y!" Grandma called from the front porch. "Come on in, now, child. You'll burn to a crisp out there!"

Mary reluctantly went into the cooler interior of the house. Drifting off into slumber on the padded window seat, she dreamed of fluffy, cream-colored ducklings chasing fat black-and-yellow bumblebees through swaying hollyhocks.

"Hurry, Mary! The ducks are hatchin'!"

Mary came instantly awake. Scrambling from the settee before her fuzzy eyesight cleared, she stumbled behind her grandmother to the nest. Tiny, wet ducklings struggled to free themselves from clinging bits of shell. Patches cocked his head quizzically from side to side, studying the strange, fuzzy creatures.

"Cain't we help them, Grandma?" Mary asked.

"No, Mary, we'll let nature take its course. We wouldn't want to hurt the babies or make them sickly."

Mary thought of Floyd. She hated to leave her baby brother to come to Grandma and Grandpop Creels', but temptation proved too great. She always had fun at her grandparents', and a week wasn't such a long time. She had kissed little Floyd goodbye and told him not to forget her.

Floyd, just beginning to pull himself up and stand on his feet for short stretches at a time, wasn't plump and strong like most babies, their cheeks glowing and little arms and legs wrinkled with fat. Floyd's cheeks were pale, and he tired easily. His eyes were blue like his father's, and his thick black hair refused to smooth down, just like Billy's, no matter how much Lindy took a hairbrush to it or slathered it with pomade.

Mary helped during school months while Jewel was away, keeping her baby brother occupied while her mother accomplished chores. Grandma Parsons had bought her new grandchild a little red rocking chair. Lindy would sit Floyd in it, tying a cotton diaper around his waist, then threading it through the back spindles, fastening him securely. Floyd kicked his skinny little legs and laughed as Mary gently rocked him or pointed out pictures to him in storybooks, reciting words she'd learned by heart.

When summer came and school ended, Jewel took over care of the baby. Mary sometimes interrupted her play with Billy to run back to the house, sharing her baby brother's sweetness with her sister.

Mary was glad Billy was out of school for the summer. She'd missed him. Jewel thought she was too grown up to run and play anymore. She spent her time either helping Mama or reading.

Mary and Billy spent a lot of their days on the hill behind the house under a huge overhanging rock, a hideaway cave, perfect for games of cops and robbers. Now that Mary visited her grandparents, Billy would find out what it was like to be home all day without a playmate.

"I wish Billy could be here to see the babies hatching, Grandma," Mary whispered. Finally the last duckling freed itself from its shell. Each one preened their wet bodies with tiny beaks until warm sunshine dried the soft down into a fluffy ball. The babies reminded Mary of dandelion heads gone to seed in the springtime. Grandma Creel gently picked up a duckling, placing it in Mary's hand. The webbed feet felt cool against her warm skin. The tiny creature nibbled at her fingers. "It's hungry, Grandma," she whispered.

"Well, we'll take care of that," her grandmother replied. She left Mary at the nest while she went after mash. Mary spent the rest of the afternoon watching the little family. Patches occasionally ventured out from the shade of the porch to sniff inquisitively at the soft balls of fluff.

When her father arrived after supper, Mary took him out to show him the new yellow puffballs. Bud's smile didn't quite reach his eyes as he listened to Mary's explanation of the hatching process, as though he only half heard her excited chatter. He seemed far away, eyes gazing at something far off.

After a while, he left her, telling her she could stay a little longer with the ducklings while he talked a few things over with Grandma and Grandpop Creel. Mary sat for a few minutes thinking of how she hated to leave the newly hatched ducklings. Yet she was homesick, and she'd really like for Floyd and Billy to see the sweet fuzzy babies.

Suddenly Mary jumped to her feet, face lit with excitement. She had a wonderful idea! She'd see if she could take one of the baby ducks home with her. Daddy would be bringing Jewel on Monday morning for her week's stay, and they could bring it back then. She ran to the house with Patches close on her heels.

Reaching the porch, Mary stopped short when she heard her father's voice raised in anger. "No! I won't accept the money, 'less you let me pay it back. I just cain't take it free and all! Besides, you know how Lindy feels about accepting charity."

"C,mon, Bud, this ain't charity," Grandpop Creel argued back. "Floyd's ours, too, ya know, and we don't want him to die for lack of money. It's high time you called the doctor in."

Floyd die? Fear chased Mary's excitement. She tiptoed to the screen door and peeked in. Her father sat with his head buried in his hands, shoulders drooping. Grandma and Grandpop Creel sat across from him, worry adding more creases to their faces.

"I know, Pop. I know," Bud murmured. "Lindy's been at me for weeks. But you know how there's always sumpthin' sneaking up to grab your money before you can even get a good look at it? We're always half between a rock and a hard place. Four kids ain't raised on air, you know."

Mary felt a stab of guilt for being a worry to her father. He always acted so happy. She never realized things weren't good.

"I just kept hopin' Floyd would perk up. You know how the little ones always seem to take a little while to adjust with earaches and cramps and all? But Floyd just don't get no better. Lindy's tried all the old remedies that worked on the others when they was babies, but none of 'em seems to help Floyd a bit."

Bud paused reflectively, coming to a reluctant decision. "I tell you what. I'll take the money if you'll let me come this fall and dig your taters. I know how it always puts your back out. And help chop your wood."

"Now, Bud," Grandpop protested, "your own farm and produce run keeps you busy enough."

"The only way I'll accept your help," Bud insisted stubbornly, mouth thinned into a straight line, "is if you accept mine."

"I declare, Bud!" Grandma Creel fretted. "You make me right proud we raised such an independent boy, but I'm afraid you've got too much pride if you'd let one of your young'uns die without accepting help!"

Crossing to the cabinet, she took down a metal Nabisco Cracker tin, fishing out a handful of bills. Turning, she caught sight of Mary standing forlornly on the outside of the screen door.

"Shh!" she hissed a soft warning. Hurrying to the door, she gathered her granddaughter up in plump, strong arms. The loving kisses she rained over Mary's face washed away some of her fear. Grandma Creel lifted one black pigtail, smoothing it down Mary's back.

"Mary, how's about you takin' one of the baby ducks home with you? I'm sure your daddy won't care." Her eyes flashed a subtle message to her son. "You can take some mash, and Billy can catch flies and dig worms to help feed it, and Jewel can bring it back Monday if your mama don't want the bother."

How did Grandma Creel know? Mary wondered. How did Grandma always seem to know?

Chapter 8

Responsibility

Dazzling October sun bathed autumn trees in brilliance, a flamboyant display of crimson reds, pumpkin oranges, and mingled yellows, emboldened by emerald evergreens and white bark of sycamores. Dry, rustling leaves, shook loose by a gentle wind, fell spiraling from the tall yard oak, swirling around Mary's small frame. Lightly tapping her shoulder and drifting to the ground, they scampered off in a tiptoeing dance. Summer had skipped into autumn, but the air had not cooled considerably.

Mary sat in the old tire swing, staring into space, scuffing bare toes in soft powdery dust. Oblivious to the charm of nature that normally entranced her, she experienced fear like a wild animal trapped in her chest. All she could see was Mama's worried face as she sat day after day in the old rocker, shushing Floyd and gently caressing his little body.

Mary sometimes stood by Mama's side, taking Floyd's little hand in her own, shocked by the hot, dry feel of it. Then she would tiptoe away and sit on the porch, too afraid to go into the yard to play.

The screen door slammed. Mary looked up. Doc came down the steps with the usual black bag in his hand. Shoulders sagging, he waved halfheartedly. Mary sat in the swing, watching in silence. The wild animal fear in her chest struggled against her ribs. Doc passed by without a word.

Old Doc Hillman was usually an affectionate, lighthearted man, teasing Mary relentlessly. His silence could only mean one thing – Floyd was really sick!

Medicines prescribed for baby Floyd in the summer did little to improve his health. His dry cough worsened. He became weaker and listless, developing a recurrent fever. Bud had gone again for the doctor.

Mary sat on, whirling slowly around in the swing. The engine of the old green sedan sputtered into life. The gears raked. The automobile roared off in a flutter of leaves. Mary ran to the house, easing the screen door shut behind her. Her mother sat at the kitchen table with her head in her hands. Her father's arms circled her shoulders. His cheek lay against hers. In the stillness, Mama sobbed softly.

The sound of her mother's crying caused Mary's eyes to smart. She sniffled. Her father turned and saw her, then came to her, picking her up and gently stroking her hair. Mary snuggled her face into the crook of his warm neck, unable to hold back tears.

"What is it, Mary?" Bud asked. "Tell your daddy what's wrong."

Between sobs, she hiccuped, "Will F-F--Floyd be all right, Daddy?"

Her father sighed, a deep, shuddering sigh. "We don't know, sweetheart. We just don't know. All we can do is pray that he will."

Mary had never heard her daddy mention prayer before. Her mother came around the table and kissed her on the cheek, pushing stray tendrils of hair from her clammy forehead. "The doctor doesn't know what's wrong with Floyd, Mary," she said. "He wants us to take him to the hospital and let the doctors check him out. But we'll have to wait until tomorrow, when we can keep Jewel home from school to stay with you." Her brow furrowed. "Or maybe I should ask Aunt Corie to come. We may be gone for a long time . . . oh, I don't know what to do!" Lindy's chin trembled, tears spilling over again.

That night, Mary awoke to see Mama kneeling by Floyd's crib, lips moving soundlessly in prayer. Silence lay heavy in the dark room except for soft sighs from Billy and Jewel and her father's rumbling snores. Light from a full moon penetrated the cheap shades, bathing her mother in a shimmering haze of moonbeams.

Mary's heart ached for her mama. She knew if anything happened to Floyd, there would be a big black hole in their lives. She squeezed her eyes tight and helped Mama pray. She hoped God would answer and make Floyd well.

Mary dozed off and later woke to the *screak, screak* of the rocker. Her mother's silhouette rocked on. Light of the waning moon glinted from tears streaming down her cheeks. Mary heard the squeak of bedsprings and looked to see her father's shadow coming to her mother's side.

Lifting the whimpering baby from his wife's arms, Bud kissed Lindy's cheek and insisted she go to bed. She complied, but lay, fidgety and unable to sleep. Floyd's weak cries twisted her heart. A palpable, black spirit of death pervaded the room.

Mary lay for a while, watching her father rock Floyd, then burrowed her head into the feather pillow, scrunching her eyes tight.

Early the next morning, Lindy and Bud left with Floyd for the hospital, after instructing Billy and Mary to mind Jewel and stay out of trouble. Lindy had decided to call Corie in to tend to Mary, but Jewel insisted she was old enough, and would stay home from school.

Mary was glad. She always felt awkward with Aunt Corie, as if the woman wished she didn't have to be there in Mama's house, wasting her time. Aunt Corie never talked, except to keep reminding Mary not to make a mess and to behave herself until her mother came home. Mary always breathed a sigh of relief whenever Mama finally returned from wherever an errand took her.

When Billy heard Jewel would stay home, he balked. "It ain't fair for Jewel to miss and not me!" he argued.

"But, Billy, Jewel's grades are better than yours," Lindy argued back.

"Let him stay, Lindy," Bud suggested. "I'll help him catch up his homework. Okay?"

"Well – okay," Lindy gave in, too upset to resist, "but I don't feel right, leaving all three of them home without someone to watch after them."

Kissing their children goodbye, Bud and Lindy climbed into the old Model T with baby Floyd. Jewel, a proud eleven and happy to be in charge, began to supervise Billy and

Mary as soon as the truck sputtered out of sight. Mary didn't mind so much, worried as she was about Floyd, but Billy was furious.

"I'm almost as old as you, Jewel, so don't you try to tell me what to do! I know what to do without you tellin' me. You ain't my boss. Mama and Daddy are!"

"Well, Mama and Daddy aren't here, now, Smarty-pants," Jewel retorted, "and they left me in charge, so you'd best listen!"

Billy stuck out an impudent tongue. The fury in Jewel's eyes sent him fleeing out the door and down the path to the toilet, turning the wooden latch into place behind him. Jewel, close on his heels, pounded furiously on the door. Mary followed in her wake, observing from the sidelines.

"Shame on you, William Robert Creel!" Jewel cried. "Actin' this way when Floyd's so sick and Mama's countin' on you!" She waited in front of the toilet with elbows askew and hands on her hips. Silence came from behind the locked door. Jewel gave up and went back inside to begin washing breakfast dishes.

Mary waited a minute or two to see if Billy would come out of hiding, but all she heard was sniffling. She followed Jewel inside and began to make the beds.

Before Mary and Jewel finished their chores, the screen door opened. Billy stood there, reddened eyes giving away evidence of crying. His eyelashes shone with the dampness of his tears. "I-I'm s-sorry, Jewel," he stuttered, ducking his head in shame. "What do you want me to do?"

Jewel's stern expression softened. She pretended not to notice the telltale signs of crying. "I'll need some kindling for fixin' lunch," she said, "but first you can slop the hogs and feed the chickens. Mary and I will gather eggs after we're through in here and maybe we'll bake a cake, if there's enough eggs."

Billy's face lit up. He scooted out the door with the slop bucket of scraps banging against his legs.

"You know how to bake a cake all by yourself, Jewel?" Mary asked in awe.

"Sure I do!" Jewel answered smugly. "I've watched Mama before. There's nothing to it." She took the egg basket from its nail on the wall. Mary followed her to the chicken house, hoping with all her heart that the hens had outdone themselves. The anticipated taste of Jewel's cake made her mouth water.

Chapter 9

A Broken Buggy and Broken Hearts

The road stretched out in the heat of the autumn sun. Bud Creel's automobile rounded the curve below the farmhouse, stirring up dust from the hard-baked clay. The vehicle rocking through the dry creekbed woke Lindy from exhausted slumber, the rough creek crossing and pungent smell of crushed peppermint signaling their return home.

Raising her head from Bud's shoulder, Lindy sighed. Rubbing swollen, blurred eyes, she struggled against sleep clouding her mind. She hadn't had a good night's rest since Floyd's birth, the day's happenings adding to her exhaustion.

An awareness of something not quite right, an aching void, began to penetrate Lindy's sleep-ridden mind. Before she could sort out her thoughts, Bud's frightened yell brought her bolt upright. He slammed the accelerator to the floor. Lindy grabbed the door handle and held on, the force of the sudden forward spurt slamming her backwards against the seat. The smell of acrid smoke mixed with the tangy scent of peppermint. Thick, black clouds boiled from every window and door of the small farmhouse.

"Oh, I knew I should've asked Corie to come!" Lindy cried in alarm. Swinging open the door, she jumped from the truck before the brakes stopped squealing. Bud passed her, yelling, "Mary? Billy? Jewel?" His hoarse cries went unanswered. Lindy's heart hammered in fear. Bud beat her to the house, bursting through the screen door. She followed him, expecting to battle a wall of flame, but only black smoke poured through every crack of the iron cookstove.

Coughing and gasping for breath, Bud grabbed a towel and jerked open the oven door. The smoke cleared, revealing a pan of blackened cinders. Batter had bubbled over and burnt to a crisp, mounds of cinders adding to the dense, acrid odor in the house.

Bud grabbed the smoking pan and carried it outside. Lindy fanned furiously to clear the air, coughing and yelling all the while for the children, who were nowhere in sight. A distant sound of wailing reached Lindy's ears, growing louder and closer, an eerie crescendo approaching the house. Lindy dropped her towel and flew to the door. Mary came limping down the hill from the orchard, both hands clasped over one knee, lips spread in a wail. Blood poured from her mouth and knees.

Billy and Jewel brought up the rear, shrill screams mixing with Mary's, an ear-piercing trio of terror. Bud dropped the pan. His boots clattered down the steps. Lindy ran in close pursuit at his heels, heart strumming her ribs, knees rubbery from fright.

"Mary, what's wrong?" Bud yelled, but the torrent of tears only increased, the wails intensified. Bud scooped Mary up, examining her all over while Lindy anxiously hovered over them, at the same time trying to calm Billy and Jewel and find out what had happened. Mary proved to have only skinned knees and a bruised, swelling forehead. The blood gushing from her mouth came from a punctured lip.

"Thank God, you're all right!" Lindy exclaimed, breathing a sigh of relief. "But what happened?"

Finding Mary not seriously injured had slowed Jewel's tears. "It was Billy's idea!" she cried.

"Was not!" a defiant Billy yelled. The veins stood out in his neck. His lip jutted out stubbornly. "Jewel wanted to do it. Not me!"

"Do what? Just tell us what happened!" Lindy ordered. Anger snapped in her black eyes.

"The baby carriage. Floyd's baby carriage," whispered Mary, lisping through her swollen lip. "They shoved me down the hill and it wrecked and I fell out." Her bottom lip trembled. Tears erupted again.

"Down in the holler?" Lindy yelled. The carriage was her proudest possession, occupying a corner of the farmhouse until she could find the time to wheel Floyd out into the sunshine. "With Mary in it?" she exclaimed. "She could have been killed!"

"I tried to catch her, Mama, but I couldn't," Jewel cried. "She went so fast!"

"I was the daddy," Billy chimed in quickly. "We was goin' to church!" Snuffling, he wiped his nose on his shirtsleeve. "Mary was too heavy, and when the buggy started downhill, I couldn't hold it."

"You had no business playing with Floyd's buggy! You know that," Lindy reprimanded, a catch in her voice. "And what was that burning in the oven?"

"My cake!" Jewel screamed. "Oh, I forgot my cake!" She ran for the house, fear of punishment forgotten. Lindy followed with Mary in tow. An acrid odor lingered in the smoky interior. Lindy cleaned Mary's wounds while Bud headed for the deep hollow below the orchard. Returning with the battered buggy, he marched Billy and Jewel to the woodshed. Billy howled and held the seat of his pants, as if punishment had already been administered, the decibels of his shrieks evidence that he could already feel the pain.

A half-empty can of baking soda on the kitchen table, among flour and other ingredients explained to Lindy the pile of ashes in the oven. She sighed, making a mental note to teach her overzealous daughter how to bake a cake, when they both felt up to it. She bandaged Mary's knees, then tackled the blackened mess in the oven, thankful that her three older children were still alive.

In all the excitement, Lindy hadn't told the children why Floyd wasn't with them, and they hadn't asked. Floyd's tired little spirit had left his body before she and Bud had even reached town. Their frightened race ended with a strange doctor in the emergency room shaking his head sadly. If only they hadn't waited. If only they'd taken their baby sooner. But it was too late for regrets.

Too late. Tears poured, hot and fast, as Lindy scrubbed furiously at the burnt batter. She didn't want to blame Bud. She wouldn't blame Bud! She knew he already blamed himself for not allowing her to call the doctor sooner.

Lindy dreaded telling Mary the awful news. How would the child understand? She didn't relish the task, but how much worse for Bud to have to break the news to the older children, whose hearts were already broken by the responsibility of causing Mary's mishap and the damage to Floyd's buggy.

Lindy's eyes traveled to the corner of the room where the buggy sat, wheels askew, frame bent out of shape, a sad picture of a once handsome carriage. But worst of all to Lindy, it sat empty – the same as her broken heart.

Chapter 10

Guilt

Bud sat in the woodshed with Jewel and Billy, unable to find it in his heart to punish his two older children for their misbehavior. He felt if anyone needed punishment, he did. He had allowed his child to die for lack of a few dollars. If only he had known how serious Floyd's illness had been. If only he could turn back time. He would give everything he had, work his fingers to the bone to save his baby boy.

No, he couldn't punish Jewel and Billy. He sat instead on the scored surface of the chopping block, wounded over the years with the bite of his ax. Billy, whimpering with fright, sat on one knee. A sulky Jewel perched on the other. Pulling them tightly to his chest, Bud experienced a fierce, overwhelming love and thankfulness for their safety and the life that throbbed in their little bodies. The worst punishment he could mete was the revelation of their brother's death. He didn't relish doling out such severe chastisement. He would rather lay the stinging willow switch to their backsides than lash their tender hearts with his news.

Bud haltingly related the bad tidings. No tears followed the children's earlier ones. Too stunned and inexperienced with the weightier matter of death, Billy and Jewel hadn't been so closely touched with such a thing in their short lives. Bud realized grief would come with time and the absence of Floyd's cherubic presence in their day-to-day existence.

Waiting until things were somewhat settled before he left in the Model T, Bud dreaded his responsibility of spreading the news to the rest of his family. His heart felt like lead. His shoulders drooped, as if the weight of Floyd's coffin already rested upon them. He left Lindy sitting in the old rocking chair, staring into space. Mary curled in her lap and Billy and Jewel flanked her sides. He knew she needed their closeness as assurance of their safety.

Bud stopped first at Grandma Parsons' farm. His widowed mother-in-law met him at the door. Bud's announcement seemed to further crush her waning spirits. Lindy's mother had begun sinking the day of her husband's death and became more shrunken and bent each day that she lived without her companion's presence in her life. Bud understood now just how she felt. Floyd's death had taken a big-sized chunk out of his soul, too.

Bud's next stop was Floyd and Corie's, where his compassionate brother-in-law offered to give the Creels the tragic news. Somehow the task of telling his own parents tore at Bud's insides more than any other. He welcomed the excuse of avoiding it. Every turn of the truck's wheels on the return from the hospital had etched Pop's words deeper and deeper in his mind, like a woodcarver's sharp knife scraping deep gouges into resistant hardwood. *We don't want Floyd to die for lack of money.*

Well, he had. And the guilt ate at Bud, knotting his stomach in pain. Corie's pinched face and skinny form followed him to the truck. An uncomfortable stillness grew between them on their way back home. Her accusing silence followed him into the farmhouse. Grabbing her sister-in-law's neck in an awkward hug proved to be the only bit of sympathy Corie showed, but she soon set to work preparing a hot, comforting supper, ignoring Lindy's protests and declining her offer of help.

"Just set a spell, Lindy," she broke her silence with a gruff gentleness. "Should'a been around to help you already. I didn't know things was as bad as this. My Floyd's plenty big enough to take care of hisself."

At the mention of Floyd's name, Lindy dissolved into tears. Corie's sallow cheeks flamed. She scrubbed harder at the potatoes. Her face twisted and two tears squeezed from her eyes. "Lindy," she mumbled, "I'm sorry about the cherries. I don't know what bedeviled me to act that way."

I know, Bud thought. Seein' your sister-in-law abundantly blessed with what your heart desired, but couldn't have. Dashed hopes can make a person so full of bitterness, it has to spew out somewhere.

Now that Lindy had lost part of what Corie envied, she was sorry she'd let anger fly at her barren sister-in-law. "That's okay, Corie," Lindy murmured. "I think I know just how you must'a felt, deprived of what you reckoned you deserved as much as me."

Corie abruptly changed the subject. "Your ma wanted to come to you," she spoke tersely, "but she's under the weather."

"She's not doin' well at all, Lindy," Bud agreed. "Her heart's actin' up, and she can hardly walk for the rheumatism."

Lindy's face blanched. "I should'a been out to see about her, but with Floyd so sick and all . . ."

"She's findin' it awful hard to keep up her work," Corie interrupted. "Floyd's talkin' about us moving back in with her and helpin' out." Frustration crept into Corie's voice. It was evident moving back into her mother-in-law's home was the last thing she wanted to do, but Bud and Lindy both knew she'd do it out of a sense of duty.

"It's not your place to care for Ma," Lindy said.

"Don't ya think I know that?" Corie returned irritably. "But you have your hands full. You cain't hardly add your ma to all you got to manage here."

Corie spoke the truth. Lindy was stretched thin. Besides that, there was no room. Even if her mother were asked to come, she wouldn't agree to it. She was a stubborn, independent woman.

Most of Corie's cantankerous behavior was directed toward Lindy. Her yearning for a child had built a wall between the two that seemed indestructible, but Floyd's death cracked that wall a little. Lindy now peeked through at the woman's sorrow. She got up from her chair, returning the brusque hug Corie had earlier given her. The action pleased Bud, but Corie didn't appear pleased. She curtly shrugged off Lindy's arms. "Got supper to git!" she growled.

Bud sighed, patting a rebuked Lindy on the arm. Glad to hear Floyd's truck grinding up the hill, he stepped out the door, breathing in a big breath of fresh autumn air. It felt good until he remembered Floyd's little lungs would never again take in a fresh breath of air. Legs weakening, he sank down on the porch stoop, head in his hands.

"Stop this!" he berated himself. "You gonna go all sissified and let your brother-in-law see ya cryin'?" By the time the truck shadowed the horizon, Bud's emotions were under control. He shoved himself to his feet. Dread carried him toward the slowing vehicle. *Now Mom and Pop know.*

Blame filled Bud up like concrete, sinking to his feet, slowing his steps, but his heart was the heaviest, nearly crushing his chest and shoving air from his lungs. His breath came in shallow gasps. He leaned against the truck for support. His heart pounded slow and hard, rocking his body in a swaying rhythm against the rusty, dented fender.

Mary ran to the door when she heard her Uncle Floyd's truck chugging into the farmyard. Pressing her nose against the metal grid of the screen, metallic odor faintly mixing with the smell of dust, she watched her father lean against the truck. His face crumpled, making her chest ache.

Uncle Floyd came around the truck, placing a big arm around her father's shoulders, saying something Mary couldn't hear. The crumples on her father's face smoothed. The two men walked toward the house, her father leaning on Uncle Floyd. Her uncle shoved a beefy hand into a pocket of his striped coveralls. Yanking out a large red-checkered handkerchief, he handed it to Bud. Mary felt a presence behind her. She looked up to find her mother watching, too.

By the time the two men reached the house, Bud's tears had stopped, but Lindy noticed the pain in his eyes was still there. She loved him, oh, so much, but why, she couldn't help wondering, hadn't he asked Grandpop for the money for the doctor sooner?

She stood back, allowing them entrance into the house. Floyd grabbed her, squeezing her tight without a word. He scooped Mary up in his arms, setting her on his shoulder. Mary felt better than she had since being told her brother had died. She watched her father go to the wardrobe and begin stuffing a flowered feedsack with clothing.

"What're you up to, Bud?" Lindy asked.

"Mom Creel told Floyd to have me bring her the young'uns for awhile, at least till after the funeral."

"No, Bud," Lindy protested. "I want them here."

Mary held her breath. She really would like to go to Grandma Creel's, but she didn't want to leave her mother. Especially with Aunt Corie!

"Lindy," her father spoke quietly, "Floyd will be laid out here until the funeral. Do you want the kids to be here?"

"You're right, Bud. I hadn't thought of that," Lindy replied with a deep, shaky sigh. "Mary, find Billy and tell him to git washed up. Jewel, git that apron off and give it to me. I'll help Aunt Corie with supper."

"Mama, can you go stay with us at Grandma's?" Mary stammered, casting a fearful glance at Aunt Corie.

"Of course, I cain't, Mary," Lindy answered. "Me and your Daddy have to stay here. Git, now, and find Billy."

Mary breathed a deep, relieved sigh. If Daddy stayed with Mama, everything would be all right.

"I'll take them right after supper, Lindy," Bud said. "You could go along for the ride, git out for a minute?"

"No, I'd best not," Lindy said. "I'll stay here and keep Corie company."

Mary's chest tightened again. Mama and Aunt Corie together — alone? "Please, Mama, ride with us," she begged.

"Go on, Lindy," Corie insisted. "The ride will do you good, and it'll git you out from under my feet so I can set this messy house to rights."

Lindy jumped up from her chair, face flushed, lips thinned in a straight line.

"Corie's right, Lindy," Bud agreed, grabbing his wife by an arm and steering her away from her sister-in-law. "Go with us. It'll do you a heap of good to git out of the house."

Mary relaxed. Mama might not get pulled bald-headed after all.

Chapter 11

Grandpop and Grandma Creel

Grandma Creel exited her kitchen door before Bud's truck rolled to a stop. The elderly woman stood on the porch, drying her hands on a clean, starched apron. Worry lines creased her plump face. Her eyes were red and swollen. As soon as Lindy climbed from the truck, Grandma Creel rushed out to meet her daughter-in-law, taking her into her arms and crooning in her ear like she did grandchildren with stubbed toes or skinned knees.

Grandma led them all into the kitchen where a percolator sang a promise of comforting brew on a burner of an immense black stove. Heaping sugar into a cup, she added cream skimmed from cow's milk, then poured in strong, hot coffee. Lindy's hands circled the cup in spite of the heat of the day, as if she needed its warmth. Grandpop kissed Lindy gently on the forehead and grabbed his son in a swift hug that made Bud catch his breath. "C'mon, kids," he spoke gruffly, "let's go to the pumpkin patch. C'mon, Bud, you go with us," he invited.

Bud shook his head, eyes downcast, hands shoved deep in his pockets. Grandpop looked at his son over the rim of his glasses. "The best medicine for a sad heart, Bud, is keepin' your mind off your sorrow," he gently remonstrated.

Bud relented and went with them out the door, he and Grandpop walking close to each other's side. Bright orange pumpkins grew between rows of dry cornstalks that rustled as they parted their way through.

"Their growth's been stunted somewhat by the heat," Grandpop explained, "but with my deep well, and the help of the Lord, I've produced a fair crop."

Grandpop and Bud stood in the center of the patch while Mary, Billy, and Jewel examined pumpkins, searching for just the right one. Bud tried to shove the thought to the back of his mind that Floyd had not lived long enough this year to see a candlelit, smiling jack-o-lantern. He recalled the light in his son's eyes and how his little legs had kicked on his first Halloween when Lindy lighted the candles. Keep your mind off your sorrow, his father had said.

Mary saw the pumpkin she wanted, the largest in the patch, one that would make a lot of light when the candle burned inside. She wanted lots of light. She waved at Grandpop and pointed to it. Then she made up her mind to ask him for a small one for Floyd. A small, perfectly round one. She would have Mama put a little candle inside it. A tiny candle seemed like the best thing for her baby brother. He had been so little himself. So little and . . . Keep your mind off your sorrow. Mary looked up and smiled at Grandpop and Daddy as they approached. The smile pinched her face and made it hurt.

That night, snuggled in Grandma's big featherbed with Jewel and Billy, Mary pulled the quilt up to her chin, listening to Grandpop's deep gravelly voice reading from the family Bible. Taking a peek as he prayed, she saw a rivulet of tears sliding down each of his cheeks.

"Lord," Grandpop added at the end of his prayer, "help Bud and Lindy see that they need to turn to you for comfort and give their hearts to you for your care and keepin'. And God, bless these dear childern real good and give them a real special happiness."

Grandpop closed the Bible, placing it back on the homemade blanket chest. "Night, young'uns," he said, giving them each a light swat across their bottoms. Grandma Creel tucked them all in, then sat back down in her rocker near the bed, softly singing songs from the ragged old church hymnal before leaning over to kiss her grandchildren goodnight.

Mary drifted in and out of sleep, the warmth of Grandma's light kiss lingering on her cheek. "Lord," she had heard her grandmother murmur as she turned away, "how I'd like to give Floyd just one last kiss." Turning her face to the wall, Mary pulled the covers over her head. Grandpop's voice echoed in her thoughts. *Keep your mind off your sorrow.* Whispering the comforting words to herself, she soon fell asleep.

Chapter 12

Going Home

The morning of baby Floyd's funeral dawned unusually warm for an autumn day. Grandma Creel brushed tangles from Mary's hair and braided two thick plaits down her back, tying them off with ribbons that matched her flowered cotton dress. She tried to tame Billy's thick locks, but as soon as she combed down the wet strands, they'd spring back up.

"Fetch me some of your hair tonic," she asked Grandpop. Shaking a few drops into her hands, she massaged it into Billy's hair. Sprouts popped back up at his crown. "Sugars, Billy!" she exclaimed. "Your hair is as hard to tame as a wild horse. You look like the offspring of a porkypine."

Mary giggled. Frowning, Jewel clamped a hand over her mouth and her cheeks reddened. Grandpop knelt down before them, stiff joints popping in complaint. He tipped Mary's face up so he could look into her eyes. "Listen, Sweetheart, don't you ever feel ashamed of feelin' a little happiness now and again. It takes a heap of it to get us through this life. Jewel," he added, "I don't believe Floyd would mind a bit us having some joy. He knows it don't mean we ain't missing him. He's probably having lots of it himself long about now."

Jewel's eyes smarted.

"All right, young'uns," Grandma announced, giving up on Billy's hair. "I guess we're all ready. We'd best go."

The solemn procession trailed out the door, piling into the wide cab of Grandpop's truck. Mary sat on Grandma's lap with Billy and Jewel scrunched in between their grandparents.

As the truck coasted out of the yard and down the hill, Mary looked out the window at the hollyhocks, standing dry and rusty-colored in the autumn sun. She wanted to climb from the truck and go sit beneath them, imagining herself listening to the hum of bees and watching the slight rolling of eggs as the ducklings inside fought to be free.

Patches ran behind the truck for a while, barking at the rear wheel. He finally gave up, plopping down in the dust and watching them out of sight.

The trip to the farmhouse proved to be a long and silent one.

Chapter 13

The Mourners Arrive

Lindy paused on her way back from the toilet, shading her eyes with her hand, hoping to see Grandpop Creel's truck in sight. They should be arriving soon for the service. She missed the children so much.

She saw the funeral line snaking around the road in the distance. Sighing with dread, she went into the house. Bud sat by Floyd's casket, engulfed in grief. "I killed him, Lindy," he said, sobbing. "I killed him as sure as if I'd squeezed the last breath from his little body with my hands."

"Bud!" Lindy ordered. "You just stop that blaming yourself! You know you did no such thing!" She ran and put her arms around her husband. Their tears mixed as she pressed her cheek against his. "Please, Bud! Please don't blame yourself. It couldn't be helped. You're just makin' matters worse."

Bud pulled Lindy onto his lap, burying his face in her shoulder. "I'm so sorry, Lindy. So awful sorry! I should've listened to you. How can you keep from hatin' me?"

"I could never hate you, Bud. Now you've got to quit blamin' yourself. You hear me?"

A car door slammed. Pulling loose from Bud's arms, Lindy rushed to the window. Parting the curtains, she saw Preacher Crookshank opening the car door for his wife. Other vehicles slowly wound their way up the hill. Lindy recognized Floyd's and Grandpop's trucks.

A warm feeling flowed through her when she saw Grandma Parsons squeezed between Floyd and Corie. Her heart ached when she noticed her mother's thinness and pale cheeks. She knew it had taken great effort for her to attend the funeral today, and she loved her more for it.

The children piled out from the cab of Grandpop's truck. Some of Lindy's emptiness ebbed. It seemed she was always busy. Her time had a way of escaping into her yesterdays, giving her false promises of being there in her tomorrows, but she vowed to give her little ones more attention than she had in the past.

If only she could call Floyd back! She'd be more than willing to once again sit up with him at nights when he cried, to neglect the housework to read him a picture book or take him out in the sunshine on a summer-soft day.

Lindy turned and looked at Floyd's little body lying in the casket. How glad she was that Bud couldn't see into her heart. She meant every word she said to him. She didn't want him blaming himself, and she couldn't hate him, but she couldn't help feeling things might be different if he'd just listened to her pleas for the doctor sooner. Lindy sighed softly, going to the door to invite the mourners in and to welcome her little family home.

Chapter 14

The Funeral

Mourners filed past baby Floyd's casket, resting on an improvised stand against one wall. With Corie's help, Bud had taken down the beds to make more room. Stacked wooden rails, cotton mattresses, and metal bedsprings leaned against the opposite wall. Lindy had covered their bulk with clean sheets. The partition for the bathing area was gone, the tub replaced by a hodgepodge of borrowed chairs.

Lindy and Bud stood near one end of the little wooden coffin, accepting handshakes and condolences from sympathetic neighbors and relatives. Vases of heavily scented, late autumn flowers, mostly marigolds and chrysanthemums picked from neighbors' yards, sat on every table and chest and covered the floor around the homemade bier, their spicy scent cloying in the crowded room.

Mary couldn't believe her eyes when Grandpop Creel lifted her up for a last look at her baby brother. Floyd didn't look anything like she expected. His sweet face was angelic. She felt that if she reached out and touched him, he would wake from his nap, blue eyes fluttering open, a smile spreading over his lips.

Grandpop sat his granddaughter down. Mary waited until the last neighbor filed past the casket. When everyone had settled in seats for the service to begin, and she thought no one was looking, she reached out and touched Floyd's little hand. The cold, hard, surface shocked her. She jerked her hand back in fright. That wasn't Floyd! Couldn't be! His small hand always felt soft and warm in hers, not hard and cold like the rocks at the bottom of their creek's icy waters.

Mary shivered in spite of the warm day. She ran to Grandma Creel, hiding her face in her bosom. Grandma squeezed her granddaughter tight. She had witnessed her first encounter with the feel of death, cruel and cold in its finality, and her heart went out to the frightened child.

Pastor Crookshank motioned for everyone to rise. Grandma Creel slid Mary from her lap and stood to her feet. The pastor closed the lid for the last time on the tiny coffin. A murmuring prayer began the service.

Lindy's breath felt suddenly cut off as the lid went down over her infant. Her chest tightened as if someone had clamped a large hand over her nose and mouth. She wanted to run and throw back the lid, rescuing her baby from the dark, cramped box. She wanted him lying in her arms where he belonged, not in the airless coffin. She wanted to see sunlight glinting off his black, shining hair, watch him kick his legs, laughing with glee.

Mary had also watched the lid going down. And almost cried out. She wished Mama or Daddy would do something, but they just sat softly crying, Mama wiping tears with a flowered hanky. Mary remembered her mother playing peek-a-boo with Floyd in Sunday school with the same hanky, humoring his restlessness.

Mary's panic stirred another memory of a time long ago when Daddy had been away in the war. She remembered the special feel of the summer day, warm sunshine and happy laughter, as they walked the short distance to the landlord's house to pay the rent. Billy and Jewel skipped ahead of Mary and her mother. The landlord met them at the door of his shed where he stacked wood for the winter.

The man stood talking around a plug of tarry tobacco, while Billy and Jewel ventured into the shed. Mary saw his sly wink before he reached out and closed the door, snapping the lock in place. A mischievous grin shoved the chew of tobacco into his jaw, making it stick out round as a jack ball. Billy and Jewel, surprised at the sudden darkness, yelled and pounded on the locked door.

Mary yelled in anger, insisting the prankster let her brother and sister out. She could feel darkness around her own body, smothery and scary, even though she stood out in open air and bright sunshine. The landlord ignored her pleas, enjoying his prank. Mary began to beat at his legs with hard little fists, crying hysterically, betrayed by Mama's laughter.

She felt the same betrayal now, frightened and powerless to help little Floyd and knowing no one else could. She began to sob and couldn't stop. Lindy turned and beckoned. Mary went to her mother, climbing onto her lap and burrowing her head in her bosom. Lindy rocked her daughter gently back and forth until the sobs subsided, except for hiccups shuddering through her little body.

The sermon ended. Everyone stood to their feet, waiting in awkward silence as the preacher helped Bud hoist his beloved burden to his shoulder. Then they all filed out the door into the bright sunshine, following Pastor Crookshank, who led Lindy behind her husband and her dead child up the steep hill to the freshly dug grave.

Birds sang. A cool breeze rippled through the trees. Brilliant sunstrokes spattered the ground with patterns of darks and lights. Lindy felt a peculiar detachment from everything, as if she were in a bad dream and needed to wake up. She would like to slip out of bed in the middle of the night to shush Floyd with one of her quiet songs.

The procession continued on until they reached the top of the hill. Bud lowered the casket beside the open grave. Everyone carried a jar of flowers to the edge of the deep hole, a colorful and unseemly contrast to the ugly mound of damp, red earth.

As the graveside service began, Jewel swiped at swollen eyes. Billy clenched his jaws tight, forcing himself to be a man and not cry. Floyd's belly shook up and down as he grieved for his namesake. Corie surprised him by reaching over and squeezing his hand. He squeezed hers back and she held on tight, her face stiff and unrevealing.

Pastor Crookshank ended the short graveside service with a prayer, barely heard over subdued sobs of adults and sniffles of younger ones. Mary couldn't cry anymore. Her thoughts kept slipping from one thing to another as the monotone voice droned on in an interminable prayer. She studied the faces of mourners, some of the women's partly hidden behind black veils. She noticed for the first time dark circles under her father's eyes.

Jewel watched a lime-green worm drop from a tree limb, descending on an invisible thread to the neck of her mother's dress. The worm worked its way across the white lace collar, tail and head meeting in a graceful loop. Lifting its length high into the air, it swayed from side to side, sniffing its direction as if blind. The worm arched forward in another slide down onto the black print of the dress material.

Jewel recalled Grandma Creel telling her once that if you let the measuring worm alone and it got your measurements, you would get a new dress. She fought the urge to pluck the worm away. Mama could use a new dress. A cow bawled in the distance over a faint stirring of leaves and gurgling of the creek below the farmhouse. The preacher ended his prayer.

Everyone's eyes riveted on Lindy as Bud led her to the casket. She knelt and placed a single flower there, then turned and held out a trembling hand to the preacher. He clasped it in both of his, sympathy and sadness making his face soft and his eyes wet.

Everyone turned their backs to the grave, following Bud and Lindy down the hill and into the coolness of the house. The contents of covered dishes brought by kind neighbors were devoured with an enthusiasm that stole Lindy's appetite. She couldn't force a bite around the huge lump burgeoning in her throat. The conversation in the room began as hushed as the hum of honeybees, but rose to a roar of forgetful abandon, assaulting her ears.

A man guffawed. A woman answered with tittering giggles. Lindy remembered the shovels of dirt falling into the grave with thuds of finality. A plump toddler sat in Floyd's little red rocker, enthralled with one of his picture books. Tears burned Lindy's eyelids. Floyd would never again rock in his little chair, excitement in his dark eyes as Mary read to him.

Lindy turned away. Her eyes fell on the spot where the handsome buggy once sat, now bent, broken, bereft, and relegated to the dusty barn loft. She looked another way, only to see another toddler taking a nap in Floyd's little crib.

She would never again watch her son's face light with delight as she played peek-a-boo through the slats when he woke from his nap. Floyd would lie beneath the mound of earth, cold and unmoving while these babies ate and played and slept. Tears ran hot and quick down Lindy's cheeks.

Caught up in her grief, Lindy didn't see her youngest daughter run out the screen door. Flying down the steps and around to the back of the house, Mary huddled under the grape arbor, hidden from sight, crying until tears refused to come. Her head nodding in exhaustion, she heard someone approaching. Jewel ducked beneath Mary's tendriled, leafy haven, struggling to lift her. She gave up and went back into the house. Bud came, gently picking his baby daughter up in strong arms, carrying her inside, and lowering her slack body on to a braided rug before the cold fireplace.

Mary slept while the sun stood high in a cloudless, periwinkle sky. She fell soundlessly into a deep dark place where her lungs struggled for air. A heavy mantle of earth covered her. She could feel the chill seeping in and knew her body was turning to cold, hard rock. She screamed for Mama or Daddy to come help, but no one came. Laughter taunted from far away, harsh and guttural, shrill and demonic. Mary screamed until she could scream no more, giving in to her hopelessness and the cold prison of her grave.

Chapter 15

After the Funeral

Mary woke abruptly, dress clinging damply to her sweating body. Her heart pounded from the terror of her dreams. Her parched tongue clung to the roof of her mouth, and her throat ached from the effort of silent screams. Everyone had gone home except Grandma Parsons, who sat in Mama's rocker, carrying on a low conversation with her daughter. Mary crossed to the water bucket, drinking deeply of a dipper of sweet but tepid spring water.

Slamming the screen door behind her, she found Jewel sitting disconsolately on the porch steps. Plopping down beside her sister, Mary playfully tugged loose the sash of her dress. Jewel jumped up and retied it, scowling. "I'm going for a walk," she said. "By myself!" she emphasized.

Mary fell back on the porch floor, studying wasps butting stubborn heads against the beaded ceiling. She got up and wandered to the tree swing where Billy slumped, listless and inactive. She gave him a shove from behind. His feet jerked up, nearly tumbling him backward. Catching his balance, he turned and frowned at Mary.

"Get a good hold, Billy, and I'll push you," she offered. Billy dropped his arms across his legs, hands hanging limp between his knees. Digging his feet into the dirt, he silently resisted her efforts. Jewel's refusal of Mary's company wasn't too painful, but she and Billy were almost inseparable. She felt betrayed.

Returning reluctantly to the house, she learned from Mama that Daddy had escaped to the garden with his hoe to dig turnips. She went to find him, only to be sent back to the house with the excuse that she needed to rest. She wasn't tired. She'd slept. What she wanted more than anything was somebody to talk to. Would her family always be like this with Floyd gone?

Mary was glad when she opened the screen door and Mama shushed her with a finger to her lips. One of the beds had been set back up, and Grandma Parsons lay napping across it. Now Mary would have her mother to herself. But Mama fidgeted nervously about the room, ignoring her.

Mary finally lay back down across the rag rug, dozing again in spite of herself. She awoke later to the squeal of screen door hinges. Grandma Parsons stood at the door, looking out across the yard. Mary went to her side.

"Mary, where's your mama?" Grandma asked.

"I don't know, Grandma. She was here when I fell asleep." Mary dug small knuckles into bleary eyes, trying to rub sleep away. She felt drugged and fretful.

"Fetch my cane, child," Grandma ordered. Worry tinged her voice. Mary ran and brought back the cane that Uncle Floyd had made from a twisted tree limb. She recalled them discovering the unusual limb one spring day.

Walking through the woods behind Grandma Parsons' home, Uncle Floyd had slashed at the tree with his pocketknife until he'd cut through the limb. Then he and Mary sat on a fallen log while he skinned away the bark.

"Ma needs some support at times," Uncle Floyd stated, whittling away at the branch, a small grunt of satisfaction displaying pleasure with his play on words.

"Uncle Floyd," Mary asked, "do you remember Grandpa Parsons?"

"Why, sure I do, Mary. He was my pa! What makes you ask that?"

"What was he like, Uncle Floyd?"

"We-ll — ." Floyd squinted up through he trees. "He was a big man, but not heavy like me — just big. His heart was big, too. He'd do anything to help anyone. Sometimes Ma'd get kind'a upset at him. Seemed like he was always off doin' somethin' for the neighbors. He'd come home all wore out and still have his own work to do. Ma quarreled a lot at him about it, but he just couldn't say no to nobody."

"How did he die, Uncle Floyd? Was he old when it happened?"

"Shucks, no, honey." Floyd stopped whittling and looked uncomfortably at Mary. "Let's see. He was — about maybe — fifty-five. Yeah, that's right. Just under fifty-five, I guess, 'cause your ma was married not mor'n a year when it happened."

"What happened, Uncle Floyd?" Mary persisted. "Did he get real sick and die or what?"

Floyd whittled on the gnarled tree branch, holding it out and turning it around, inspecting its smoothness. "Well, whatta ya say, Mary? Ya think Grandma will like her cane?"

Mary felt the smooth surface of the hickory branch. "Sure, she will, Uncle Floyd. It's real nice."

"Then we'd best be gettin' it back to her, and be gettin' ourselves to supper. My stomach's so empty, it's gnawin' on my backbone." Floyd shoved his immense weight up from the log with the help of the sturdy cane and headed toward the house.

"But, Uncle Floyd," Mary complained, "you never said how Grandpa died!"

Floyd stopped dead in his tracks, turning in anger. "Mary, don't your mouth never quit?"

Mary's lower lip trembled. Uncle Floyd had never before said an angry word to her. Floyd knelt before her in contrition. "I'm sorry, Mary. Listen, honey, it's just something I'd rather not talk about. Okay?"

"All — all right, Uncle Floyd," Mary whispered. She grabbed her uncle around the neck, squeezing it tight. They continued on in silence to the house where Grandma Parsons made a big, happy fuss over her new cane.

Grandma Parsons started down the steps and Mary followed, almost afraid she'd want her to go away like everyone else, but her grandmother gave neither assent nor dissent. She slowly made her way up the hill, Mary keeping pace beside her.

I'll ask Grandma about how Grandpa died, Mary decided. "Grandma?" she ventured, "How come Uncle Floyd got mad at me when I asked him how Grandpa died?" She hoped her question didn't make her grandma mad, too, but she had to know.

Grandma Parsons stopped for a minute, breathing hard from exertion. Her eyes searched the sky for a long while, so long Mary began to wonder if her question would be answered. Finally, the old woman looked down at her granddaughter, placing a palsied hand against her cheek and studying her face. Mary felt the tremor of cool, leathery fingers against her skin.

"Land sakes, child!" her grandmother murmured. "You can sure ask a bunch of questions sometimes." Her rheumy eyes bored into Mary's. "Honey," she said, stroking her hair, "if I tell you, can you keep it to yourself and never say nuthin' about it to Floyd? He was hurt awful bad when it happened and never really quit blamin' hisself, though it couldn't be helped, I don't suppose."

"I promise, Grandma. Cross my heart and hope to die! I promise."

Grandma Parsons resumed her climb, words coming in breathless snatches. "Floyd and your grandpa had gone huntin', promising me squirrel for supper. They was gone a long time when I heard Floyd yellin' and screamin' for help."

Grandma's voice quavered. "I run to the door and saw Floyd comin' stumblin' along with his daddy across his back. Your grandpa was bleedin' purty bad. I ran to help him. I was never so scairt in my life, Mary."

Exhausted, the old woman stopped once more, leaning heavily on her cane, looking off into the distance as if she saw the whole thing happening again. Just when Mary began to think her grandmother had forgotten her, she resumed her story. "Grandpa had been shot and was already gone. There wasn't nuthin' me nor nobody else could do."

"Did Uncle Floyd shoot him, Grandma?"

"Yes, darlin', your Uncle Floyd did shoot his daddy, but it was an accident — an awful, senseless accident. He saw a squirrel and made the gun ready. The squirrel disappeared, and he tried sneakin' around the tree to sight him. He was so busy looking for that crazy creature, he didn't watch where he was going. He tripped over a big, ol' twisted root and dropped his gun. It hit the ground and went off."

Grandma's voice caught. Mary looked up. Her grandmother's eyes narrowed, looking into the past. Her teeth dug into her lower lip to control its quivering. "Shot Grandpa right through the neck. Didn't kill him though. That's another thing makes yore Uncle Floyd feel so bad. He thinks if he'd done things different, his daddy'd still be alive. But he did all he could.

"Your grandpa was a big man, a heavy weight even for Floyd, but he got him across his back somehow and ran all the way home with him. Still he says maybe he should'a tried to stop th' bleedin' some way, or just left him there in the woods and ran for help. But nuthin' could'a saved his daddy, 'ceptin' a miracle. I guess the Lord wanted your grandpa for some reason. I ain't goin' to try to outfigure my Maker. I don't blame God, and I don't blame Floyd, but I sure do miss your Grandpa."

"You still miss him, Grandma?"

"I sure do, honey, and it's been nigh onto eleven years since he was dead and buried."

Mary walked in thoughtful silence beside her grandmother. Eleven years? Eleven years was a long time! Longer than she had lived. Would her family miss Floyd that long? She hated to think of things going on like they were now if they did. She felt sorry for Uncle Floyd. A person felt bad enough when someone you loved died, but to blame yourself, like Daddy did, now that would be awful hard, even though you couldn't help causing their death.

She wondered if Grandpa Parsons knew about little Floyd and his death and if they would find each other in heaven. Wouldn't he be surprised to see what a nice grandson he had?

Mary wished she could have known her grandfather, even for a little while, but she didn't want to leave her mama and daddy and everyone else just yet to see him. She hoped he'd understand if she didn't come along too soon. She was sure heaven was a nice place and she sure missed Floyd, but she was afraid of dying, especially after touching her brother's cold, hard hand.

Poor Uncle Floyd! She couldn't blame him for getting so upset with her questions. Death was bad enough without being there when it happened and not being able to stop it. She never wanted to see anyone die or be buried again.

Mary and her grandmother finally reached the gravesite. Lindy knelt with her head in her hands beside the fresh mound of earth. The old woman touched her daughter's shoulder with a gentle, gnarled hand. Startled, Lindy jumped and turned.

"Lindy, honey, why don't you come to the house so's we can talk? I'll have to go home soon." Grandma's breathless voice sounded sympathetic and troubled.

Lindy got to her feet. "Ma, I hate it because I caused you to come searchin' for me up this steep hill. I meant to git back to the house before you finished your nap." Placing an arm around her mother's waist, Lindy gently helped her down the hill, Mary following behind.

Chapter 16

Coping

Lindy set the filled coffeepot on the stove where it perked a jaunty tune. The day was still warm. She knew the fire would only serve to make the interior of the house hotter, but a warm cup in your hand seemed to have a certain comfort to it. She needed that comfort now. Her mother sank down in the rocker with a weary sigh, patting her lap for Mary to climb up. She rocked rhythmically while she talked.

"Lindy, I know how bad you're hurtin'. You know I lost two little ones myself, one before you come along and the other between you and Floyd. And then when your daddy left me, I didn't think I could stand it. The house was so empty, and everywhere I looked I saw something to remind me of him."

She shifted her burden from one leg to another, thin varicose arm wrapped around Mary's neck, hand stroking her granddaughter's cheek. "It was so hard not feeling needed anymore. You was gone and Floyd was pert near grown and had things of his own to keep him busy. Then he was soon gone, too, with Corie, and there was no one to cook for or clean up after.

"There wasn't no use havin' a big garden or cannin' a lot of food just for me, and there was no one to talk to about your day and things that happened to you, or just to put their arms around you and tell you they loved you. I'd catch myself talking to Daddy just like he was still there in the house with me, pretending he'd answer me. I felt for a while like I was losing my mind. Still do sometimes."

Grandma Parsons stopped talking and sat silent for a moment, staring pensively at the floor, rheumy eyes revealing the pain of introspection. Mary lay back in the curve of one arthritic arm, looking up at her grandmother with wide, liquid eyes.

Why, I've never thought of Ma having feelings like that! Lindy thought. Her guilt of neglecting her mother grew.

The rocker started up again. The sad, shallow voice started up with it. "The house was so quiet, and the things your daddy and I used to do together wasn't that much fun anymore without him to share them. And the work! I couldn't keep up that big place, and I hated callin' on Floyd or Bud for help. I knew they had lots of their own work to keep them busy. When Floyd and Corie moved in, I thought things would be better, but lonesome as I got before, I missed having time to myself."

The thumping stopped. Grandma leaned forward, tilting the chair on the rocker's tips. Mary's arms gripped her grandmother's neck to prevent sliding to the floor.

"And, Lindy, Corie made it plain she hated bein' there, not havin' a place of her own. That woman got beneath my skin like a batch of chiggers after berry pickin'. I just had to scratch where I itched! Well, when Bud went away to war, Corie was on Floyd like a flea on a dog's back to git her out of there. I guess I did make it a little hard on her. Lord knows I didn't want to, but her rough tongue just whetted mine." The rocker thumped back in place.

Lindy could appreciate her mama's lack of patience with Corie's sharp tongue, but from her years at home, she knew it didn't take much honing to make her mother's razor-sharp either.

"For once, I was on Corie's side," Grandma continued with a mischievous smile. "I helped her reason with Floyd, tellin' him I could take care of myself, and that you needed to git away from here. I saw how the farm was pulling you down. Floyd gave in, and Corie and me welcomed the parting of our ways. But now my old heart's actin' up and the place is falling down around my ears. There seems to be no answer to it all. There's times when I wished I'd git my living over with and go on home to meet your daddy. I ain't got the strength for life, and I'm not needed here no more anyways."

Lindy rushed to her mother's side, catching both the old woman and Mary in a tight hug. "I need you, Mama!" she cried. "We all need you."

"And your young'uns need you, Lindy, and so does Bud. That's where you're better off than I am. You still got a whole passel of folks needin' you. Your life will be full — too full for grievin' much."

Mama, you sly old fox! Lindy thought with a warm twist of her heart. She knew what her mother was trying to do. You just couldn't outwit Mama. "But Mama, I miss Floyd so much. I cain't just forget him."

"Do you think I've ever forgot my young'uns? Sure, you miss him! You always will, but you cain't just give in to grief and let the ones that's left suffer. They don't quit needing till you're ready to go on agin. You've got to pick yourself up and get goin', like I did, and keep your family on its feet. Then, when and if you git as old as I am, and everyone's done gone and left you, then's when you can start to feeling sorry for yourself. Then's when you can afford to, but now you just cain't. There's not time nor room for it. Now me, I got the time."

"Oh, Ma." Swiping tears away, Lindy placed a cool hand on each side of her mother's sunken cheeks. "You're still needed, Ma. More than you think." The softness of her mother's face was a contradiction. Her flesh looked parched, like onionskin, but felt like baby's flesh. Lindy's heart splintered as she realized just how old her mother really was. She didn't want to think about losing her, too. But she knew it couldn't be long.

Lindy made a sudden decision. "Ma, if I asked Bud and he agreed, would you come and live with us?" Lindy slid her hands down and over her mother's thin quivering lips to stop the protest she knew she was about to make.

"I know we don't have much room," she persisted, "but if Floyd would help and we could git a little lumber, we could add on a room for you. Please don't say no, Ma. I need you. I really do need you!" Lindy tried to forget her growing weakness, for her mother's sake. Mary sat squeezed between the two of them, dark questioning eyes glistening with hope. Grandma Parsons reached up and took Lindy by the wrists, pulling her hands away. "Lindy, ain't that coffee done yet?" she asked testily.

Lindy's hands fell to her sides. Turning quickly away, hiding anger and disappointment, she poured the strong brew into two cups. Grandma Parsons squinted at her daughter for a moment, then shoved Mary off her lap. "I tell you what, Lindy," she said, using her cane to pull herself to her feet, "I got a proposition for you. If you'll get Bud and Floyd to agree on what you said, I'll sell my farm and you can use the money to build that room. But only on one condition — that you and Floyd take what's left after puttin' away enough for my funeral and divide it to use as you see fit. I won't be beholden to nobody."

"If that's what you want, Ma," Lindy answered, "but it's going to be a long time off before you're needing a funeral."

"Pshaw! No use patronizing me! We both know I ain't got long." Grandma Parsons smiled. "Corie's gonna love you for this, Lindy. She was dreadin' moving back in with me. And, Lindy?"

"Yes, Ma?"

The old woman leaned closer to her daughter, whispering in her ear. "I'll thank you even more than Corie. The Lord knows I was dreadin' it, too!"

Lindy smiled for the first time since Floyd's death. "Ma! You rascal!" she scolded. "Shame on you!" But Lindy knew how her mother felt. The time spent with her sister-in-law before the funeral was like living in a cocklebur patch — a pretty sticky situation!

Lindy was instantly ashamed of her thoughts. Corie had worked hard and never complained or asked for a thank you. Cockleburs weren't all bad. Their loyal attachment wasn't easy to shake and, on close inspection, the bloom that produced their prickly burrs was a beautiful sight. She had been given a close look at her sister-in-law this week and saw something she'd never noticed before. Corie, brittle on the outside, like a thistle, had a soft inside.

Chapter 17

Bud Rebels

Bud took Grandma Parsons home that evening. Lindy rode along, seeking an opportunity to talk to him in private about her mother moving in. She dreaded his response. She knew he liked her mother, in spite of her curt ways, but she wasn't sure he liked her well enough to live with her day after day, especially in their crowded little home.

But on the way home from Grandma Parsons, Bud surprised Lindy by agreeing to her plan without any argument. "I'll go to town first thing in the morning and put an ad in the paper to sell her farm," he said. He turned the truck around and drove back to Grandma Parsons to help her fix up the ad. Lindy tried to talk her mother into moving in right away, but she refused.

"I've made it alone this far, Lindy," she argued. "Floyd's got me plenty of wood cut and hauled in and I can spend the time until the farm sells sortin' through stuff and deciding what to do with it. There's a few things I'd hate to part with, and I may store them at Floyd's until the boys git my room built. Most of the furniture, I guess I'll let go with the house, 'ceptin' my bed and dresser and my old rocker. That should outfit the room real good. I don't need much."

Lindy looked forward to the time when her mother would come to live with her, but she saw it as a mixed blessing. She felt so drained and tired, yet she knew she could face her mother's death far better if she put forth effort to make her last days a little more comfortable.

Floyd's death had taught her a valuable lesson, and a painful one. Some things were more important than clean floors and done-up dishes. She meant to see her mother to her grave with a lighter burden of guilt. If Floyd's death meant anything, it had made her better appreciate those she loved and get her priorities straight. She fell on her knees that night, reacquainting herself with the God she'd neglected so in the past.

"Lord," she prayed, "you've just got to give me strength and nudge me a little when I forget. I just cain't make it through this valley of death without your help. Please let Bud see that he needs you, too."

When Bud came in from outside, she asked him if he would read some scripture before they all went to bed. He glared at her and stomped back out the door, slamming it hard. The children sat stunned, staring up at their mother.

Lindy forced down disappointment and began reading. Her weak voice, after a few verses, became strong and sure. She wouldn't give up on Bud. She'd just keep praying and reading the scriptures each night, no matter how he reacted. He'd soon come around, she was sure.

Chapter 18

Christmas

Christmas Eve finally arrived. The Creels had somehow made it through the months since Floyd's death, and were now spending the night at Grandpop and Grandma Creel's. The beds overflowed the same as Grandma's cupboards, laden with fruit and cream pies, tall moist cakes and huge gingerbread Christmas cookie cutouts sprinkled with colored sugar.

The night seemed eternal for Mary. She propped herself on one elbow behind her mother's sleeping back, studying cavorting shadows of flame dancing across the walls and ceilings.

After what seemed hours, Mary's eyelids became heavy. Her hand propped beneath her chin tingled with sleep. Her head slipped, jolting her awake. Lindy awakened, catching her daughter staring into the darkness, the firelight's ballet reflecting eager excitement in her black eyes.

"Mary!" Lindy admonished gently. "Lay down now and go to sleep, child. Don't you know Christmas never comes while a young'un's awake?"

Mary was abashed. She didn't know! What if she had lain awake the whole night, unaware she would spoil the whole thing? She snuggled down under the covers, scrunching her eyes tight, rubbing her arm awake and willing herself to sleep. Only seconds passed with Mama's callused hand gently rubbing her back until she was lost in dreams of curly-haired dolls and bright-colored crayons.

In spite of Mary's scarcity of sleep, an internal alarm nudged her awake the next morning in time to creep into Grandma Creel's high bed. She snuggled close against her grandmother's bed-warmed softness. Excitement shivered up and down her spine, mingling with goosebumps raised by the cold linoleum on her bare feet.

Grandma stirred. Mary's icy feet against her warm legs aroused her from deep dreams. Groggily, she slipped an arm

71

around her youngest grandchild, tucking the flannel quilt around the small body. She didn't question Mary's presence in her bed, but pulled her slight, shivering frame close. This was an event that had become a sweet ritual from the time Mary had been old enough to toddle on unsteady feet to her side. The morning was still dark, lighted only by flickering shadows from dying embers of the stone-lined fireplace.

Grandpop's soft, musical snore was a sweet serenade of bass accompaniment to Mary and Grandma Creel's shared morning closeness. His mouth hung open in the dim firelight. Mary could see the straggly growth of salt and pepper stubble sprinkled over his weathered face.

"Good mornin', Mary," Grandma whispered into her granddaughter's ear, nuzzling the soft flesh of her neck.

"Mornin', Grandma," Mary whispered back in eager excitement. "Can I go see the presents?"

"Wouldn't be fair, Mary," Grandma replied. "Billy and Jewel wouldn't like you goin' ahead of them. Cain't you hold your taters?" Her warm lips touched Mary's cheek.

"Grandma!" Billy yelled, peeking around the door. "Christmas is here! Hurry! Get up!"

"Billy Creel! Did you peek?" Grandma admonished. "You was to wait for the rest!"

"I couldn't wait, Grandma! I just couldn't. I didn't go in though. I only looked to see if there was presents under the tree! And there is!" He jumped up and down. Jewel joined him, giggling. Bud and Lindy stood framed in the doorway behind them, smiling.

"No fair!" Mary pouted. "I asked to go and Grandma said no!"

"Wh — whuh!" Grandpop's fuzzy exclamation interrupted his snore. He raised from a prone position, rubbing his eyes to clear the sleeping fog. "What ain't fair, Mary?" He struggled to the side of the bed, big feet protruding from legs of flannel underwear. Groping blindly for a pair of worn corduroy slippers, he stretched and yawned, arching his arthritic back until it popped like castanets. Leaning across Grandma, he tweaked Mary's nose. "I'll tell you what ain't fair, Mary. All that quarrelin' wakin' a man from sleep. And then to open your eyes and find a varmint in your bed. That's what ain't fair!"

Mary giggled. Grandpop playfully slapped her rump. "C'mon, child! You're holdin' up the works! Best wait till I poke up the fire, though," he advised. Shuffling his feet, his hair sticking up like rooster feathers, he crossed the room. Mary, Billy, and Jewel giggled, pointing at the drooping flap of the unbuttoned panel on the seat of his longjohns.

Grandpop turned and glared menacingly at them. "And just what do you think is so funny?" he growled. Gales of laughter followed him as he exited the room.

Grandma pulled back the layer of quilts. "Come on in, young'uns. Land sakes, it's cold! It's a wonder the fire hadn't froze up on such a cold night!"

Billy and Jewel scrambled beneath the covers, giggling and squirming, chasing the chill of the cold room by their cozy snuggling. Bud and Lindy sat at the foot of the bed, smiling at the children's happiness.

When Grandpop returned, Grandma Creel reached for her Bible on the bedstand. Shushing the fidgety children, Grandpop squeezed in beside Mary, barely clinging to the edge of the mattress. "Now, young'uns, let's all forget the gifts for a while," he admonished, "and listen to Grandma read to us about the first and best Christmas Gift ever."

A solemn silence settled over the bed groaning with its familial burden. Grandma Creel's hushed voice, reading from the second chapter of Luke, reminded everyone what Christmas really meant, the birth of the Christ Child, God's most precious gift to mankind, heralded by angels and worshipped by lowly shepherds and gift-bearing Magi. Lindy's heart ached with memories of baby Floyd. She wondered if she dare dream again of another child to lay in Floyd's bassinet, now stored in the dusty, junk-filled attic.

Yes. Yes, she would! she decided.

Mary thought of her baby brother, too, memories mingling with wondrous stories of the baby Jesus and His gentle, God-filled mother. She had asked for a golden-haired dolly and crayons and a huge, thick coloring book, and now she'd ask God on this blessed Christmas morning for another sweet brother that she hoped would stay with them forever.

But even though they'd only kept Floyd for a little while, she was glad they'd had him. She still kept his memory in her heart and would never forget his baby sweetness. He must be happier today than he had ever been, celebrating Jesus' birthday in heaven, with all the angels singing "Happy Birthday!" in their sweet voices. She could imagine Floyd joining in, healthy and whole, his earthly sickness all forgotten.

Mary's nightmare of death and the grave had tormented her until Miss Jenkins told her Sunday School class how a dying person's spirits return to God the second they leave the body and of how they wait happily in heaven, free from sickness until their loved ones join them.

The old house, warmed by the blazing fire, crackled and popped like Grandpop's arthritic joints. The seven persons crowded in the high, iron bed felt double warmth — that of the fire and that of family closeness and love.

Grandma ended the reading of the Christmas story. Everyone bowed their heads — everyone except Bud. Lindy glanced up, noticing Bud's rigid back, his eyes staring straight ahead, his mouth a hard slash in his face. Her father-in-law's prayer filled the room, asking God's blessing on the day and thanking Him for His Son Jesus. Then his voice trembled as he asked God to touch the heart of his son and cause him to accept His love-wrapped gift.

Lindy sneaked another look at her husband's cold, stern face. She couldn't keep the tears from squeezing from between her eyelids. She recalled the storekeeper's gentle admonition about attending church and his promise of prayer for Bud's escape from sin. They attended church every Sunday now, but Bud stubbornly refused to go, resisting all their pleas. "I want nuthin' to do with the God who took my baby away!" he stated flatly.

As Grandpop ended his prayer, Lindy added her own petition: *Lord, please let Bud see how much you love him.*

You watched your own Son suffer and die like little Floyd, when you could have saved Him, but you let Him die so people could go to heaven.

She wanted so much to go to heaven when she died. She was glad Floyd was there now and not lying beneath that cold mound of dirt back at the farm. If Bud could only hear Pastor Crookshank tell of heaven and realize how happy Floyd was. But he wanted nothing to do with God or Pastor Crookshank and his Sunday meetings.

Please, God, Lindy prayed, *can you put a want-to in Bud's heart to go to church with us? If he did, then maybe he'd learn to love you.*

"Amen!" Grandpop Creel's voice rumbled. The covers flew back. Lindy immediately forgot her sad contemplation as they all followed the children in their mad dash to the tree.

The first thing beneath the pine-scented tree to meet Mary's eyes was a doll with shining curls, one that looked exactly like the one she had seen in Mr. Cranshaw's store. The cotton body felt so soft and baby-like. Golden curls ringed a china head adorned with long-lashed blue eyes that open and shut just like a real baby's.

How did Mama and Daddy know exactly the kind of doll she wanted, right down to the red velvet cloak and bonnet? Naming it Heidi, after the girl in her favorite storybook, she kept it by her side all day. That night at home, she stored it, safe from harm, in the wardrobe in a boot-box Daddy gave her. The boots, ordered from a Sear's wishbook, he proudly wore.

"Heidi," Mary whispered in the doll's ear before closing the lid on the box, "I'm going to keep you forever and ever. I'll never let anything happen to you. I promise!"

Chapter 19

Disaster Strikes

Billy sat on the floor a few days after Christmas, watching Mary play with Heidi. That's all she wanted to do anymore. Play with that dumb doll! Bored with his cars, he jumped up, running to get his snowsuit. He knew Mary would put the doll down long enough to go play in the snow. She loved the outdoors, especially in the wintertime.

Outside, bare branches of forsythia and wisteria drooped to the ground in glistening arcs of crystal white. The farmyard glinted like diamonds under brilliant rays of a pat-of-butter sun. The enticement of the outdoors would make Mary lose interest in that old doll. He hurried to her side. "Mary, let's go ride down the hill in my new sled," he offered, anticipating her agreement. "I'll let you ride first, and I'll pull it back up."

Mary looked up, considering. "Ask Jewel," she said, dismissing Billy while combing Heidi's curls.

"She won't go!" Billy grumbled. "All she ever wants to do is read!" Jewel lay across her bed, absorbed in Louisa Alcott's Little Women, borrowed from the school's library for the holidays. Billy cajoled and wheedled, but Mary turned a deaf ear to his pleas.

"C'mon, Mary!" He begged. "Please go outside with me. You can play with that silly old doll anytime."

"Heidi's not silly!" Mary retorted. "She's mine and I love her."

Lindy looked up from her sewing in time to see the doll flying across the room. She sat in stunned silence as it struck and shattered the wardrobe mirror, cracking the glass and breaking the doll's head into countless pieces.

Jewel looked up from her book in surprise. Terrible silence reigned for a few breathless seconds. Billy stood rigid with shock. He hadn't meant to hurt the doll. He just wanted Mary to go sledding.

76

Mary's pitiful wails brought her mother to her side. Jewel remained rooted to her bed, a sympathetic look on her face. "Billy!" Lindy scolded. "Whatever made you do such a mean thing?" Her explosive words brought on a fit of coughing.

"I - I'm sorry, Mama. I didn't mean to break it." Billy knelt by the broken doll, crying, frantically attempting to fit all the shards of the head back together. Realizing the futility of his task, he jumped up and ran out the door, slamming it behind him. Plowing his way through the drifted snow to the toilet, he locked himself in and wept.

He would give anything to undo his wicked deed, but it could never be undone. Never! And now Mary would hate him forever. And Jewel, too, and Mama. Maybe even Daddy when he found out. He would be thrashed, too, but he deserved it. A good thrashing might make him feel better.

Billy heard Mary's wails coming from the house. He remembered her excitement when she saw the beautiful doll sitting beneath the tree in Grandma and Grandpop's living room. She showed little interest in the books and crayons that were usually a love of her life. She played with the doll all day, even sitting it beside her at the breakfast table.

Billy sat on the closed toilet seat, cold, miserable, and uncomfortable, wishing for a friendly soul to rescue him, but doubting if anyone in the house wanted to be his friend. Why hadn't he listened to Grandpop Creel? Grandpop was right. When we don't shorten our tempers, they're like our dogs biting a neighbor because we keep them on too long a chain.

I sure wish I had shortened my temper before it bit Mary! Billy lamented. He sat in the toilet, mixed odors of disinfectant and excrement nauseating him. He recalled how Marshall Crimmons, a friend at school, teased him one day on their trip to the outhouse behind the school building.

"Did ya know the Devil lives in that old deep, dark hole just waitin' for mean children to sit down so he can pull them down where he lives and keep them there forever?"

Billy laughed off the tale at the time, but all the same he was glad the hole had a lid to be let down, just in case. He was glad, too, that he had dressed to play in the snow. The chill crept into his bones in spite of the snowsuit and boots.

SCRUNCH! SCRUNCH! Someone approached through the crusty snow! Was it friend or foe nearing his hideaway? He heard Mama's familiar cough. A tap rattled the latched door. A fearful sob tore loose from Billy's throat. He choked it back and got up to lift the latch, dreading what waited for him on the other side of his sanctuary.

A stern Mama stood before him, sympathy and anger fighting for prominence in her face. "Billy, you've done a hateful thing," she remonstrated. "But Mary says she knows you didn't mean to. Still, you'll hafta take your lickin' like a man. You know that?"

Billy's chin dropped to his chest. Twisting his gloved hands together, he whispered almost too low for Mama to hear, "I know, Mama." He didn't relish the whipping or returning to the house to face Mary's woeful forgiveness. He'd almost rather she'd be mad.

Lindy reached out and took her repentant son by the arm. He hung back as they headed for the house, delaying his punishment as long as possible. Mama's whippings didn't hurt as bad as Daddy's, though, and anything was better than being yanked down in that black hole by Satan himself.

You got to get a shorter chain! he reminded himself.

Chapter 20

Forgiveness

At first Mary had been mad at Billy. Awful mad! But she'd seen the look on his face as he knelt before the wardrobe, trying frantically to make her beautiful, shattered doll whole again. Mama had said he would suffer every time his broken image looked back at him from the cracked mirror. If Mama could forgive Billy, so could she, though it would be an awful hard thing to do.

Miss Jenkins told them once about Jesus, and how mean men had beaten Him and fastened Him to an old cross with big, ugly nails. But before He died, He'd looked up to His Father in heaven and asked Him to forgive the men because they didn't know what a bad thing they were doing. Miss Jenkins said people who loved God were to forgive the same way. Well, Mary would try. She wanted to be as much like Jesus as possible.

Tenderly placing the headless doll in the shoebox, she smoothed the soft, red velvet. A tear splashed onto the bright red cape, spreading a crimson stain. Had Mama's heart hurt this bad when she'd seen Floyd's dead little body in the casket? Probably worse. Heidi was only her pretend baby, and she'd had her for just a few days. Floyd had been a living, moving real baby, and Mama had held him and learned to love him more every day during the long, tiring months of his sickness.

Mary gave Heidi a loving pat and closed the lid on the box. Placing it back on the wardrobe shelf, she hurried to pull on her snowsuit. The snow was deep and so beautiful! She grabbed a handful and pelted Billy with it. He giggled and ran out of reach, falling down and making a snow-angel before she caught up with him. Mary fell by his side, creating her own snow-angel in the whiter-than-white snow.

Through a window, Lindy watched her children. Smiling, she sat down and resumed sewing with a deep sigh of contentment.

Chapter 21

Summer at Last!

The blustery breath of March blew away winter's chill. Driving winds and pouring spring rains once again packed the roadbeds, softened to a mush by winter's deep freezes. After the spring thaw, Grandma Parsons' farm sold. She moved in with the Creels, temporarily sharing Mary's bed, while Bud and Floyd hammered and sawed far into the nights to finish her room.

Spring soon overheated into another sweltering summer, bringing an end to school days that kept Billy's free spirit imprisoned and itching for release. He and Mary roamed the fields and woods in abandon, swinging on grapevines and wading the cool creek, searching for elusive crawdads and darting, silvery minnows.

Bud loaded the Model T to the hilt on warm, feathery-soft, summer nights — blankets, pillows and poles, carbide lanterns and bait, Lindy's picnic basket stuffed with fresh-killed, fried chicken and homegrown green beans, seasoned with pork fat from hogs Billy had helped his father slaughter. Homemade bread and frosty, iced lemon tea perfected the picnic. Jewel, Mary, and Billy climbed into the bed of the pickup, laughing and singing silly songs as they splashed through shallow waters of Rushing Creek and down the dusty road toward the river.

Grandma Parsons never joined them, claiming the night air was poison, causing her rheumatism to act up. She even stayed home on Sunday mornings now, reading her Bible and listening to preaching on the radio, while Bud fished and the rest of the family attended Sunday School. "My back just cain't take the long sermons and the hard seats," she complained.

At the riverbank, the "Ch-rumph!" of long-legged frogs in the gathering dusk kept beat with humming insects. The pungent smell of carbide, used to light the lantern, mingled with the river's fishy odor and campfire smoke.

Lindy sang softly in her high, sweet soprano, "Shall we gather at the river, where bright angel feet have trod . . .," Bud's voice picking up the tenor. The frogs stopped chorusing long enough to admire the sweet blend of voices, then joined in, adding rich bass to gospel hymns. Their songs, mixed with insects' strumming, became a charming symphony, lulling Billy into sleep. He started as the tip of his pole dropped, sinking into the water.

Lindy had already carried a sleeping Mary to the blanket spread on the soft carpet of grasses by the firelight's glow. Tugging off the little scuffed shoes, she slipped the knot from her dress sash so she could sleep comfortably.

"Ready to sleep under the stars, Billy?" she asked. He shook his head, stifling a huge yawn. He fished on, struggling to stay awake. He had a reason other than his love for fishing to avoid sleep. He always sat on the front fender of the truck on the way back to the farmhouse, holding the lantern high to guide his father through the dark night.

Someday, Bud kept saying, he'd have to get the old truck's wiring fixed, but Billy secretly hoped he never did. He felt real important, like the engineer of a train or the boss of a westward bound wagon train, sitting on the hood in the darkness, holding the swaying lantern. His legs straddling the headlamp, he held on with his free hand. Bud always drove slowly over the bumpy road while Lindy quarreled and fretted, afraid Billy would be bounced off and run down by the sightless vehicle.

"Aw, he's a strong young'un, Lindy," Bud would chuckle. "His legs are gripped tighter around that headlamp than your cannin' tongs on jars you lift out of boiling water."

Lindy couldn't help but remember Bud's insistence that Floyd would be all right when she begged him to get the doctor, but she said nothing.

Billy wasn't worried, though. He assured his mother he wouldn't fall. Like Daddy said, he was a strong boy. But he didn't blame his mama for worrying. He'd probably fret, too, if it was someone else out there straddling that headlight. So he kept a careful grip. He didn't want to cause his mother any more sorrow. And he didn't want to die. Who would want to die when living was so much fun?

Chapter 22

A Surprise for Mary

With July came the fulfillment of Lindy and Mary's wish — another baby in their house — one just as sweet as little Floyd. Mary had been to visit Grandma and Grandpop Creel. She sat playing in the yard with Patches when Daddy came to pick her up. He seemed extra happy, swinging her high in the air, then catching her in a bear hug as she came back down. Grandma and Grandpop watched them, their faces crinkled with smiles.

"Guess what, Mary?" her father teased. "Guess what's waitin' at home?"

Mary guessed and guessed. A new dress? A puppy? A kitten? Bud shook his head each time, laughter bubbling from his throat, eyes shining like Billy's clear blue, glass marbles. Finally he told her his secret. "It's a baby brother, Mary! A little baby brother! Six-and-a-half pounds of him."

Mary was so excited, she stuttered. "W-Where did you get him, Daddy? What's his name?"

Bud exploded with laughter. "Why, from Doc Hillman's old black bag, Mary. Don't you know that's where babies come from? And his name's Walter. How about that?"

Walter? Walter. Jesus would be better, but Walter would do, just as long as there was a baby. And she had been right. Doc Hillman did bring Floyd in the black bag!

"But, Daddy, where does Doc Hillman get the babies?" she asked. Grandma Creel came toward the truck, carrying Mary's small parcel of clothing. Bud remained speechless.

"From God, Mary!" Grandma answered for him. "We all come from God. Ain't that right, Bud?"

"Git in the truck, Mary," Bud ordered, subdued and angry. "If you want to see your new brother, we'd best hurry back home."

Grandma stood waving as they pulled out, a tiny pucker of a frown creasing her usually cheerful face.

Mary couldn't wait to get home. It seemed the truck crept slower and slower. Impatience swelled inside her until she thought she would burst. Another baby! And his name was Walter. She hoped he would be as sweet as Floyd — but not get sick and die like Floyd. God had once again answered her prayers. It had been a long, long time, forever, it seemed, but she'd just kept praying.

Miss Jenkins read in Sunday School class the story of a woman named Hannah who prayed for a baby, and about how God answered her prayers, but she'd had to wait. Remembering Hannah, Mary had waited, too. She was glad the wait was over. This was one time she wished she'd been home instead of at Grandma Creel's.

She would loved to have seen the look on Mama and Daddy's faces when Doc Hillman opened that black bag and handed the new baby to Mama. She bet her mother was really surprised. And Grandma Parsons would love having a baby on her lap when she rocked in her old chair. That was about all she did anymore, rock and sleep and read stories to Mary and Billy. She'd become so crippled she could hardly walk, even with her cane, and it was hard and painful for her twisted fingers to turn the pages of books as she read. Mary had to turn them for her.

Mary loved her Grandma Parsons, but she was so quarrelsome lately, she avoided her as much as possible. She hoped the new baby would cheer her grandmother up.

Chapter 23

Life and Death

Grandma Parsons never got to enjoy rocking Walter. Lindy found her in bed the next morning, life's warmth gone from her shrunken body. It seemed life was always traded for death. Lindy's joy over her baby mixed with sorrow.

She remembered how, on the day of Floyd's funeral, her mother had wished she could go on to be with her husband. Now her wish had been fulfilled. *Oh!* Lindy suddenly had a thought; she was with Floyd, too! She'd left part of her family to go be with others. Lindy would miss her mother, but was glad her rheumatism and pain were over.

After a while, Bud and Lindy moved into Grandma Parsons' little room with Walter, and Jewel was given their bed for her own. It felt strange to Mary to have her bed to herself. She would wake up at night, missing Jewel. Dark shadows moved about like strange creatures on the prowl. Mary pulled the covers tight around her neck and squeezed her eyes shut to keep out the scary visions, but dark shapes still loomed behind her eyelids.

Sometimes she'd get up enough courage to run from her bed to Jewel's, snuggling against her sister for comfort. Jewel never scolded Mary, but slipped an arm around her waist, snuggling her frightened sister's head beneath her chin. The night monsters slipped away, and Mary slept.

Chapter 24

Mary Goes to School

"Hold shhtill, Mary!" Lindy scolded, lisping around pins sticking from her mouth like porcupine quills. Mary tried, but the excitement of new school clothes made her wiggly and squirmy. Since early morning, she had stuck like a cocklebur close to her mother's side while she nursed little Walter and rocked him back to sleep, then began ripping out seams of the colorful, patterned feedsacks.

Lindy had saved the feedsacks all summer, washing and storing them on a shelf for the grand occasion of Mary's first year in school. Mary knelt on a chair by the kitchen table, watching her mother place the patterns this way and that on the narrow sacking, finally fitting all the pieces in.

The scissors flew, snipping through the material in record time. The table had been cleared for the noon meal, a welcome rest for Lindy's aching back, but Mary thought the meal would go on forever. Why did her mother have to be so slow in sipping her coffee? And why two cups?

At last, the second cup emptied, Lindy sat down at the treadle machine with instructions to Mary and Jewel to clear the table and begin the dishes. In the meantime, Walter woke from his nap and had to be changed, fed and tied in the little red rocker where he kicked and chewed at a wooden clothespin. Jewel called Mary time and again from her mother's side, back to her neglected chore of drying dishes.

Now at last Mary stood on the kitchen stool, turning slowly around so her mother could pin the last hem in place. Bud came through the door from his produce route, arms piled high with leftover vegetables. He whistled a long, low wolf whistle at Mary in Lindy's feedsack creation. "You'd best watch out, girl, or all the boys will be follerin' you home from school!" Blushing crimson at her father's good-natured ribbing, Mary fidgeted even more.

"Mary!" Lindy intoned. "Please hold still just a second. I'm almost through here." Sighing in relief, she thrust the last pin in place, then stood back and surveyed her handiwork with a critical eye.

Mary stood perfectly still, watching her mother's intent face for sign of approval. When a satisfied smile touched Lindy's lips, Mary jumped down and ran to the old broken mirror in the corner. Her usual melancholy memory of how the cracks had gotten there dissipated somewhat with the thrill of seeing herself in her new school dress. She couldn't remember ever before having anything that hadn't been passed down to her from Jewel.

Holding the full cotton skirt out by her sides, she twirled, watching her distorted image. The splintered reflection made her appear as if she needed to be put back together, like one of Mama's jigsaw puzzles.

Was she as pretty as Daddy said she was? Would the boys at school like her? Her arms fell to her sides. The whirling skirt collapsed around her skinny legs. She didn't think so. She was tall and skinny, not short and cute like Jewel. Her nose was big like Grandma Creel's. A large nose looked okay on Grandma. She was old and Mary thought she was beautiful anyway, and would love her no matter what she looked like, but she wished she had a button nose and curly hair like Jewel. She pulled a strand of her poker-straight hair over her shoulder. Mama usually braided it each morning to keep it from tangling.

"Well, sugars, Mary!" she would exclaim. "Have rats been sleepin' in your hair?" Mary shuddered. She'd seen the big, ugly rats scurrying through the trash dump, beady eyes and bristly gray fur sending shivers up and down her spine.

One good thing about getting taller than Jewel, though, she wouldn't have to wear hand-me-downs anymore. Now she could have dresses of her own, dresses never worn except by chicken feed that filled the sacks before Mama emptied them. When she went off to school she would be her own self, not a faded copy of her sister.

What would it be like to sit in the one room schoolhouse, learning reading, writing, and arithmetic? Would she be as smart as Jewel, or would she find things

86

hard to learn like Billy? Daddy said Billy was smart, but kept his smartness hidden beneath tomfoolery. Billy didn't like sitting still, unless he was fishing or watching for crawdads in the cool, shallow creek on warm spring days.

Lindy or Bud had punished Billy more than once for playing hooky. He soon learned to find excuses for staying home, waking up with a funny-sounding hoarseness or returning home wet and dirty from falling in a mudhole when they lived in the little rented house close to the school.

"Let's get that dress off, Mary," her mother said. "I guess you're all ready for school now."

Was she? Mary wiggled carefully out of the dress as Mama pulled it over her head. She was so excited, she didn't know how she could bear it until school started, yet so scared, she dreaded it, too.

Chapter 25

Lindy

Lindy dreaded Mary entering school. Her babies were growing up too fast. "Like weeds," she told Bud. "And some day, just like we pluck weeds outta the garden, some lovestruck young man or woman will pluck our young'uns right outta here and they'll take root somewhere else."

"But, don't forget, Lindy," Bud reminded her, "how them weeds spread when we ain't lookin'. Why, we'll have grandyoung'uns all around us in no time. This old house will be full!"

Lindy smiled. She certainly hoped so! But she'd better have more energy when the time came. She wanted to be a good grandmother, but she hardly had the energy to be a good mother.

Sighing, she headed toward the cellar for potatoes to peel for supper. She felt a little guilty thinking of how things might ease up when all her kids were in school. Still, she'd miss them something awful! And she wondered how Mary would adapt to her new environment.

"Aw! She'll do fine, Lindy," Bud told her when she voiced her uneasiness. "Mary's a smart young'un, You needn't worry about her!"

But it wasn't grades Lindy worried about. Mary was such a quiet, backward child. It would be very hard for her to make friends in school. And making friends was just as important as making good grades. Maybe more important.

Chapter 26

Mary Finds a Friend

Summer finally lazed its way into fall, and school began. Bud was right. Lindy discovered she had nothing to worry about. Mary liked nothing better than learning. The one-room schoolhouse held children from grades one through six, so Billy and Jewel were right there with Mary to make it easier. Even though she was shy, one little girl named Nella Borden singled her out, making it impossible for them not to become friends. Nella, short and chubby with a mass of golden curls framing her round face, was full of life and never seemed to stand still for a moment, a trait that kept her in constant trouble with the teacher.

Nella didn't learn as well as others, a fact that didn't seem to bother her at all. "Nella Marie Borden!" Mrs. Holstan would exclaim. "You don't hold still long enough for a new idea to settle down on you!"

Nella merely giggled and continued on in her whirlwind. Mary found out, after a few weeks of companionship, that Nella was an only child. Her father had been killed in the war. "But I can't remember him," Nella confided. "I wish I could, but I was too small when he died, and he wasn't home much after I was born."

Nella's green eyes clouded for an instant. Her full, pink mouth drooped. Mary wanted to put her arms around her friend, but backwardness tied them to her sides and froze her tongue.

Nella's remorse didn't last. Her eyes soon brightened like sun popping out from behind gray clouds. Running and giggling, she shouted for Mary to hurry and grab a swing before they were all taken. She jumped in the nearest one. Shoving with her feet, she pumped chubby legs until she flew high into the air, then swooped back toward earth.

Mary watched in admiration while waiting her turn for a swing. But before one could be relinquished, Nella put her feet down and skidded to a stop, running toward the school steps.

"C'mon, Mary, let's play jacks," she yelled, plopping down on the top step and scrabbling in a dress pocket for the ball and jacks. "You first!" she offered, grabbing Mary's hand and stacking the jacks in her open palm.

Mary studied the jacks scattered on the concrete stoop of the school building. She calculated the best way to play her hand, then threw the ball for the bounce. Swooping up her first set, she grabbed for the ball, but Nella snatched it from midair before Mary could catch it.

"Nella! What are you doing?" Mary yelled. "That was my ball!"

Nella's green eyes rounded with excitement. Leaning over, she whispered in her friend's ear. Mary turned and saw Leonard Freshour watching her. A group of boys stood around him, grinning and poking one another in the ribs. Mary turned beet-red from the collar of her dress to the top of her head.

"He likes you!" Nella teased.

"How do you know?" Mary retorted, cheeks burning.

Nella giggled. "'Cause! He's told everybody but you! Oh, here he comes!" she shrieked. Mary jumped up from the steps and took off around the schoolhouse, pigtails flying.

Leonard and his friends ran behind, laughing and teasing. Nella followed, skipping and giggling. The ribbons at the tips of Mary's braids fluttering in the wind proved too much of a temptation. Leonard reached out and snatched one, his friends cheering him on. The sudden stop jerked Mary backwards. Her head hit the ground with a jarring thump. Leonard stood over her wringing his hands, red hair tousled and chestnut eyes watery. Nella angrily shoved Leonard aside. Mary sat up, rubbing the swelling knot on the back of her head.

"I-I'm sorry," Leonard stammered. "I didn't mean to make you fall." Shoving a crumpled note into her hand, he flew away, subdued friends close on his heels. Mary tucked the note in her pocket, refusing Nella's request to see it.

"Oh, please, Mary! Pu-leeze!" Nella begged, jumping up and down, hands folded in petition. "C'mon! Read it and see what it says!"

"No!" Mary refused, hardly able to wait for the schoolbell to ring so she could read the note in privacy. Recess finally ended. The children trooped resignedly back into the school building. Shoving past them, Mary rushed to her seat. Pulling the note from her pocket, she smoothed it out on the desk. She colored red all over when she read, I LOVE YOU! scribbled in bold, crooked, crayon letters.

Leonard slid into his seat across the aisle. Mary sneaked a look his way. Grabbing up a book, Leonard sat with his head bowed over it, seemingly engrossed in the story. Sliding a sideways glance at Mary, he caught her looking. He smiled sheepishly, showing off a gap where a front tooth was missing. His blush caused the spatter of freckles on his face to stand out in vivid relief, matching carrot hair standing up in a cowlick at the crown of his head.

Mrs. Holstan rapped a ruler on her desk, causing Mary to nearly jump out of her seat. "And just why were you not in your place, young lady?" Mrs. Holstan asked.

Mary turned to see Nella scampering to her seat. "I'm sorry, Mrs. Holstan," Nella said, hand over her mouth to muffle giggles. She had read the note over Mary's shoulder! Feeling as if all eyes in the room had seen words meant just for her, Mary quickly folded the paper and stuffed it back into her pocket, hoping Mrs. Holstan wouldn't ask to see it. She felt her heart stop until the teacher turned to write on the blackboard. The staccato rhythm resumed, gaining speed and volume as she thought again of the bold, black letters.

He loves me! Waves of pleasure washed over her. Remembering her father's earlier prediction, she straightened from her habitual slump, pulling her braids over the shoulder closest to Leonard. Smoothing the plaits, she noticed a ribbon missing. Had she lost it when she fell?

Psst!

Mary looked in the direction of the sibilant whisper. Leonard's outstretched hand lay beneath the desktop. There

91

in his open palm curled the missing ribbon, wrinkled and dampened with sweat. Grinning at her, Leonard shoved his prize into a pant's pocket.

"Mary!" Mrs. Holstan repeated loudly. "Are you paying attention? I asked you to get out your primer."

Nella's giggles brought a warning frown to the teacher's brow. The afternoon dragged by until Mrs. Holstan dismissed school. Mary couldn't wait to get home and tell Mama she had a boyfriend, but she wasn't showing her love note to anyone — no matter how much Nella begged.

Lindy smiled at her daughter's good fortune, but she became more puzzled and frustrated each day as Mary's hair ribbons began to disappear and the sashes of her dresses had to be constantly re-stitched to ripped waists. She couldn't imagine what sort of games her usually subdued child joined in at school that kept her dresses torn and ribbons missing.

Love has its price. Mary was glad to part with the ribbons as long as Leonard grabbed her by the sash in the wild chase around the schoolyard, claiming a prize for his growing collection. Nella pouted, jealous that Leonard interrupted their recesses under the maple on the hill, where she and Mary played house.

Nella's Christmas doll with moving eyes and pink porcelain cheeks made Mary a little jealous herself. The doll was a painful reminder of Heidi, who lay headless in the shoebox at home. Her rubber doll with painted-on eyes, carried to school each day, seemed a poor substitute for beautiful Heidi.

Chapter 27

Secrets

Billy came rushing in the door after school one afternoon, too excited and out of breath to appreciate the aroma of baking cornbread. "Mama!" he yelled. "Mama! Where are you?"

Lindy turned from the stove. "I'm right here, Billy. No use to yell. I ain't deaf, you know." She poured brown beans from an iron pot into a bowl. Walter, tied in the little red chair, kicked his legs and whined for attention.

"Mama," Billy panted, ignoring Walter. "Marshall Crimmons wants me to spend Saturdays at his house. I can go home with him after school and spend the night, and they'll bring me back to Sunday School. Daddy won't have to take me or bring me back. Please, Mama, can I? Please?"

"You mean every Saturday, Billy? I don't know if we can let you do that." Lindy peered into the oven, checking the cornbread. It was a nice golden brown, with bacon fat sizzling around the edges.

"But, Mama! I got to! I just got to!"

"Billy, we need you here weekends to help with the work. You cain't just go traipsin' off to someone else's house. Besides, Mrs. Crimmons won't want you on her hands all the time." Cutting the hot, crispy cornbread into squares, Lindy piled them on a plate. Steam escaped into the air.

"She says it's fine, Mama. Marshall done ast her. And, Mama, Jewel said she'd trade chores with me. She'll do all mine on the weekend, and I'll do all hers through the week. Oh, please, Mama!"

"No, Billy! Put it outta your mind. It ain't gonna be!"

"Mama?" Jewel followed Billy through the door, Mary trailing behind. Placing her books on the table, she came to her mother's side, stretching up to whisper in her ear. Billy watched Lindy's face. Lindy looked at Billy in wonder, then at Mary, squatting down beside Walter in his little chair.

"Are you sure, Jewel? Mrs. Crimmons said it was all right with her?"

"I'm sure, Mama. You know Russell, Marshall's older brother? He talked to me at recess and said it was fine, that his mama said to tell you to not worry none at all about letting Billy come."

"Well, Billy, are you sure you'll do all Jewel's chores? She does an awful lot around here."

"Not all of them, Mama," Jewel said. "Just the chores out-of-doors, like feeding the chickens and weeding the garden and things. I'll still do my inside work." Billy's head bobbed up and down in agreement, eyes lit with expectancy.

Lindy smiled. "Well, we'll see. I'll have to talk to your daddy. Now get the table set, Jewel. Mary, you come help. Billy can watch Walter a while."

Bud arrived home shortly, standing over the enameled pan, washing up for supper. Lindy, warmth and secrecy shining from her eyes, held a whispered discussion with him. Bud looked astounded, then turned to Billy with a big smile. "So, Billy," he said, drying his hands on a towel, "I hear you want to spend the weekends with Marshall Crimmons. That right?"

"That's right, Daddy." Billy jumped up from Walter's side. Walter began to wail. Mary ran to him. Untying the diaper confining him to his chair, she lifted him free. Jewel watched her father, intent, listening expectantly to the whispered conversation between him and her brother.

"Well, I guess you can go, Billy. But you've got to keep your promise about the chores. You hear?"

"Yippee!" Billy yelled. Walter gurgled with glee, waving his arms in the air. Lindy smiled. Jewel smiled back.

"You mean Billy gets to stay every weekend, Mama?" Mary asked. "That's not fair! He won't be here for me to play with!"

"Now, Mary," Lindy admonished. "It won't be forever. Get your hands washed, you and Jewel, and you'all can eat while I feed Walter."

Mary's lower lip trembled, but she washed her hands and sat down at the table. Billy ate with enthusiasm, but she shoved food around on her plate, watching him with a frown.

The next weekend, at Sunday School, Mary stood waiting as the Crimmons' truck pulled into the church yard. Billy rode in the back with Marshall and Russell.

Cross and sleepy, Billy dozed a little through the devotional services. Mary sat on one side of her brother, Marshall on the other. She kept poking Billy to wake him until he jabbed her angrily with his elbow. She sniffled, and he dropped his head in shame. Pulling a stick of gum out of his pocket, he stuck it under her nose. She turned her head and smiled at him through tears. Billy smiled back, then laid his head back against the seat and closed his eyes once more while Mary unwrapped the gum.

"HALLELUJAH!"

Jolted awake, heart hammering, Billy saw Tom Hawkins, the town drunk reformed by religion, racing around the church, Bible held high in the air. Every few steps, he'd leap and shout again. Since his conversion, Tom had never missed a meeting. His face, once reddened and splotchy from his unhealthy habit, now shone with an inner light. He stood to his feet often, witnessing to the grace of God in his life.

Tom's Bible, worn from constant use, always rode under his arm. He could recite chapter after chapter from its pages without missing a word. His gentle wife sat watching him with tears and pride in her eyes. His children were better behaved and neater in appearance. Their eyes didn't look so hollow anymore and once-bare feet now sported new shoes, benefits from Tom's job of mailman, acquired when Mrs. Crooney's son relinquished the post.

"He's sure to make a preacher some day," Billy heard Grandpop Creel, seated in the row in front of them, speak in Grandma's ear.

Grandma Creel nodded sagely, pale blue feathers on the crown of her Sunday- meeting hat bobbing in silent agreement.

With the weather turning cool, all the Creels sat in the front of the truck on the way home from church, packed like canned sardines. Jewel sat between her mother and father. Mary sat on her lap. Lindy held Walter on one knee. Billy occupied the other, attempting to hold his weight off his mother's lap as much as possible. He had begged to ride in the back, but Lindy said no. "I'm afraid you'll get sick, Billy. It's too cold."

"But, Mama, I rode in the back of Marshall's truck here this morning, and I didn't get cold."

"That you did!" Lindy countered. "But that ain't the same kettle of stew. They don't have nearly as far to go as we do, and this is our truck, not theirs. I don't have say over their truck, but I do ours, and I say you ain't freezin' back there and comin' down with pneumonia. I don't want to hear no more or you'll not go to Marshall's again!"

Billy clamped his mouth shut. He didn't want to hurt his chances of staying the weekends with Marshall. He shifted his weight, holding on to the dash so that his mother's frail knees didn't bear the full weight of his body.

The truck had hardly quit rolling the first Sunday after Billy's overnight stay before he jerked open the door and jumped from his mother's lap, racing to the house like something wild chased at his heels. Rushing to his bed, he lifted the mattress, deposited his secret, and sank into a kitchen chair, all out of breath. When the rest of the family came through the door, Lindy smiled a secret smile at her son. His father patted him on the back.

"You're a good boy, Billy," Bud said. Jewel giggled, then refused to answer when Mary wanted to know what was so funny.

"Mind your own business, nosy Mary," Lindy said, smiling to soften the words.

Billy saw hurt in Mary's eyes. "C'mon, Mary. Let's go swing!" he invited.

"Billy!" Lindy yelled. "Not till you get outta them good Sunday clothes!"

Billy caught Mary's splintered reflection in the wardrobe as they hurried to change. Mary looked happier. Billy felt like he couldn't be happy unless she was happy. He thought about the boot box in the bottom drawer that held her doll. He never remembered the doll without guilt gnawing at him. He talked fast now to keep Mary from thinking about it, too.

Every once in a while, Mary took the box from the wardrobe and sat studying the dismembered doll. She never mentioned to her brother that he was to blame for Heidi being headless, but Billy didn't need anyone to remind him. He couldn't forget what his temper had done. It had been a hard lesson, but it had helped him learn better control. He only regretted that Mary had to be the object of the lesson.

Chapter 28

Heidi's Gone!

Slipping into an old dress, Mary took off her shoes, then hurried out the door with Billy, glad to have him home. Why did Mama and Daddy allow him the rare privilege of spending every Saturday night with his friend, Marshall?

When the Crimmons' truck pulled into the churchyard that morning, she saw Billy nudge Marshall in the ribs. He whispered some secret in his friend's ear that made them both grin and join in a friendly game of shoulder-punching until Mrs. Crimmons climbed from the cab and gave them a stern look.

Mary's badgering Billy about it proved useless. She gave up, spending the afternoon playing cowboys and Indians with him until Lindy called them in for supper. Their play had been greatly curtailed with her brother's weekend absences. Sometimes, at school, they joined in games of "Kick the Can," "Red Light-Green Light," or "Andy Over," but usually Billy and Mary went their separate ways. It felt good to have the afternoon together.

Mary's love for school woke her each morning with such an eager excitement she could hardly eat breakfast. While her mother combed her hair, she balanced impatiently on first one foot, then another. "Goodness, Mary! Do you have ants in your pants?" Lindy complained. "Now try not to lose these ribbons today. You hear?"

Mary tried to stand still, but it seemed like Mama braided slower and slower every morning. Now there were no more long and lonely days stretching ahead of her while Daddy dropped Billy and Jewel off at school in the Model T on his way to peddle produce. Walter had been some company, but napped most of the day, and Mama had always been busy with endless chores.

Mary loved the alphabet and putting words together in the school primer until a story emerged. She loved the smell of chalk and sweaty cloakrooms and the perfumed smell of Mrs. Holstan when the teacher bent over her desk to examine her work. She loved playing with Nella, but most of all, she loved Leonard and the chase around the schoolhouse at recess. Not one word ever passed between the two, but as their penmanship skills grew, the love notes that passed between them grew.

Another passion of Mary's school days was the construction paper and watercolors Mrs. Holstan supplied for art period. The paper had such a woodsy smell and Mary loved drawing and cutting and pasting. One afternoon after school, reaching for her sweater from the cloakroom hook, she noticed a pile of the paper on a top shelf. Such beautiful colors! And such a big stack! She looked around and found no one else in the cloakroom with her. Grabbing a few sheets from the top of the pile, she shoved them into her tablet.

That evening, Mary sat in the floor cutting colored chains and gluing them in a circle to place over Walter's neck. "Where'd you get the paper, honey?" her mother asked Mary glanced at Jewel, who sat engrossed in a book. Billy frowned over homework at the kitchen table. "Mrs. Holstan let me have it," she answered in a quiet voice. What she took was hardly noticeable. Mary was sure it wouldn't matter. There was such a big stack of the colorful paper. The next day, she slipped a few more sheets in her tablet, and the next day a few more. Mama never questioned her about it again.

Time flew as September chased warm days into chilly October, and October with its cool breezes and colorful leaves caught up with November. Mary awoke one morning to see snow everywhere, covering fallen leaves with a pure white blanket. Winter winds blew drifts across the road, piling them high against the barn and farmhouse.

Lindy stuffed Mary and Billy into snowsuits and tugged mittens and boots on their hands and feet. Bud had to stop his Model T in the middle of the road on the way to school to shovel a path through the occasional high drifts while Mary and Billy and Jewel pelted each other with snowballs, laughing and running through the white, wonderful world.

Snow always brought a feeling of Christmas in the air. Mary sat one evening at the kitchen table, laboriously printing a letter to Santa Claus, the radio tuned to a station where Santa read letters from wishful boys and girls.

"Ho! Ho!" Santa Claus bellowed in a deep gruff voice that reminded Mary of Grandpop Creel. "Have all you boys and girls out there in radio land been good girls and boys this year?" he asked. "Have you helped your parents and not told a lie or took anything that wasn't yours?"

Mary cringed. She had tried hard to help her mother, and she wanted to be good, but sometimes she forgot. Had she told lies or took anything that wasn't hers? She sucked in her breath with sudden remembering. The candy she'd sneaked into her dress pocket at Mr. Cranshaw's store that spring when the storeowner and Mama were busy with her order! It was just a small piece, but it seemed to grow bigger and bigger until it weighted her dress down. She was sure Mama and Daddy could see the telltale bulge of her pocket in the truck on the way home.

When they reached the house, Lindy carried Walter inside while Bud hoisted the chicken feed to his shoulders and stored it in the woodshed. Mary threw the evidence of her sin in the creek. It floated away from sight, but her guilt didn't float away with it. She hoped a fish ate it up before anyone saw it.

And the construction paper! She had stolen it, and then lied to her mother about where she got it. Several sheets rested now inside her tablet. She slid it beneath her primer, looking around to see if Mama watched. Lindy sat sewing, paying no attention.

"Remember, boys and girls, lying and stealing is a bad thing to do, and Santa is watching you. So you'd better be good!" The radio seemed to have eyes, boring through the books and discovering the paper hidden beneath them. Mary finished her letter, hoping Santa wasn't aware of her sins. After all, there were a lot of children out there. Just in case, though, she wouldn't take any more papers. And she would take what she had back to school and return it to the stack on the shelf first thing in the morning.

Before Mary had a chance to replace the paper the next morning, Mrs. Holstan walked into the cloakroom. "Mary," she asked, "do you know who's been helping themselves to the supplies?" Mary flushed bright red. Before she could stop herself, she shook her head.

"Well, Mary, the paper has been disappearing," Mrs. Holstan told her. "Can you tell me why?"

"Nella." Mary's throat was so dry the name came out in a squeak. She couldn't believe she'd said it.

"Who?" Mrs. Holstan asked.

Mary wanted to confess, but her courage failed. Mrs. Holstan waited, arms crossed over an ample bosom, tapping a ruler against her cheek. Mary answered once again with her chin on her chest, "Nella took it."

"Are you sure, Mary?" the inevitable question made Mary break out in sweat. Now's your chance, something seemed to say. She raised her head and looked into Mrs. Holstan's eyes, but the traitorous words jumped right off the tip of her tongue before she could bite them back.

"Yes, I'm sure. See, she even gave me some." Mary pulled the papers from her tablet and handed them to the teacher. She tried to relieve some of her guilt by excusing Nella's thievery. "She didn't know it was wrong, Mrs. Holstan. She thought you wouldn't care since there was so much paper. She just loved to have it to work with at home."

The teacher stood looking at Mary for a long moment, holding the proffered paper. Her eyes softening, she sighed, handing Mary a few sheets before sliding the others back on the shelf. "Mary, if everyone took all the paper they wanted, we wouldn't have enough for all the students. Do you understand?" Mary nodded. Tears ran down her cheeks.

"I'm going to have to talk to Nella about this," the teacher warned. "You know I have to, don't you?" Cold shock ran over Mary. Her tongue, so quick to betray her friend only seconds before, now stubbornly refused to voice her repentance and free Nella of suspicion.

That night, the usual joy of cutting and pasting had disappeared, fleeing with Mary's honesty. She sneaked the paper back the next day, even though the teacher had given it to her, but she couldn't bring herself to reveal her dishonesty to Mrs. Holstan. Nella glared at her from teary eyes at recess, refusing to play. Mary ran to hide behind the girl's toilet, wishing she had the nerve to confess.

Mary eventually won back Nella's friendship by sharing her elderberry jelly-and-butter biscuit with her each day, but guilt still stabbed her now and then, especially when she heard Santa ask his question over the radio, "Have you been good girls and boys today?" She reasoned that if she worked real hard at being good from now on, Santa would know how sorry she was and bring her the gifts on her list. Maybe he wasn't even as all-knowing as everyone claimed. This thought eased her guilt.

But that weekend when Miss Jenkins taught the Sunday School class about the Ten Commandments, Mary's guilt ballooned again. "Thou shalt not steal" stood out above all the rest. When the teacher also explained the meaning of bearing false witness, Nella's look of accusation turned Mary's cheeks fiery red. She was so ashamed of what she'd done, she went up front right after class and confessed.

"Mary, I'm glad you told me, but don't you think you should tell someone else?" Miss Jenkins coaxed.

Mary slowly nodded her head, numb with embarrassment. Hurrying out the door, she ran to Nella. Nella's forgiving spirit made things right between them, but Mary knew she had to clear her friend with Mrs. Holstan, no matter how difficult her confession. She went first thing in the morning to the teacher.

"I'm proud of you, Mary," Mrs. Holstan said. Squeezed against the teacher's full bosom, Mary inhaled a wonderful, deep breath of lovely perfume.

"I suspected you took the papers," Mrs. Holstan said, "and when I talked to Nella, I knew so. She was so hurt because you had betrayed her. Just remember, Mary, 'What a wicked web we weave when first we practice to deceive.' We weave the web with our falsehoods, then are caught up in our own trap."

Mary would never lie again. Never! Or steal. She went home that night and wrote another letter to Santa with a lot of XXX's and OOO's after her name. She admitted her sins, but explained how she had made everything right. She carried the letter to the mailbox with a promise in her heart that if her Christmas wish were granted, she'd be doubly good next year. She knew Santa Claus had a big workshop with lots of hardworking elves, but she wasn't sure they knew what Heidi looked like. She would be satisfied if they came close, but she would never forget Heidi or throw away the body that lay in the shoebox.

Mary raised the flag and hurried back to the house to open the wardrobe for one more look at Heidi. The box wasn't there! "Mama!" she cried. "Heidi's gone!" Her mother seemed to have no idea what had happened to the box, or even seemed concerned with Mary's loss. "What good was the doll anyway, without a head?" she asked, drying Mary's tears with the corner of her apron.

"But, Mama," Mary sobbed, "I wanted to keep her forever and ever."

Lindy sighed and rubbed Mary's back. After supper, she sent Billy and Jewel outdoors for a while.

"You stay, Mary," she ordered. "I want to talk to you." Kneeling down by Mary's side, she said, "Honey, I know you wrote to Santa, but there's someone else you need to believe in. Don't you know Jesus is the one who forgives sin? If you do somethin' wrong, He's the one you should tell you're sorry."

Mary was crestfallen. She didn't know why Mama was telling her this, but she was right. If God had given the Ten Commandments and then gave His Son for anyone who broke them, she should ask Jesus to forgive her. She nodded her head, and she and Lindy bowed their heads together.

Afterwards, Lindy patted Mary gently on the shoulder. "If you ever do wrong, Mary, straighten it out quick. Then ask Jesus to forgive you. He will, but you mustn't be doin' that wrong again. If you're really sorry, you'll try hard not to."

I will try! Mary told herself. I'll try real hard.

Chapter 29

Redemption

The wait for Christmas seemed interminable, but the holiday arrived at last with a flurry of baking and cleaning, tantalizing smells, secrets, and laughter. Spicy pine, cinnamon scents, and joy filled the Creel home, a great change from the sad year before when the raw memory of Floyd's death dimmed the candles and lessened the appetites. Walter was just beginning to crawl. It took everyone's attention to keep him from overturning the fragrant, heavily decorated tree or getting too near the hot, crackling fire.

Christmas Eve passed by on sluggish feet, taunting those trying their best to tightly shut their eyes and force themselves to sleep. Billy tossed with excitement, impatient for morning to arrive, feeling as if he would pop if he couldn't hurry and share his long-kept secret with Mary. He watched the flickering shadows of the fire joyfully dance the hours away. At last he slumbered. Shushed giggles, rustlings of paper, clink of cup and saucer, and aroma of hot coffee from the next room never penetrated his deep dreams or those of his sleeping sisters.

Listening to Grandma read the Christmas story the next morning, Billy squirmed until his mother reached out and tweaked his ear. He tried harder to listen, but experienced relief when everyone bowed their heads for prayer. This time he waited and let Mary be the first to see the tree and the gifts around its base. He noticed her disappointment as her eyes fell upon the blackboard with her name chalked on it.

Mary sat with a frozen smile on her face while Jewel squealed over a silvered mirror and brush. Billy loaded his cap guns, filling the air with loud bangs and the acrid smell of gunpowder until demanded to holster them. A sheriff's star gleamed brightly from his shirtfront. His chest had swelled when his father pinned on the badge of honor.

Walter gooed over a rubber frog whose buggy eyes just fit his drooling mouth, and Lindy kissed Bud on the cheek in appreciation for the new cake tins and housedress. Grandma Creel unwrapped a new teakettle, and she in turn handed Grandpop a new shiny axe, purchased with her cache of egg money.

When the last gift had been opened, Billy ran to the kitchen. Hurrying back with a package tied with red ribbon, the wrapping slightly askew, with an overabundance of tape, he handed it to Mary as proudly as if it were wrapped in gold wrappings with silver ribbons. She stared at it with a puzzled look. "Go ahead, Mary. Open it! See," he said shyly, pointing to the nametag, "it's to you from me!"

"Open it, Mary! Quick!" Jewel giggled with excitement. Everyone's faces beamed as they watched Mary tear the wrappings away, exposing the boot box that had disappeared from the wardrobe. She looked up at Billy with a puzzled frown.

"C'mon, Mary!" Billy jumped up and down with suspense. "Hurry up and open the box."

Mary lifted the lid. She caught her breath. Heidi reposed on a layer of white tissue paper, whole and beautiful, eyelids closed on smooth cheeks. How could Billy have fixed the doll so well? Not a crack showed on the china face. Mama must have helped him. Mary looked up at her mother with a question in her eyes.

"Billy bought the new doll head for your doll, Mary," Lindy explained. "He spent his Saturdays makin' money helpin' Marshall clean and stock Mr. Cranshaw's shelves."

Mary turned and looked at Billy. A smile stretched the width of his freckled face, displaying the gap where a tooth was missing. "I — I — saw an ad — advertisement in one of Mama's catalogs," he stammered with a mixture of pride and embarrassment. "This company sold doll parts to repair broken dolls, and one looked just like Heidi. I wanted to get it for you because I broke her. Daddy sent my money away and Mama wired the head back on."

Mary wanted to run and hug Billy, but timidity glued her to the floor. She smiled at him through happy tears, forgiving him completely for destroying Heidi. The doll

105

looked new, more precious than ever for having been lost for a while. Maybe that explained why Walter was so special to all of them. Walter could never replace Floyd, but his being there sure helped.

Grandpop's gravelly voice intoned a blessing on the food at the breakfast table. Mary added her own special thanks to God for Heidi and for Walter. She hoped she got to keep the new doll forever — and Walter, too.

Mary could hardly wait to show Heidi to Nella. She was so proud of Billy for his efforts to redeem himself. Mary decided she needed to make amends with Nella for the terrible accusations made about her. How could she enjoy Heidi when she didn't deserve her? She promised herself that when school began again after Christmas, she would let Nella be the first to play with her doll. Until then she would keep her safely wrapped in the boot box — just in case.

A spasm of coughing interrupted Lindy's dinner. She excused herself after the meal, lying down to rest while Jewel and Mary cleared the table and washed the dishes. She slept for a while. When she awoke, Mary sat across the room in an upholstered horsehair chair, watching her.

Lindy managed a weak smile. "I feel better now," she said. "Trying to keep Walter out of everything and helpin' with all the Christmas doin's has just plumb wore me out."

Mary sat, quiet as a mouse, in the rose-colored chair with Heidi in the box on her lap. Subdued clatter of dishes from the kitchen mingled with Jewel and Grandma Creel's laughter. Grandpop and Daddy sat in the next room, drinking coffee and eating pumpkin pie. The low murmur of conversation floated though the doorway.

Lindy beckoned for Mary. Climbing down from the chair and into the bed, she curled in her mother's arms. Lindy held her with a fierce possessiveness that frightened Mary.

Walter came crawling into the room, the rubber frog dangling from his mouth, eyes wide, searching for his mother. Laughing, Lindy pulled him up into the bed.

"Mama," Mary whispered, squeaking Walter's frog, "are you gonna get up now?"

"In a minute, Mary," Lindy whispered back. "Right now I just want to lay here for a while and hold my precious young'uns."

Mary snuggled close to her mother. Walter lay beside her, blue eyes looking up into his mother's face. Reaching a little hand up, he touched her cheek.

"Bud! Bud!" Lindy cried, startling Mary and frightening Walter so badly he began to wail. Bud ran into the room, Grandpop behind him. Grandma Creel and Jewel followed close on their heels. Billy's capguns could be heard going off on the back porch. "Feel Walter's hands," she insisted. "Do they feel hot to you?"

Bud placed a gentle, callused hand on Walter's hands, then his forehead. His troubled eyes met Lindy's, and she began to cry.

Chapter 30

Sorrow Renewed

Even though he knew the children sat on the front stoop listening to him, Bud couldn't hold back harsh sobs raking his throat. Walter became congested shortly after Christmas. Bud took no chances this time. He called Doc Hillman out right away. The doctor gave Lindy liquid medicines and chest rubs with implicit instructions for Walter's care. The baby seemed to improve with the arrival of spring and summer, but Walter found it difficult to breathe in the hot humid air of August.

Doc didn't want to take any chances either. He instructed Bud and Lindy to take the baby to the St. Clair Hospital in the city. Lindy sent Bud after Corie to stay with the other children. Anxiety shone in her black eyes as she stood watching him drive the truck away down the dusty hill.

At the hospital, Lindy refused to leave Walter's side. Bud returned home to ask Corie to stay on a little while. She complied without complaint. Just a few days later, Bud and Lindy made a second long trip home from St. Clair, their dead baby lying in the morgue in preparation for burial.

Lindy wiped away Bud's tears in infinite tenderness, her own eyes dry from shock. She had prayed for the baby. Why had God not answered her prayers? Corie worked quietly in the background, polishing and scrubbing the already spotless house, expression unreadable. Smells of bleach and polish mixed with aromas of fresh-cooked pintos, cabbage, and cornbread that no one had an appetite to eat.

Doc followed Bud and Lindy in from the hospital as soon as he could get away. He now sat mutely by, pulling at his drooping mustache, looking helpless and drained. Bud knew the doctor had done his best, but sometimes best just wasn't good enough.

"Why, Doc? Why?" Bud questioned angrily. He knew deep down the doctor wasn't to blame, but he had to vent his anger on someone. It was only a few days past Walter's first birthday.

Doc rose from his chair, sighing deeply. His dragging steps took him to the window overlooking the hills beyond the house. Gray, dirty clouds, bloated and heavy with rain, obscured their crest. The relentless dry heat of the summer before had not returned, but a sultry humidity lay low in the damp air, making breathing a chore. Lindy's labored breaths filled the silence left by Bud's anguished question.

Doc turned and spoke hesitantly. "I have no answer for your question, Bud, but how's about we get an autopsy on the little one?"

Seeing the start of angry shock on Lindy's face, Doc rode right over her unvoiced disapproval. "Now, now, Lindy, I know it's a hard thing, but think for a minute. Maybe there's a link between Floyd's death and this one's. If you plan to try again, wouldn't it be good if we knew what we're facing?"

Bud looked at Lindy. Her tortured expression knotted his insides. He knew what she was seeing, the same as he-the tiny, precious baby sliced asunder, the sanctity of Walter's little body invaded by a cruel knife and probing hands. Yet he had to agree with the doctor. Best to know before the next time. He didn't think he could bear this kind of grief again. For sure, he wanted to spare Lindy of it.

A fit of coughing shook Lindy. She crossed to the screen door and spat into the yard. Bud could see the children watching her with fear in their eyes. He knew he should go to them, give them some comfort, but he sat unmoving. Lindy returned to his side.

"Lindy, honey, it's whatever you say," Bud left the decision to his pale, trembling wife, "but I think maybe Doc's right. We cain't afford to let this happen again if it can be helped." Lindy's tears erupted. Bud knew she would let them cut her own heart out if the frail, still little form they had left at the hospital could be well and at home again.

"How can I give him up to bein' cut apart and pieced together like an old cloth?" she cried, bent double with grief.

Suddenly Corie spoke. "Yea, though I walk through the valley of the shadow of death, thou art with me," she recited in a monotone voice, staring at Lindy with a direct gaze. Then she resumed polishing. The other three occupants of the room stared at her for a long, charged moment.

Lindy's body seemed to deflate. She nodded at Doc Hillman. "All right," she choked in a small voice, then turned and buried her head in Bud's shoulder. Her sobs set off another spasm of coughing.

Bud could feel the violent trembling of his wife's slight form. Her hair falling against his cheek smelled fresh and clean.

Chapter 31

A Hint of More to Come

A nasty suspicion had been shoving its way into Doc's mind. Lindy's cough opened the door wide to let it in. He hesitated for a moment, then decided he'd better wait until he had the results of the little one's autopsy. No use piling more grief on the Creels than they could handle.

He patted Lindy on the shoulder, then glumly shook hands with Bud. Weariness and despair sapped his strength. At times like this, he wished he'd stayed on in the drugstore like his father wanted him to. Saving lives was a wonderful thing, a gift from God, but the ones death snatched from his hands were a mighty hard burden to bear.

"Bud," he said before leaving the house, "Lindy's still got a nasty cough. I'll give her some cough syrup for it, but as soon as she's up to it, I'd like you to bring her in to my office. Has she had this cough since I doctored her last?"

"Off and on," Bud answered. "Seems winter brings it back, and all the dampness in the air ain't helped her none this year. I told her she should see you, but she said it was just a bad cold and she would soon shake it."

"That's probably all it is," Doc replied, "but we'd best see that it's taken care of. All right, Bud?"

"Sure, Doc. I'll see she comes in, soon's the funeral's over and she can stand the trip."

Doc dreaded going past the children on the porch. When he opened the screen door, they all turned and looked at him. The sad questioning in their eyes let him know they were fully aware of every word that had been spoken.

"Bye, now, young'uns," he said as he descended the steps. His eyes searched for the spot where Lindy spat. He saw what he dreaded seeing — sputum tinged with flecks of blood. With dragging steps, he approached the green sedan. Climbing into the car, he waved dispiritedly at the sad trio sitting side by side on the porch stoop in the muggy August heat. The image of their solemn faces haunted him all the way back to St. Clair Hospital.

Chapter 32

The Proverbial Straw

Doc stood by the graveside, studying Lindy, attempting to determine her inner strength. Worry lines creased his brow. How could he tell this broken woman his suspicions? The stoutest soul could only bear so much sorrow, and sorrow seemed to be stacking up on the Creels. He tugged at his mustache, turning his attention from Lindy and the tiny casket to the roiling pewter sky.

The storm threatened to break, swelling clouds promising relief from the sweltering heat, yet pushing the humidity down until the air was suffocating. Doc ran a finger around his starched white collar, rubbing sweat from his prickly neck. Others stood about wiping perspiration from wet faces with sodden handkerchiefs. Doc hoped the storm held off until this sad affair was over. A downpour would only add to already dampened spirits, and the narrow creek that ran below the Creel's farmhouse would overflow, blocking everyone in until it dropped. He knew from past experience that Bud and Lindy would just want to be alone after the funeral.

His gaze returned to Lindy. She was a bright woman, despite her lack of education. Had she suspected what he left unspoken? He mentally kicked himself for not being aware of the first baby's problem and not putting more importance on Lindy's frequent colds. He was sure now, having the facts and looking back, that the same disease that had invaded this little one's body, snuffing out life before it could have even a good-sized taste of it, had caused the raging fever and coughing spells in little Floyd.

How would Bud cope? Lindy would probably have to be institutionalized and, even though Bud or none of the other children showed any symptoms, it was possible they were all infected.

"Lord, spare them a little of this old world's troubles," Doc prayed as the preacher intoned, Ashes to ashes and dust to dust. "Let at least Bud and the other three young'uns be well. And give Lindy and Bud fighting spirits. They're both going to need it for what they'll have to go through, if I'm right and Lindy has been the carrier."

Lindy's soft weeping blended with her occasional cough and the clearing of throats of the other mourners. Spades of dirt falling into the grave onto the lowered casket thudded loudly in the silence of the brooding storm.

"The Lord giveth and the Lord taketh away. Blessed be the name of the Lord." Pastor Crookshank ended the service with a prayer. Bud gently helped Lindy to her feet. Doc didn't always understand God. Why would He give something and then take it away, just when you were real attached to it? Was there reasoning in all this?

Everyone returned to the house in muted conversation, watchful eyes turned toward Lindy, who stumbled blindly between Bud and Floyd. The oppressive, weighted clouds, suddenly split by a loud crack of thunder, opened up, adding their weeping to the day. Great drops of liquid spattered the dry ground as the mourners rushed to the house to escape the sudden deluge.

The house proved hot and suffocating, humid outside air forced in by the storm. Bud and Corie began closing windows against the rain, allowing space to let in cooler air.

Doc watched sheets of rain streaming down the windows. Did all of heaven cry with them over the dead baby? Corie passed by him to shut the last window. That was one good thing that had come from the Creel's sorrow. Corie Parsons had put aside some of her cantankerous attitude and had begun to show an awkward tenderness that seemed foreign to her personality. Doc helped her with the stubborn window. A slight grimace touched her face. He interpreted it as a grateful smile.

Bud came toward him, hands in his pockets and a lick of black hair, plastered flat with dampness, escaping down his forehead. "Bud," Doc spoke in an undertone, "I've got to leave soon. I want you to bring Lindy in as soon as you're able." He fidgeted with his mustache, twirling one end in a tight corkscrew. "I don't know how to say this, and I hate to say it now or ever, but you'd best make it tomorrow. It could be she's the source of the babies' sickness."

Bud stood staring at him, water dripping from his hair. He turned and looked at Lindy, then back at Doc. Doc saw the disbelief in his eyes, then watched his face crumple.

"No, Doc!" Bud choked. "Not Lindy! Say it ain't so. I cain't take no more of this. I just cain't take no more!"

He leaned with one hand against the wall, shaking his head. Slamming the flat of his hand against the wall, he walked out the door into the pouring rain. Lindy saw him go. She jumped up from her chair, puzzled and concerned, watching her husband disappear around the house.

Chapter 33

Broken Hearts

Lindy stood by the truck cab watching as Bud slung the cheap suitcase, purchased from Ben Franklin's Five and Dime, into the bed. He looped a piece of baling twine through the handle and then around the spare tire to keep the suitcase from sliding around on the long trip to the Beckley Sanitarium. Mary, Billy, and Jewel stood side by side, faces glum. Lindy knew, by the redness of their eyes, that they had all spent a greater part of the night in tears.

How hard this must be on my babies! she thought. What will happen to them? There's so much work to be done, and Jewel only ten. Bud leans on me more'n the kids sometimes. And how will I ever stand bein' separated from my little family? Hot tears blurred her vision. She promised herself she wouldn't cry, then broke the promise. How could a person bear the pain of a broken heart without tears?

Turning from his task, Bud saw the tears streaming down his wife's face. "Aw, Lindy!" he moaned. He took her in his arms. The children began sobbing and ran to their mother's side, throwing their arms around her waist. Bud opened up his arms and gathered them all in. Lindy was afraid—more afraid than she'd ever been in her life. Please, God. I don't want to leave my young'uns, she prayed. They need me! Please keep them safe and let me come back home to them real soon.

A spasm of coughing shook her body. Bud tightened his grip around her and the children. She knew he fought tears of his own. His eyes were black hollows, his cheeks pale. The future looked so bleak and hopeless. How would Bud manage? He'd have to divide himself between the sanitarium, the children, the farm, and his produce run. He always depended on her to keep things going — too much, sometimes, she thought. How would he cope if something happened to her? Where would he find the strength?

Lindy's thought evoked a memory of a scripture Pastor Crookshank had based his sermon on the last Sunday she had been able to attend services. "My help cometh from the Lord . . . ."

But Bud hadn't heard the sermon, and He didn't know God like she knew Him. His rebellion built prison bars around his heart that kept God on the outside. But Lindy knew God's love could melt those bars of hatred and resentment so that His Holy Spirit could walk right in and rescue her husband. She would spend her lonely days praying for that and for her children.

The truck crawled down the hill, seeming almost reluctant itself to carry her away. Lindy waved to the three brave soldiers until they were more than out of sight. The picture she would carry in her mind during her convalescence was one of six arms waving high into the air, sweet flags of love and hope, and Corie's face peeking through her lace curtains. Faithful, irascible Corie.

Chapter 34

Comfort

The fall and winter following Lindy's confinement had been bleak at the Creel's home. Inclement weather interrupted regular visits to the sanitarium. But spring finally came and then summer. It was now autumn again, and Mary was spending a weekend at Grandma and Grandpop Creel's. She walked close by her grandmother's side through the woods, daydreaming about Leonard. Summer had been long and lonely before school began.

Mary and her grandmother had been up before the sun that morning, getting necessary chores done so that they could have time to go in search of piquant fox grapes growing wild in the woods behind the house. The skies, a spectacular vastness of gentian blue, boasted small tufts of clouds floating free and lazy. The spongy forest floor yielded up a pungent, woodsy odor beneath the feet of the old woman and her sedate, dreamy granddaughter. Strident calls of blue jay and chattering of chipmunks only added to the peace of the autumn morning.

An abrupt chatter of a squirrel sounded from a tall poplar. Before Mary could sight the creature, Grandma stooped to the ground, grabbed a rock and sent it sailing through the air. The squirrel seemed frozen for a moment, only its bushy red tail quivering, then toppled from its perch and fell with a thud.

"There!" Grandma Creel exclaimed, standing with her hands on her hips, surveying the creature lying on the ground. "That'll teach ya to bark at me, ya varmint! I'll make you into squirrel stew."

Mary stood awestruck, staring at the patch of blood staining the back of the furry creature's head. Grandma turned to Mary, her face beaming with pride. "Well, c'mon, child! Don't just stand there starin'. Go git your supper!"

Mary ran toward the fallen squirrel. A flash of black and white hurtled past her. Patches had begun the walk with them, but then soon wandered off on his own, snuffing at the ground in his joyous search of something to chase. Close by, he had heard the squirrel's shrill chatter.

Grandma chuckled. Her pet carried the squirrel to her. A grin stretched on each side of his catch. His tail beat the brush around him. She stooped and patted the old dog's head. "You're a fine boy, Patches! Yessiree!" she bragged.

The dog's tail increased to full speed. His tongue licked the hand of his owner. Mary wondered if Patches might not live on forever. His youthful puppy spirit belied his age. The threesome headed home, Grandma carrying the squirrel by its bushy tail in one hand, a bucketful of fox grapes in the other. Mary carried a basket filled to the top with more grapes. The sheen of tan hickory nuts peeked out beneath purple pods.

The meaty smell of the squirrel stew laced with herbs and fresh garden vegetables simmering on the old black wood stove made Mary's mouth water in happy anticipation. She peeled sweet onions and sliced juicy ripe tomatoes. Rows of gleaming jars filled with jelly from their day's picking lined the utility table in the corner. The deep purples contrasted pleasingly with a red-and-white checkered oilcloth. A hickory-nut cake sat cooling on the windowsill.

Grandma Creel expertly flipped hot corn cakes to a delectable golden crispness in bacon fat spooned into a crusted iron skillet. She hummed as she worked, and her humming in the homey kitchen made Mary wish she could live with her Grandma and Grandpop Creel forever.

Home wasn't the same at Mary's house since her mother had been hospitalized. Her father had lost his joy in life. He moped around the house and hardly ever whistled or sang anymore or teased Jewel and Mary like he used to. He'd lost interest in fishing, staying home more often instead of rising early to peddle his vegetables.

When he did go out, he usually came home with the rancid smell of liquor on his breath, something Mary had never before experienced. It made her think of Tom Hawkins before his conversion. She began to pray more earnestly for her father.

If only Mama could get well and come home! Mary thought. Things just weren't the same without her. It seemed her father was lost. They all felt a little lost. Home just wasn't home anymore.

Billy and his father had begun to bicker between themselves at times, and Jewel had become silent and tired, burdened down with all the responsibilities. Mary and Billy helped some, but no one could turn out the work their mother had. Mary often wondered how her mother had managed so well when all the time she'd been so sick. Aunt Corie and Uncle Floyd had tried to help at first, but rarely visited anymore. Her father's sour reception and bitter attitude scared off any visitors.

Each time they visited the sanitarium, Mary's mother cried when they left, promising them she'd be home soon. She said if it weren't for the fact that she was afraid of infecting the rest of them, she'd just walk right out of there and come on home anyway. "No such thing!" Daddy replied. He wanted her well.

Patches' joyful barking put an end to Mary's sad reflections. Grandpop Creel came through the door with his lunch bucket in his hand. He worked hard at the lumber mill, but was whistling and smiling as he winked at Mary and went over to Grandma to plant a kiss on her wrinkled cheek. Mary blushed, but it was a good blushing. She wished she could see Mama and Daddy once again showing their love for one another.

"Child, whatever in the world are you so solemn about?" Grandpop asked, bending down, gnarled hands resting on his knees, tilting his head back to look at her through thick bifocals.

Mary jumped up and threw her arms around her grandfather's neck. Grandpop rubbed a bristly cheek against hers, then handed her his lunch pail. He watched with humor in his eyes as she opened it to see what was hidden inside.

Grabbing a fistful of penny bubble gum, Mary squealed in delight. Then she kissed her grandfather's bearded cheek.

"Land sakes, Dad!" Grandma Creel chided him. "You keep on and you'll spoil that child." But Mary knew by the soft way her eyes looked at him that she really didn't mind.

"Umm! What's that I smell?" Grandpop asked, sniffing the aroma of squirrel stew and cake.

"Hickory-nut cake, Grandpop! And squirrel stew!" Mary giggled. "Grandma knocked a squirrel clean out of a tree with a big rock!"

Grandpop chuckled. "Well, Mary," he said, "you never know what you'll come home to for supper with a fine woman like your Grandma." He gave his wife a swat on her backside. She jumped around from her frying pan, threatening him playfully with her spatula.

"Behave yourself, old man," she admonished. "Git your hands washed for supper. You, too, child."

Grandpop and Mary went giggling to the washstand on the porch. Mary's heart swelled, nearly bursting with the love she felt for her grandparents. Her times with them created fond memories to carry back to her dismal home.

"Grandpop," she whispered, "I'd like to live here forever. Really I would!"

Grandpop looked down at her from his height. Despite his grin, something in his eyes looked like a hurting. "Mary," he said," always remember this. When things git too bad, call on the Lord. He'll help you right good if you'll let Him. He's helped me and your grandma many a time, and everyone knows from His words in the Good Book that He has a special love for little childern."

Tears spilled over from Mary's eyes. Grandpop took the towel from her hands and dabbed at her wet cheeks. "Things'll git better, honey. They's bound to. Jest be good and say your prayers and trust in the Good Lord."

"What're you two doin' out there?" Grandma called from the kitchen. "This squirrel'll be comin' alive and eatin' up the nuts in the cake if you don't hurry and git in here!"

Mary giggled hysterically. Shaking his head, Grandpop chuckled. It sure was hard to stay sad around Grandma. She never let problems rob her of the joy of living.

After supper, Grandpop reared back in his chair and patted his stomach. "Wasn't that a fine supper, Mary?" he asked. "Sure was, Grandpop," Mary agreed. It was about the best supper she'd ever eaten — almost good enough to make her not mind washing up the dishes.

Chapter 35

Miss Jenkins

Miss Jenkins noticed Mary's growing sadness. The child, now nine years old, absorbed Sunday School lessons with a seriousness the other children didn't show. I wonder, she contemplated, if it's time?

She prayed that week for God's guidance, then stood waiting outside the church the next Sunday morning when the Creel children climbed from their father's truck. Bud had never failed to fulfill Mary's request at the train station the year of his return from the war. He made sure the children were in Sunday School whenever possible.

"Good morning, Mr. Creel!" Miss Jenkins greeted Bud. "Won't you join us for Sunday School today?" Mary looked up hopefully at her father.

"Thanks anyway," Bud replied. "I ain't dressed for the occasion and the fish should be jumping outta the creek for worms today. Our supplies are running low. Maybe some other time."

Mary's face fell.

"How's your wife?" Miss Jenkins asked.

"'Bout the same," Bud answered flatly. "Went to see her yesterday. She's pretty low in spirits. She's missing her family sumpthin' awful."

"I'm sure she is, Mr. Creel. We've been praying for her recovery." She paused, looking thoughtful. "Mr. Creel?" she ventured. "We're starting a revival — a tent revival — in the baseball field tonight. Won't you please come and bring the children? We'd love to have you."

"Oh, please, Daddy!" Mary begged. "I've never been to a tent revival. Can't we come?"

Jewel and Billy chimed in with Mary. Bud, fidgeting, looked angrily away. "We'll see," he spoke curtly. The church bell pealed out a welcome. "Now you'd best hurry to your seats," Bud said. "You don't want to be causing a ruckus going in late."

"Good day, Mr. Creel." Miss Jenkins put her arm around Mary's shoulder, walking with her toward the church. A motor revved. Tires spun angrily in loose gravel. She turned to see the set expression on Bud's face as he made a hurried and indignant exit. He didn't even return his parents' greeting as they passed him in the driveway.

In Sunday School class that morning Miss Jenkins read John 3:16, then carefully explained the plan of salvation to her little group of children. She told them how being good wasn't enough, about the shepherd and the sheep, and how Jesus was the Good Shepherd and the Door of the sheepfold. "We are all God's sheep, and the only way to Him is through the Door, His Son Jesus Christ," she explained.

She saw a growing awareness in Mary's eyes. She left class that morning with assurance that the time was indeed right. But she would have to be patient and let the Holy Spirit do his work in the child's heart.

That night Miss Jenkins watched the gathering congregation with anxious eyes, but the service began without the Creel's vehicle pulling into the field. Swallowing disappointment, she opened her hymnbook and joined the singing. Music soared on the night air, causing the sawing of crickets to pause for a moment, as if the insects listened.

Mosquitoes had a tasty feast that night, but no one seemed to mind. Only one soul was out of tune with the wave of joy passing through the little congregation. Miss Jenkins could hardly keep her mind on the service for thinking about Mary and the destitute situation of the Creel family. They had been plagued with problems that would have brought many a heart down. She wondered how Bud Creel bore them without looking for strength from God.

Tears streamed down the teacher's face as she knelt in the sawdust during prayer, pouring out her heart to God. She prayed not only for Lindy's healing, but also for Bud's redemption and that of his little brood. Little Mary was especially on her mind.

Billy's spirits seemed not too dampened by his mother's absence and his father's growing addiction. On Sunday mornings he and Marshall Crimmons kept up their usual shoulder-jabbing and giggly whispering, until they earned painful tweaks on their ears by Marshall's mother.

Jewel sang in the choir each Sunday and helped keep the young ones in order. She was developing a responsible, calm maturity that attested to the authoritative position she'd had to assume in the motherless Creel household. The Creels' problems had forced her into early adulthood. At twelve years of age, she seemed as capable as any young mother in the church, perhaps more than some. Responsibility lay well on Jewel's adolescent shoulders. She didn't mourn her position, but stoically accepted it as her duty.

Mary seemed most affected by her mother's absence and the emotional distance and moral upheaval of her father. The little girl's emotions, Miss Jenkins felt, ran deep. The child became more withdrawn and despondent as the months of her mother's convalescence passed.

When the call came that night for special prayer requests, Grandpop asked the congregation to remember his daughter-in-law for healing. Miss Jenkins beseeched the church to also pray for Bud's heart to be softened. She left the tent at the end of the service with a heavy heart, but was intercepted on the way to her car by a tug on her arm.

"Miss," Tom Hawkins spoke kindly, awkwardly fingering the leaves of his Bible, "don't lose sight of your faith. Why, look what God has done for me! My woman prayed for many a year before I lost my stubbornness and turned in the right direction for help. It might take time, but we'll just keep praying, and Bud'll see the light. Sometimes it takes a heap of troubles for a man to sit up and take notice of where he is in life. Just maybe God will use the troubles old Satan's flung at Bud to wake him up to his need."

Miss Jenkins shook her head in doubt. "I spoke to him this morning. He seems so hard! I think he blames God for everything that's happened to him."

"Well, prayer has softened many a hard heart, little lady. We're praying, all the good people of Victory Church are praying. Now that's a lot of prayer! I don't reckon as how any man's heart can withstand all that softening, do you?"

Tom's lopsided grin filled Miss Jenkins with an assurance, lifting doubt. "Of course! You're right, Tom. Thank you for reminding me of the Lord's mercy and grace." Shaking Tom's hand, she fairly waltzed to her car.

Miss Jenkins marveled at the change in Tom Hawkins. At one time, she would have feared the man. She knew that his family had many an occasion to fear him. But, oh, how he'd repented of his awful deeds! And the change in his family was evidence of the change in his soul. If God could do that for a habitual drunkard like Tom, why, converting that gentle Bud Creel should be an easy task!

Miss Jenkins fell in bed that night, exhausted but at peace, after entreating God on the behalf of Bud Creel and his three children. She lay with a scripture of hope, Hebrews 11:1, on her mind, *Now faith is the substance of things hoped for, the evidence of things not seen.* She hoped for Bud Creel's salvation, along with little Mary and Billy and Jewel's. She hoped for their presence in the tent revival as a family. Her faith would become substance, if only she believed, and the evidence of her prayers would be seen if she didn't let up. Miss Jenkins smiled and snuggled a little deeper into her pillow.

Chapter 36

Bud and Mary

The evening progressed entirely the opposite in the Creel household than in Miss Jenkins' house. Bud Creel lay sleepless and miserable. He tossed and turned for what seemed hours, worrying over his problems, worse than a toothless hound worried a bone, but he could see no solution to his misery.

He finally gave up, slipping stealthily from his bed and out the door, grimacing at the lament of rusty hinges giving away his exit. He headed toward the barn where a hidden supply of whiskey called out to his thirst for forgetfulness. He needed the fiery, numbing brew to burn his problems from his mind. Only then could he sleep.

Mary lay awake, thinking about what Miss Jenkins had taught them in Sunday School that morning. The lesson had buried itself deep in her heart and nibbled at her off and on all day. She had been praying for her daddy to find God, never realizing she needed an experience with Him herself. She had always loved God and tried to be good, but now she knew she had to dedicate herself to Him through faith in Jesus and His death for her.

She wanted to become one of Jesus' little sheep. She had always thought He died only for those who didn't love God and were wicked and mean, but now she knew no one could be good enough to go to heaven. Only Jesus could be the way through His death on the cross and His resurrection.

She wanted so much to attend the tent revival, but Daddy had cut short her pleadings, telling her he didn't want to hear her mention it again. She heard the complaining of the door hinges and knew where he headed. Turning her face to her pillow, she muffled her sobs. Oh, how she wished Mama could come home! Daddy was always so happy before she left, even with all his problems. It was like Mama was his sunshine and, without her light, he couldn't see his way around the things that fretted him.

Mary heard feet padding across the linoleum. She tried in vain to hold back the tears. Jewel slipped into bed beside her, pulling her close with a smothered sigh. Without a word, she smoothed Mary's hair back and stroked her forehead until exhaustion overcame sorrow and she slept.

Out in the barn, Bud couldn't sleep. Thoughts raced through his mind like bugling hounds, hot on the trail of prey, twisting and turning this way and that until he felt he'd go crazy with their frenzy. He lay against a bale of hay, chasing the worry-hounds with gurgling swigs of whiskey.

He worried about Lindy, so many miles away, and her sickness he felt so responsible for. She'd had a hard life, so much to do on the farm keeping her worn down. He'd known she didn't really want to move back there when he'd come home from the war, but he'd put his wants ahead of hers. The sick babies kept her from resting at nights and worried her through the days.

He hadn't been much use to her until she'd already lost her strength. She blamed herself for the boys' deaths, and he guessed she had passed her sickness on to them, but he didn't hold her accountable for it. The guilt was all his. He should have seen to it that she had an easier life, should have been better to her, helped her more.

He couldn't forget how he'd shrugged off her pleas for calling out Doc Hillman for poor little Floyd. That was something he'd never forgive himself for. Maybe calling Doc sooner couldn't have helped. It didn't save Walter, but at least he could fall asleep at night without the ugly guilt eating at his insides like a half-starved animal.

How he was to manage the medical bills? Or the power and food bills? He owed Mr. Cranshaw a small fortune, and he kept slipping behind on his power bill, not to mention the gasoline needed to visit Lindy. He didn't get to see her nearly as much as he'd like, still his debt to the gas station was piling up like heavy winter snows in a blizzard.

And the work on the farm kept slipping behind. Jewel was just what her name implied. She never complained, just like her mama, and did all she could, but with school and homework and all, it wasn't enough. Billy and Mary helped, but their small efforts barely dented the mountain of work.

How did Lindy ever manage to get so much done? He sure hadn't appreciated her enough. He mightily hoped he'd get a second chance with her. But the way his luck had run in the past, he held little hope for her recovery. Seems God had it in for him. And then that highfalutin' Sunday School teacher with her prissy ways had the gall to invite him to a tent revival! When did she think he'd find the time, even if he had a hankering to go, which he didn't! He tilted the bottle higher, draining the last dregs from its recesses.

The liquor finally accomplished Bud's intentions and lulled the worry-hounds to sleep. He slept with them, snoring loudly to comforting sounds of the milk cow in her stall. But he slept too deeply and too late. Jewel was up the next morning before him, and she knew where to find him. She had known since that terrible morning when he hadn't been in his bed, and Billy had stumbled over him in the dark barn.

Bud tried after that to stop his drinking but, despite his vows, turned more and more to the traitorous comfort of the bottle. He felt shame for his sullen, snappish ways, but couldn't seem to control his feelings. Billy often became the brunt of his bad humor, taking up his slack and bearing up under his faultfinding.

Jewel carried on in her quiet, efficient way, doing what she could. Bud knew he had shocked and shamed her that first morning when she'd followed a white-faced Billy back to the barn and found him sprawled among the hay and empty bottles. But she never said a word. She merely accustomed herself to the changes in him and acted as if things were as normal as ever.

It was Mary who made him feel guilty. She cried each time he failed in his struggle with his drinking. Mrs. Holstan sent home a note once saying that she wasn't keeping up with her work. Mary sits staring out the window most of the time, like she sees things we can't see, the note said. Bud never went to see the teacher, afraid of what she'd suspect. He was glad she couldn't see what Mary was most likely seeing. His shame was bad enough. Mary's sad, reproachful eyes shot arrows of remorse through his heart every morning when he returned from the barn. He'd vow to himself he'd never go near the bottle again, but always broke his promise.

Jewel had slipped into the barn early that morning, shaking him awake. He felt as if he'd spent the night on the cold, hard floor of a cave with a family of disgruntled bears.

Bud stretched and yawned, a foul taste gagging him. He staggered to his feet, holding his hammering head. Cursing the strident crow of the cock that had at one time encouraged his singing, he kicked at it when it crossed his path, sending the indignant fowl squawking across the yard.

He was glad when he'd dropped the kids off at school. Now he could go back to the quietness of the house. The jarring ruts of the road pained his head till he could hardly see to drive.

Coasting down the steep hill, the truck backfired, adding to his misery. Yet the silence of the children on the way to school had seemed louder to him than the backfire of the Model T, paining his heart.

Parking the truck, Bud headed toward the house. He hadn't been a good husband and now he couldn't be a good father. He slammed the screen door with a vengeance he immediately regretted. Sinking down in Lindy's old rocker, he sobbed until he was all cried out.

The sun's rays lengthened across the linoleum. He decided he'd better shake off his gloom and make some use of the day, and the best use he knew was a letter to Lindy, a good long letter telling her they were all fit as fiddles. No use fretting her with things she couldn't help.

Bud sat at the kitchen table laboriously printing out recent happenings. Finishing the letter, he foraged through a cigar box for a stamp, licked it and pressed it to the corner of the envelope. He missed his woman so much, but he guessed it would be a long time before she could be at home with him and the kids, even if she did get well. This last thought sent a shiver of fear riding down his backbone.

Chapter 37

Bud and Tom

Finishing his letter, Bud looked up at the kitchen clock. Where had the morning gone? Seems he never had time anymore for things needing done. He hurried from the house toward the mailbox, hoping to beat Tom before he happened along to pick up the mail, but the sound of the government vehicle pulling the hill below the farm let him know he hadn't made it in time. He picked up his pace, each step setting off a pounding in his head.

He didn't want to meet up with Tom this morning. He'd skipped breakfast and was still in rumpled clothes from the night before. Bits of hay clung to his uncombed hair, and his eyes were bloodshot and swollen. Besides, he was in no mood to listen to Tom Hawkins' spiel about what the Lord had done for him when He'd saved him from the bottle.

"Ain't nuthin' to it!" mumbled Bud, hurriedly shoving the letter into the box, slamming the lid shut and raising the flag with an angry jerk. "He just got scared when he thought God was speaking to him. Thinking a voice was coming down outta the blue would sober up the drunkest man. He's a hypocrite, just like that proper talking Miss Jenkins."

Bud tilted his nose in the air and wiggled woman-fashion as he turned back from the mailbox. "Won't you join us for the service this morning, Mr. Creel?" he imitated the teacher in a falsetto voice. "Her and her almighty ways! Sitting in Sunday School, singing and praying to a God who couldn't care less what happens to the lot of us. Wait till troubles come her way and then see how loud she'll sing or how low she'll bow!"

In his angry reverie, Bud couldn't remember if he'd raised the flag. Hurrying back to check, he saw Tom's jeep coming around the curve, stirring up plumes of dust. Resisting an urge to run, he forced himself to walk calmly toward the house, ignoring the jeep as it skidded to a stop at the mailbox.

Tom stuck his head out the window, yelling a good-natured greeting at the top of his lungs. "Good morning!"

The lusty greeting set off fireworks inside Bud's brain. Growling beneath his breath, he continued on his way with a curt, backward wave of his hand, but Tom wasn't about to be daunted in his mission. He called again. "Wait up, Bud! I want a word with you."

Bud couldn't have suffered more if Tom had turned a washtub upside down over his head and pounded it with a splitting mall. Gritting his teeth in pain and frustration, he turned back toward the jeep. Tom's ear-to-ear smile burned his chest with savage fury.

"What in this whole wide miserable world does that man have to be so happy about?" he growled. "I oughtta shove my fist right through the window and knock that silly smile off his foolish face!" Getting a grip on his emotions by the time he reached the jeep, he stood glaring in silence at the beaming mailman, not bothering to return his greeting.

Undaunted, smile firmly in face, Tom held out the stack of mail. He couldn't help but notice Bud's disheveled appearance. A sour scent of overnight whiskey and rancid body odor wafted through the window. Tom's heart went out to the man. No one could know any better than he how rotten a next-morning hangover could be.

"Glad I caught you, Bud." Tom tried to act as if nothing were out of the ordinary. "I've been meaning to have a talk with you. Listen, how's about coming down to our tent meeting some night? Had a good service last night."

"Haven't got time!" The abrupt answer cut Tom short. Bud sifted through his mail. Just what he had expected! Some advertising circulars — as if he had any money to spare on foolishness — and three bills. At least there was a letter from Lindy. He held the coveted letter in his hand, but jammed the rest of the mail into his hip pocket.

Bud knew the power bill was behind, and the feed bill was long past due. The third one from the gas station, he guessed, was a demand for payment on the hefty deficit. He'd already cut down on his trips to see Lindy, but still the bill crept up to gigantic proportions, even with his parents taking turns driving to the sanitarium. Having to ration his visits to Lindy only added to his guilt and increased his hatred toward God.

"Bud, listen," Tom spoke kindly, climbing from the jeep and crouching on the roadbank. He felt animosity from the brooding man like a brewing storm, but he sent up a silent petition to One who had never failed him. He would just open his mouth and let God fill it. "Bud, I know things have been bad for you. And I also know you've taken to drinking. But take it from a first class fool that's woke up to his foolishness, there's no help nor hope in that bottle. You need hope, Bud. Hope comes from God. And you need help. Help comes through God and His people."

"Oh, yeah?" Bud shot back. "Where was God when my two young'uns died? Where was God when Lindy got sent off to that sanitarium, leaving behind her three young'uns that need her so bad? And where's God when I cain't pay these bills?"

Bud last question ended in a yell. He yanked the envelopes from his hip pocket and shoved them under Tom's nose. "God ain't helped me yet with help nor hope nor money, but at least when I get good and soused I can forget my misery for a while!"

Tom didn't flinch. "But that's just for a while, Bud. Tell me, when you get over your hangover, do you find your heartache over your boys eased any, or do you have any more hope for Lindy's cure, or does what you spend on that sour mash pay your bills? I know liquor don't come free. I've wasted lots of money my family needed on that foul stuff."

"So? I'm so far in debt now a little more cain't hurt. And how's going to church gonna heal Lindy or bring back my boys or bring in money to pay the bills? Tell me that!"

"It might not, Bud. I'm sure it cain't bring back your boys, but you could go to meet 'em some day. And you could trust God for Lindy's healing. No, it won't pay your bills, but then again, sometimes a touch from God can bring about a lot of good things. Why, look at me! Since I've accepted the Lord and quit the bottle, I've got this good job, and my family is happier. My health is better, too."

"And you think God gave you your job, do ya?" Bud spat in derision.

"Not think, Bud. Know! Know for a certainty. And that's not all He's given me. More'n I could ever tell you. Most of all, peace of mind and riddance of a lot of guilt. Why, I sleep like a baby at nights now!"

Bud jumped up. "I sleep fine!" he protested a little too loudly, forgetting his headache. He stuffed the bills back into his pocket. "I got no guilt. If there's a God, He's responsible for all my problems. Not me!" He waggled his finger in Tom's face and hissed, "I don't never want to hear such talk from you again! Hear me? If you want to stop and pass the time of day, fine, but don't be givin' me words that are as useless as a water trough full of holes. I ain't got time for such nonsense!"

Bud stomped off toward the house, once more aware of the explosion inside his head. In his anger, he didn't notice the piece of mail fluttering to the ground, fallen from his back pocket.

But Tom noticed. He picked it up, ready to call Bud's attention to his loss, but a flash of inspiration hit him. He smiled once again as he tucked the bill from the Eckhart Gas Station in his shirt pocket. He climbed back into the jeep, whistling a merry tune as he continued on his way, jouncing over the country road to his next stop.

Tom could hardly wait to put his plan into action and witness the outcome. It sure wasn't Satan's imp who had sat on his shoulder and whispered the idea in his ear. Nope! He knew just where the idea had come from. And he knew it wouldn't backfire. But it sure might be a test of his patience to wait for the results.

The remainder of Tom's route flew by in record time as he occupied his mind with prayers and thoughts of Bud and his little batch of children. Hadn't he told Bud that God gave help through His people? That's where they had failed. Their prayers had been sincere, but they'd neglected to put legs on them. Just how far could an amputee prayer get? With a little nudge from God, he'd been reminded of that fact, and he meant to make sure those prayers were equipped with stout legs that would run to accomplish their task.

"Just be patient with me, Lord," Tom prayed. "I'm a mite new at this, but I'm willing to learn. I sure am willing to learn!" Stopping off on his route at the home of Bud's parents, he had a good long discussion with them about their son and his little family. Loaded with facts and figures, he continued on his way, stopping here and there on his mail route to hold a discussion with various individuals. The last person he talked to was Pastor Crookshank. He departed his presence with a good warm handshake and a warm happiness bubbling up from deep down within.

Chapter 38

Love Conquers

Tom arrived at the tent meeting a little early that evening, leaving his wife and children sitting on the folding chairs while he took Pastor Crookshank aside for a private conversation. After an emotional, spirit-filled service, the visiting evangelist delivered a soul-stirring message of God's love and judgment.

Marshall Crimmons' older brother, Russell, couldn't wait for the sermon to end. He left his seat and ran for the altar. His move seemed to unglue his father's feet from the sawdust floor. Mr. Crimmons followed, crying his heart out.

The service ended with a lot of backslapping and hugging and tears, especially between Mrs. Crimmons and her new husband and son. Marshall was proud of his father and brother, but his bashfulness and fear held him in the back of the tent with his head buried in a songbook as if it were the most interesting book he'd ever encountered.

Before closing the service, Pastor Crookshank made an announcement of Bud's financial needs, then passed the offering plate. Men and women dug into their pockets, piling the plate high with hard-earned money. Not many had much to spare, but they were willing to tighten their belts for a neighbor in need. Miss Jenkins, deciding to forego the new dress she'd been eyeing in the latest Sear's catalog, doubled her usual weekly contribution.

Some, a little more affluent, dropped a more substantial donation into the plate. When the amount was tallied and announced, Grandpop Creel hugged his wife and blinked his eyes. Tears flowed into his white beard.

The next morning, Tom was out early before heading to the post office to begin his route. He pulled up to Eckhart's Service Station with Mr. Creel's bill in his pocket. "Didn't open this, Clyde," he stated, "so I don't know what's inside, but you know what Bud Creel owes you, and I'm here in behalf of the Victory Church of Rushin' Creek to clear the debt. And whatever the total is on the bill inside this envelope, I want to add another ten dollars over and above that to Bud's credit, so he can go see his wife a little more often without the worry of where the money's comin' from."

With gas prices what they were, ten dollars would go a long way toward pleasing Lindy with her family's visits. Tom jumped back into his jeep with crusty old Mr. Eckhart staring after him in awe. He made another stop at the Cranshaw store, where the bill was paid and another ten dollars allowance added by a delighted Mr. Cranshaw.

"Tom, I'm ashamed it took a young Christian like you to make a veteran like me realize the church's responsibility toward Bud. I've prayed for the man for years, but I never gave a thought to supplying his need. The Good Book says where two or three agree, it'll be done. How's about you and me kneeling right down here on this old floor — watch your britches. I oiled it this mornin' against the dust — and agreeing that Bud will make it out to our revival?"

Two women, who had never attended Victory Church, or any other for that matter, happened into the store. They looked at each other in amazement. Two grown men on their knees right in the middle of a business establishment in the middle of the day, talking out loud to God? What was the world coming to?

Tom's last stop was the feed store. Then he began his mail route, pulling up at Bud's mailbox singing so loudly that anyone within a half mile could benefit from his rendition.

"I must tell Jesus all of my trials. I cannot bear these burdens alone." Tom opened the box and shoved in the mail, then topped the pile with a fat envelope addressed to Bud Creel from Friends at the Victory Church. Bold capital letters underneath declared, *GOD LOVES YOU!*

Pulling out from the mailbox, Tom continued on his way with, "Jesus saves! Jesus saves!" riding through the air on joyful waves, traveling right up to Bud, hoeing the garden. The chords pierced Bud's heart, cutting like a knife. The earlier rendition of Tom's "I Must Tell Jesus" had caused him to strike so hard at the earth with the hoe, the handle splintered in two.

His temper flared and he cursed bitterly, flinging the broken hoe across the garden, crushing a tomato plant in the process. He stomped furiously down the road to the mailbox, tears of exasperation streaming down his face. He had reached the bottom of hopelessness. Despair settled down like dark, oppressive clouds just before a cloudburst as he opened the lid to the box that was sure to bring more unpaid bills and no hope. The words of Tom's song rang over and over in his mind. "Jesus saves! Jesus saves!" "I must tell Jesus. I must tell Jesus. I cannot bear these burdens alone."

The improvement in Tom's life was evident. Could there maybe be something in what the man said? Had God changed his life and turned it around? Yet Lindy had trusted God and what had it got her? Nothing but trouble. "If there's a God He'll have to show me He cares!" Bud mumbled. "I've not seen any sign of that yet."

Retrieving his mail from the box, he noticed the fat envelope, with no stamp or postmark. The inscription, *GOD LOVES YOU*, leapt out at him, an almost audible reply to his challenge. Ripping the envelope open with trembling fingers, he found a large wad of bills wrapped in a yellow piece of paper, more money than he'd seen at one time in his life. He opened the paper, finding it to be his lost gasoline statement.

"So that's where it went!" he whispered. He knew he had taken it from the mailbox the day before, but when he missed it and retraced his steps, he assumed the wind had blown it away. He had bid it good riddance. He knew he couldn't pay it anyway. The bill was now marked, "Paid in Full", and even more to his amazement, his account was credited with ten dollars toward further gasoline.

Two other papers lay folded on top of the stack of money. He found one to be a receipt from the Cranshaw's Grocery, also marked paid in full with ten dollars to his good. The third receipt from the feed store stated the same. He sank to the ground, completely drained of strength. He slowly counted the bills, then recounted them.

One hundred dollars! And his three largest bills paid! Why! He could pay up the electric before they shut it off and get in some much needed groceries, have gas to visit Lindy, and — and money left over!

Bud jumped up, energy renewed. He rushed toward the house. He would go to town right now! No, first he'd write Lindy — no, no — he'd take the kids out of school!

Yes! That's what he'd do. He'd get the groceries today, keep the kids out of school tomorrow and go tell Lindy the good news in person. His mind jumped from one thought to another. Then he heard the sputter of an automobile around the bend, dancing over the rutted road from the neighbor's mailbox.

"Praise Him! Praise Him!" Tom's exuberant song floated over the fields. Bud recalled his contrary thoughts on the way to the mailbox. "Show me, God!" he had declared. He stopped short in his tracks, the money clenched in his sweating fist. He remembered his exact words, *If there's a God, He'll have to show me He cares!*

Bud began to sob, trudging slowly and thoughtfully toward the house. He stood before the cracked mirror of the wardrobe, staring at his broken image. That's how he felt, all torn apart, broken, and in pieces. Could God make him whole? He opened the wardrobe and laid out the best clothes he had. He shined his shoes while water heated for a bath.

When Bud arrived after school to pick up the children, they could hardly believe their ears. He told them they would have to hurry if they wanted to finish their chores in time to attend the tent meeting that night. The chores were accomplished in record time.

Chapter 39

A Promise Broken

Bud's apprehension sent butterflies flitting through his stomach. He backed his battered truck in between neighbors' vehicles parked in the revival field. His heart thudding against his ribs seemed loud enough for the children to detect. Even though he had driven the truck into the creek after supper and washed off the accumulation of dust, it still was the worst looking vehicle there.

The tent flaps were rolled up to let in the cool evening air. Bud was dismayed to see the seats almost filled, though it wasn't time for the service to begin. He had come early, hoping to find a seat unnoticed before the crowd arrived. Turning off the engine, he scowled as the muffler announced their arrival with a loud, belching backfire.

Heads swiveled and eyes bulged in unbelief at the sight of Bud Creel sitting in the truck in his Sunday best, black hair slicked down with pomade.

The children piled out, skipping and running toward the tent. Pastor Crookshank came toward the truck. Bud's nerve left him. He slid down in the seat. He could see Grandpop and Grandma Creel waving and smiling from their seats. Miss Jenkins sat near them. Her pleased expression infuriated him.

"Welcome, Mr. Creel!" the pastor extended a large hand. "We're so glad you've come!"

Bud pretended not to see the hand, studying the steering wheel with red-faced concentration as if the words he searched for might be scratched in the worn black enamel. "Didn't come to attend the service, Pastor," he lied, backing down from his earlier resolve.

He just couldn't face that crowd gathered inside the tent, knowing they were aware of his poverty and had contributed to his need. He was grateful for their help, but felt lower than a whipped dog's tail in the humiliation of not being able to provide for his own. He swallowed the lump of pride in his throat that threatened to choke him.

"I just wanted to let the church know how grateful I am for your care of me and mine," he said. "I'll pay back ever cent soon as I'm able. I wouldn't even accept it, but my kids, they got needs I just cain't meet right now."

"Of course, Mr. Creel. We understand. We all come to a place where we need help at some time or other. But the money is yours free and clear, a gift from the Good Lord. It's not a loan. We couldn't accept a penny of it back. But we would like for you to attend our service tonight."

Tom Hawkins approached the truck with his Bible in his hand. Delight overflowed his face, splitting it in two with that perpetual grin. Bud's face reddened. He fought the tempting impulse to roll up the window in order to cut off the man's cheerful greeting. Foolsome smile! he thought. No one can always be that happy!

Continuing his inspection of the interior of the truck cab, studying the gas gauge and speedometer in consternation, he ignored the postman's outstretched hand. Tom, a little flustered, retained his smile and spoke heartily. "Glad you came, Bud!"

"Well, I see there comes our evangelist," Pastor Crookshank said. Excusing himself, he hurried across the field toward a car coming into view.

"Better get out and grab a seat, Bud," Tom offered. "They're filling up mighty quick."

"Tom." Bud gritted his teeth. "I didn't come to take part in the service. Mary's heart was set on coming, and Billy and Jewel kept after me, too." His finger traced haphazard patterns in the dust on the dash. "I know you had a big part in seeing I got the money." He slid a sideways glance at Tom. The big smile, beaming brighter, spread rancor through him.

Was that smile frozen on the man's face? Couldn't he just once not look so all-fired happy? Irritation increased Bud's pressure on the steering wheel. He jumped as the horn

140

blared. Tom's smile turned into a startled expression. Heads swiveled once again inside the tent.

Mary watched the exchange between her father and Tom with anxious eyes. A cloud of sawdust stirred by her nervous scuffing settled over her highly polished shoes. Grandma Creel reached out and caught her granddaughter's hand in a gesture of comfort.

Miss Jenkins' eyes closed in what Bud figured was supplication. A flush crept up his neck above his stiffly starched shirt collar and traveled on up into his hair. How he wished he'd stayed at home!

He could go now, but the kids would be disappointed. Why didn't Tom leave? The accidental blare of the horn had accomplished one good thing. It had wiped the silly smile right off the man's face for a split second. Bud fought the insane urge to lay on the horn once more. Better not. He'd made enough of a fool of himself for one night.

It'd be the last, though. No matter how much the young'uns harped on coming back, he wouldn't give in to their whining again. With an effort, he thanked Tom for his thoughtfulness and repeated his rejection of the offer to join the congregation.

"I'll just wait right here for my young'uns," he said. "It'll give me a chance to snooze a little. I've had a hard day." He rested his head against the seat back, hoping Tom would take the hint and leave.

Tom thought to offer to bring the children home after the service, but an invisible hand seemed to close over his mouth, stifling his proposal. A knowing smile touched his lips. "Sorry, Lord," he murmured. "Of course, You're right!"

"What's that?" Bud asked.

"Hrumph!" Tom cleared his throat and extended his hand once more. "Nothin', Bud. Just thinking out loud. Well, I hope we don't get too loud for ya to get that nap."

Bud didn't like the twinkle in Tom's eye. Hardly able to ignore the outstretched hand, he reluctantly shook it, unprepared for the electrical warmth of the grip. He slid lower in his seat, hoping to force an end to the visit. Tom turned toward the tent, whistling, "Jesus saves! Jesus saves!" so cheerfully that frogs in the nearby creek seemed to take up the tune.

Bud imagined the echo of the song in the frogs' chorus until he rolled up his windows in frustration, but the sound carried too well on the evening air. Soon the murmur of worship heightened, floating out over the field to cover the frogs' imitation of Tom's song. Bud feigned sleep, wishing it was later in the year so darkness would fall around him. He could still see rebuke on his children's faces with his eyes shut. His misery worsened as the interminable minutes stretched into unbearable lengths.

He finally opened the door quietly in the gathering dusk, slipping from the truck and through the maze of vehicles to the creek where he crouched on a rock, watching soft beams of a rising moon brush the waters with golden ripples. A light warm wind arose, stirring willows overhead. The music of wind through swaying fronds and singing waters lulled Bud's mind from his plight and drowned the preacher's message. He felt the deepest peace he'd known since he'd taken Lindy away.

Bud remembered his plans for the next day. He had seen the teacher at the service. He would corner her right after the amens were said and let her know he would be keeping the kids out of school. Skies burning with flames of red just after the sun dropped from sight promised fair weather on the morrow, and he intended to make good use of it. Stretching out on the warm rock with his hands locked behind his head, he made plans for the anticipated trip.

They'd all get up early the next morning and get the chores out of the way, then drop by the North Pole Ice House before heading toward Beckley. The old tub filled with chunks of ice would chill one of the best watermelons in the patch. Jewel could pack a picnic lunch with slices of salted ham hanging in the smokehouse.

They'd swing by Cranshaw's and pick up some Orange Crush and those little twin chocolate cakes Mary liked so well with white icing swirled all pretty around the top. Bud smiled and shifted on the rock. He might even go really generous and have Mr. Cranshaw throw in some Three Musketeer bars. His kids deserved a little relief from the eternal skimping.

"Ah, Lindy!" he whispered, sighing with pleasure. A mosquito whined near his ear, and he smacked at it, chuckling at the thought of Lindy's reaction to their windfall. He could just see her face. She was the same as he, so stubbornly independent, but he felt sure she'd swallow her pride for the children's sake, even if it did go against the grain somewhat.

Muted sounds from the tent suddenly exploded into shouts carrying all the way to the creek, silencing the frogs and covering the murmur of ripples washing over the rocks. Bud's mind was drawn from his musing. Curiosity led him up the creekbank in the darkness. The sight he saw stopped him dead in his tracks. His little Mary stood before the altar with the congregation gathered around her, each hugging her in turn, shouting and praising God.

Miss Jenkins stood on one side, softly clapping her hands, her head raised, gazing in rapture toward the roof of the tent. Tears streamed down her face. Jewel and Grandma Creel flanked Mary's other side, smiling through their tears.

Billy and Nella sat near them on the front row. Billy kicked up puffballs of sawdust in agitation. Marshall Crimmons sat beside him with his head hung low and his perpetual impish grin gone. In its place was a look of serious contemplation.

Tom Hawkins and Grandpop Creel nearly walked the seat backs as they ran around the church aisles. Other people engaged in hearty backslapping and cheek-kissing, and all the while praises rolled out past the tent flaps in waves until Bud could almost see them dancing toward him.

But one thing astonished Bud more than anything in the emotional drama unfolding before his eyes. The picture would be forever emblazoned on his mind and heart. His baby daughter stood there, meek but joyful, timidly shaking hands and shyly accepting embraces and pats on the head — around which shimmered a soft ethereal halo of light. Bud rubbed his eyes and looked again.

"Just a reflection of the light," he reasoned, but of all the heads in the church, the golden, angelic halo only encircled one, that of his youngest daughter, crowning her with a beautiful luminescence, making her face glow and accentuating her shiny black hair. A verse of scripture came to Bud's mind, echoing in his father's resonant voice, "This is my beloved Son in whom I am well pleased."

Along with the voice came the picture from the old family Bible of Christ standing in the muddy baptismal waters of Jordan River with John by His side, a pure white dove descending from the heavens to sit on His shoulder. Was Mary now one of God's children, a little lamb led into the Shepherd's fold, and God was showing His approval of her meek surrender by this miraculous halo?

"Nonsense!" Bud sputtered, shaking his head in an effort to dislodge his fanatical imaginings. It was only a trick of his eyes. Coming from the shadows of the creek so suddenly into bright lights from the tent had caused an illusion. Yes, that would easily account for the hazy glow about Mary's head.

Of course, that explained it. There was a natural explanation for all the mysterious happenings people embellished to try to invent for themselves a God. Well, let them be fooled by their needy imaginations! He was too smart to be caught up in fanatical spiritualism. Bud decided to drop his resolve to speak with Mrs. Holstan. He hurried to escape the troubling scene.

"They're my kids. I'll do as I like!" he declared to himself. Slipping to the truck, he roared the engine into readiness for a quick exit, firmly rolling up the windows. He tooted the horn impatiently to hurry the kids along. They rushed to the truck and climbed in, a parade of well-wishers in step behind them.

Bud leaned across his children, pulling the door shut at the same time he gassed the truck forward. Speeding away in a haze of dust, he left the procession wide-eyed with surprise in a wake of blue exhaust. The billowing, acrid fog of heavy oil smoke smothered the congratulatory smiles.

Chapter 40

The Good Shepherd's Comfort

The trip home from the tent meeting progressed in silence, the vehicle whipping around each curve at high speed and jolting unmercifully over the ruts. Well aware of her father's anger, Mary wisely held her tongue. Billy and Jewel did the same.

Mary's spirits, dampened somewhat by Bud's attitude, could not be completely drowned. The soft circle of warmth enveloping her shielded her from too much disappointment. In the hasty trip over the rutted road, the Good Shepherd cuddled her safely in comforting arms. The jarring ride and her father's evident disapproval of the night's events could not jolt happiness from her heart or shake loose the rapture of her encounter with the Holy Spirit.

Mary could still see the vision that welcomed her when she raised her head from the wooden altar. The roof of the tent had folded back like the flaps on a cardboard box. She saw Jesus in the clouds, followed by a great flock of contented sheep. One small lamb rested contentedly in his arms. He smiled down on it with a look of love that took Mary's breath away. She knew beyond a doubt she was that lamb, protected in the arms of Jesus, the Good Shepherd, from anything that might try to destroy her soul.

Daddy's wrath could not touch her. She would love him and pray for him until he became one of those sheep obediently following the Master into the sheepfold, safe from all problems, safe from hurts and worries that caused his anger and ate up his happiness.

Mary could hardly wait to tell Mama what had happened. She found it hard to fall asleep that night. Her father headed for the barn without entering the house or speaking a word.

The three children dressed quietly for bed and turned out the lights. Disappointment lay over the room like a heavy blanket. They knew for sure what tomorrow would bring in place of their anticipated trip to see Mama. Mary wanted so badly to let her mother know of her experience. She didn't sob into her pillow this time with bitter tears, but with tears of hope and faith — faith for her daddy's salvation. Mary's eyelids fluttered.

-hope for Mama's happiness . . .

She snuggled deeper into the blankets.

-that she'd be free from sickness. . .

Mary slept, curled in a cocoon of peace.

Mary slept soundly until suddenly awakened. She sat up and peered into the darkness. Her heart felt as if it had stopped beating. Then it leapt into her throat. Mama stood in the doorway, smiling like she already knew all that had happened.

Mama looked different. The hollows were gone from her cheeks. Her eyes were bright and full of life and love. Color tinged her face with a healthy glow, and her beautiful hair, once limp and dry, had regained sheen and fullness, falling straight and shining down her back. She walked as if on air to Mary's bed. Mary tried to open her mouth to speak, to tell her mother how she had been changed and made happy, but no sound came. She began to cry. Mama's cool hand reached out and wiped the tears from her face.

"Mary," she spoke softly, tenderly stroking her cheek, "I'm so glad for you! I want you to help your daddy. Don't give up on him. Right now his troubles are bigger than he is. Help him. Try to be patient with his anger. He's a very angry man because he's lost so much, but you can help him give that anger over to God. Others will help but it depends on you. And don't worry about me, Mary. I'm doing fine!"

With a kiss Mama was gone. Mary wanted to wake Jewel and tell her all about her dream, but she couldn't move, couldn't speak. The first thing she remembered the next morning was her vision of Mama. She told Billy and Jewel all about it. Billy looked confused and hurried out the door to the barn with the milk pail swinging against his legs.

"Mary, that was a good dream," Jewel told her. She stirred biscuit dough in a large ironstone bowl. The kitchen was already filled with mouth-watering aromas of sausage browning in a skillet, coffee perking on the stove and the astringent scent of freshly cut pine kindling piled in the woodbox near the stove.

"Mama told you right. We've got to help Daddy. When he gets hateful and mean, I just try hard to remember him like he used to be and ignore as best I can what he's like now. It's not really Daddy. He doesn't want to be like he is. That's why he drinks, Mary."

Jewel rolled biscuit dough flat on a floured cloth with a green quart Mason jar, then began cutting circles of the soft doughy mixture, placing them in a pan greased with bacon fat. Mary washed her hands and took plates from the pine cupboard.

"Mary, I had a dream, too," Jewel told her. "I guess we were thinking about going to see Mama today. I can't wait until she's home again. We'll have to help her all we can, so she won't get sick again. We know how hard it was for her, now, don't we? Will you promise to help, Mary?"

Mary swallowed hard and nodded her head. It would be hard to keep her promise. She wished she were like her sister. Jewel and work got along fine, but she and work were, if not bitter enemies, at least not on the best of terms. She'd rather daydream or swing high in the old oak tree with wind blowing her hair and rustling leaves while she pretended she could touch the clouds with outstretched toes.

She liked to draw pictures and read, putting herself in the stories. She could waste away time lying in the yard and watching the wind drawing animals with white chalk clouds on a blue construction-paper sky. Work was boring, but she really would try harder if it would help Mama be at home with them. She rushed to make her bed without Jewel reminding her, straightening usually ignored wrinkles. She didn't dawdle over dusting, but raced over the room, even brooming cobwebs from corners of the ceiling.

The table set with a hearty breakfast, Jewel and Mary worked efficiently together, slicing thin portions of ham and spreading thick slabs of bread with mustard for the picnic.

147

Billy came back into the house with a pail of milk. "Just as well stop what you're doing," he said, voice quavering. "You were right, Jewel. Daddy says he's too sick to go see Mama, but maybe we can go tomorrow. And he said to forget about church tonight. He's not taking us no more except on Sundays. And he says don't wait on him, he's not eatin'."

No one felt like breakfast. A sullen Billy sat in the rocker staring out the window while Jewel gathered the scraps. Then he stomped back out the door with slop for the hogs. Mary heard him venting his anger at the rooster. She figured he would rather yell at Daddy. Jewel sighed and began wrapping ham sandwiches in waxed paper for their school lunches. Mary helped. There would be no picnic today. No cold watermelon or Orange Crush or Three Musketeer bars. No chocolate cakes. No nothing. Especially no Mama.

Mary stood in the center of the kitchen, staring morosely at the floor. A heavy weight lodged in her chest. She wanted to run to the barn and beat Daddy with her fists. Was his bottle more important than Mama? How would Mama feel if she knew he'd rather spend a night with his bottle than a day with her?

Her dream returned in full reality. She could almost smell the fresh soap scent of her mother's skin and sniff the fragrance of her sun-dried clothes. The only thing that kept her from running and screaming toward the barn was the memory of her mother's gentle exhortation to help her daddy.

But how? Mary sat down in the rocker to slip on her shoes. She didn't know how, except to pray. A good thought came to her. Daddy didn't act much like a daddy anymore. But she had another Father who loved her so much He sent His Son all the way to earth to suffer just for her even more than she suffered now. A little of the weight lifted. Daddy wasn't the only one who needed to know her heavenly Father. Billy needed to know Him, too. God was a Father who would never let His children down.

148

Chapter 41

Billy

Even though Billy almost hated his father for telling him they weren't going to see Mama, the last bit of news came as a welcome relief, though he tried not to show it. He had dreaded going back to the tent meeting. He squirmed all through the prior service, punching Marshall with sharp knuckles when he suggested they follow Mary to the altar.

Russell, Marshall's recently converted brother, must be trying to talk that nonsense into his head. What Mary did was fine for her, but not for him. He wasn't a sissy! He wasn't embarrassing himself that way! Still he had concentrated hard on mounding piles of sawdust on the tent floor in an effort to fight off a strange desire to run to the altar and fall on his knees beside his sister.

His heart had thumped so loudly, he was glad the noise in the tent covered it. He was sure glad he hadn't given in to his crazy notion. He would have hated to face all the boys at school after doing something that dumb! He saw yesterday how the bigger boys teased Russell. But Russell just laughed away their teasing and carried his Bible and read it at recess anyway. He wouldn't let friends copy his papers anymore, and he refused to join in the fist fights behind the wellhouse. Yeah, Russell was a real sissy now. Billy sure didn't want to follow Jesus if that was what it did to you. He didn't want the boys laughing at him!

Another thing that had really surprised Billy the night before was Mr. Eckhart's attendance at the tent meeting, along with two strange ladies he had never seen in church before. Russell told Marshall that they had come out of curiosity because of things going on in the community, like Mr. Cranshaw and Tom Hawkins praying right in the middle of the grocery store floor.

They must've had something awfully important to pray about, Billy thought as he hurried toward the pigpen with the hog slop. The hogs jumped up from their wallow and shoved at one another, eager to get to the trough. Their frantic squeals brought Bud stumbling from the barn. Billy stood watching his drunken father trying to brush hay from his rumpled clothes. How could he face them this morning after telling them they couldn't go see Mama?

A breeze blew across the wallow, carrying its stench on the damp morning air. Billy knew his father wasn't aware of him watching. The drunken man staggered to the back of the barn to relieve his stomach of its contents. Billy stood, watching him wipe his mouth on his shirtsleeve, deeply shamed and glad his mama and sisters couldn't see what he saw. His father looked up suddenly, catching sight of him. Billy knew he could see the accusation in his eyes, but he didn't care anymore. He dumped the slop into the hogs. They fought each other, biting and shoving to grovel in breakfast meant for the family.

Daddy's no better than our pigs, Billy thought. Swilling slop and yelling at us all the time. Billy fought his tears, ignoring his father's plea for him to wait for him. He ran back to the house with the bucket banging his legs. He slammed the door behind him and leaned against it, panting. Mary and Jewel stood staring at him with puzzled faces.

"Why, Billy!" Jewel exclaimed. "Was the Devil on your trail?" Billy kept his answer to himself. A devil was on his trail. Then he immediately felt ashamed of his thoughts. He remembered his dream of Mama. She had come to his bed last night, smoothing the unruly shock of hair back from his forehead in her old familiar way. Her hand felt cool and comforting.

Mama placed a tender kiss where the hair had been while he tried to reach for her. He wanted to throw his arms around her neck, but they remained immobile at his sides. Mama disappeared, but not before she whispered in his ear, "Oh, Billy, try hard not to hate your Daddy. He needs your love now more than ever before. And always remember, Billy, how much I love you."

He turned in his sleep to the wall, the dream slipping from his mind until Mary had revealed hers.

Okay, Mama, he told himself, wishing his mother was there to hear him. I'm trying. I am! But it's awful hard when Daddy doesn't try, too.

Chapter 42

Too Late

Bud leaned against the barn, watching his son running from him toward the house as if fleeing from the Devil. You've got to get a grip on things! he warned himself. For Lindy and the kids' sake, you've got to pull yourself up by your bootstraps and act like a man!

He ran a shaky hand over the stubble on his face. His chin trembled. He clamped a hand over his mouth in an effort to stop the quivering. "Lindy," he whispered, "I'll do better. I promise you. I promise you and the kids. We'll see you tomorrow, for sure."

Bud came home from taking the kids to school to find Tom Hawkins waiting on his doorstep. "Bud," Tom hesitated, wringing his hands. "Sit down, man. I got bad news for you." He scooted over, patting the stoop.

It has to be bad, Bud thought. This was the first time he'd seen Tom Hawkins without that foolish smile decorating his face. Lindy! His knees buckled. He sank to the stoop beside Tom. "Doc Hillman got a call from the sanitarium this morning, Bud. He told me to stop on my route and tell you that he'd be here soon as he could. Pastor Crookshank will be coming with him."

Tom didn't have to say more. Bud forgot his animosity and fell into the man's arms. His heart split in two, fresh hope rushing out in a torrent of despair.

Tom's childlike faith was badly shaken by Lindy's passing. He had no pious platitudes to offer. He could only offer his presence. He forgot his mail route for a while to stay with the grieving man until Doc and Pastor Crookshank arrived. He knew the neighbors would understand and forgive his delay when they heard of Bud's tragedy.

Tom let Bud pour out his grief until he emptied his emotions. Then he led him into the house where he stoked up the fire still smoldering from the untouched breakfast. He put on a pot of coffee, heaping up the spoon with grounds to make it strong, then went to the spring and filled two buckets with water to heat for Bud's bath. Bud was ashamed, knowing he was in no condition to go visit his dead wife after his night's binge.

Tom took the washtub off its nail on the wall. Bud remembered how he had scoured it clean to hold the watermelon and ice for the picnic. His docility turned to rage. He lashed out at Tom. "You said you'all were praying for my wife! Is this how God answers your prayers? Where's your miracles now that you talk so much about?"

Pastor Crookshank walked through the door with Doc behind him just in time to catch Bud's question and to see the look of utter helplessness in Tom's eyes. He knew Tom's young Christian faith, though strong, was not yet strong enough for facing this battle alone. God had sent reinforcements just in time.

"Bud, God knows best," Pastor Crookshank soothed, taking Bud by the hand. "He answers prayers as He sees fit. Maybe this is Lindy's miracle. She's suffered a long time and you know she was ready to go. I know it's hard for you, Bud, but think of it on Lindy's behalf. She's a lot better off now."

Pastor Crookshank held his tongue on telling Bud that he needed to be ready to meet his wife. The man must be well aware of his condition. Bringing it up would only add to his animosity and suffering. Time would bring about a better moment for pointing out shortcomings. Better yet, let the Holy Spirit do it.

"Bud," Doc spoke up, "I've sent for Corie and Floyd and your mom and dad. Floyd's going to drop Corie off here and then go on to the school to pick up your young'uns. I figured your parents would want to go with you to the sanitarium, so we can all ride together in my car. Corie and Floyd's offered to stay with the children until we get back."

Pastor Crookshank's heart went out to the children. He hoped this blow coming so soon after Mary's conversion wouldn't knock her off her spiritual feet. If she leaned on the

Lord, it would make her stronger. If she blamed Him, it would cripple her salvation. He had seen many people blame God for things that were a product of Satan.

A car splashed through the creek below the house. Tom pulled back the curtain and looked out the window. "Here's Floyd and Corie now," he said. "I'd better get on my way with the mail." He gripped Bud's hand in a warm grasp. "If there's anything I can do, let me know. I'll be praying for you and your family."

Bud recalled the harsh words he'd spoken to Tom, the cold treatment he'd given him. Tom should have been offended, but he only came back at him with kindness. Evidently the man had really had a change of heart. He nodded assent. Tom slipped out the door, speaking a few words of sympathy to Floyd and Corie as they passed him on the way in.

Pastor Crookshank and Doc Hillman offered their consolations to the couple. Floyd seemed overwhelmed with grief. His sister's death had hit him hard. Lindy had been the only immediate family he had left after his mother's passing. Corie's eyes were red-rimmed, but she entered the house with a no-nonsense attitude. In record time, she emptied the buckets of steaming water into the tub in the back bedroom. She laid out fresh towels, washcloth, and soap, wrinkling her nose in disgust as Bud passed her on the way to his bath.

"Fool man!" she hissed after the door closed behind him. "Them young'uns is having a hard enough time without his adding to it by nipping at the bottle!"

Floyd hung his head and went out the door to go after his nephew and nieces. Pastor Crookshank, at a loss for words, asked Corie if she'd like some coffee. She declined with a pursed mouth, attacking a stack of ironing in a corner of the room.

"Corie," Pastor Crookshank asked, sipping at the hot coffee, "did you hear little Mary was converted at the tent meeting last night?" Corie looked up in surprise. "Bud brought the children, but he refused to attend the service. He sat and waited in the truck until it was over."

Corie appeared to be absorbed in her ironing, but he knew she hadn't missed a word. The woman had never had a knack with children, but Mary had always been her favorite from what the child's grandmother had said. Corie's eyes blinked rapidly, moisture building up around the lower lids. "Poor young'un!" she muttered. "She's gonna need what comfort she can find. She loved her mama so much, and she's so young."

"Well, Corie," Pastor Crookshank said, "the Lord can be a great comfort in times of distress."

"Amen!" Doc agreed. Corie ironed furiously, huge drops of godly sorrow spotting the shirt under the iron. Pastor Crookshank thought of all the times Lindy had requested prayer for her brother and sister-in-law.

Corie hung the shirt on a hanger just as a car pulled up. Hurrying to the door, she let Bud's mother and father in. Bud came from the bedroom, dressed for his trip. Grandpop and Grandma Creel appeared to have aged overnight, yet their concern centered on their son.

Bud sobbed as his mother held him. "I promised Lindy I'd see her tomorrow," he told her. "I guess I'll keep that promise sooner than I figgered."

Grandma Creel looked over Bud's shoulder at her husband. Pastor Crookshank saw the plea for help in her eyes. Grandpop Creel shook his head in dismay. Without a word, he placed a tender hand on his son's shoulder, giving it a comforting squeeze.

Floyd's truck pulled up outside. Corie ran and opened the front door. Three stunned children spilled from the cab, filing in past their aunt. Mary and Jewel ran to their daddy, who broke out in fresh mourning at the sight of his motherless children. Billy stood by the door, sullen and miserable, watching his father from lowered eyes.

Pastor Crookshank knelt before him and took his hands. "Billy," he spoke softly, "I know how bad you're feeling, for I've been there myself. Lost my own mother when I was but a young'un. Death isn't singular to any one of us. It comes to all of us in time."

Jewel and Mary listened intently to the words of comfort offered by their pastor. Bud stooped with his arms around his girls, listening, too. "The comforter soon finds himself to be the comforted," the preacher continued. "Yet somehow we make it through. I'm here as living proof of that. Grief cuts, bruises, and wounds worse than anything, but, Billy, you know how a wound takes time to heal?

"Well, the healing of this will take time, too. It'll fester and your heart will bleed, but one day, if you'll let God be the Great Physician, the pain will pass and the wound will heal over. The scar will always be there, but it will eventually lose its ugliness, and you'll only feel tenderness when memories touch it. Those memories become a good feeling, a beloved touch. Can you believe that?"

Billy glanced up at his father, but remained silent. Great tears welled up and rolled down his cheeks. He jerked a hand away and swiped at them.

"Billy," Pastor Crookshank said, taking a clean hanky from his hip pocket and pressing it into the boy's hand, "maybe you can't accept what I'm saying now, but remember it. Hold on to it when you hurt too much." He turned and looked at Bud.

"You, too, Bud. All of you." He included all of Lindy's family with a sweep of his hand. Remember, God is the Healer, the Holy Spirit a soothing balm. And fellow Christians can swab the wound with caring and bind it with love. Love is the answer to all life's calamities. God's love."

Bud frowned. Pastor Crookshank knew his words, for the time being, only served to alienate the man, but little Mary drank them in like liquid hope, slaking her thirst for comfort like a long, cool drink of fresh spring water.

"Well, we'd best be going," the preacher said, struggling to his feet. He felt assured Mary's salvation would survive the blow, though the days facing her would be filled with trials and testing, but he doubted if she would find much help in this troubled little home, except perhaps from Jewel. Yet he knew God would send someone her way to help absorb the shock of her grief. Unlike Bud, Mary would be open and receptive to her heavenly Father's resources.

The pastor wished he could make Bud see that to fight against God was to commit suicide of the soul. It was like holding a live coal in your hand and refusing to let go. You were the one who suffered the burn. In this case, though, three small children felt the pain, too. That was very evident in their eyes as their father told them all goodbye.

Mary thought over the things Pastor Crookshank said about waiting. She remembered when her Daddy was away. They waited, though sometimes it was awfully hard, but one day his ship came home. She'd just have to wait for the pain to go away. And she'd have to wait on her daddy, too.

Mama had always said that someday their ship would come in. She guessed Mama's had, if heaven was like everyone said. Now, without her, they were all on a battered ship sailing in troubled waters. What she must do with all her might was to try to convince Daddy to make God the captain of their ship, so they could all find safe port in the storm.

Cars began arriving, the house filling up with friends and neighbors who had heard the sad news of Lindy's death. They came bearing warm condolences and dishes heaped with hot and cold food. Mary felt enfolded in their love. She wished her daddy were there to feel some of it. Her heart ached for him to be comforted.

Chapter 43

Mary and Nella

"I missed you, Mary," Nella said when Mary returned to school after her mother's funeral. "I was awful sorry to hear about your ma dying." Mary fought to control her tears. She didn't want any of the other students to see her crying.

"Did you feel this bad when your daddy died, Nella?" she asked her friend.

"I can't remember, Mary. I was too little. But it hurts awful bad sometimes, anyway, just not having a daddy."

"Sometimes I forget Mama's dead," Mary whispered, fidgeting with the bow on the neck of her dress. "I think she's still in the hospital and I can go see her. Then I remember. That's when it hurts the worst."

Nella sat on the school steps looking at Mary, not knowing what to say to make her feel better. "Want'a play jacks, Mary?" she offered.

"Not now."

They sat in silence, staring at their feet.

"How about swingin'?"

"Nope."

"We could play house under the tree in back."

"I don't feel like it."

"Well, fiddlesticks, Mary!" Nella jumped up, hands on her hips. "No wonder you feel awful! If you just sit there and feel sorry for yourself, you'll never feel any better!"

Mary's eyes flashed. "I got a reason to feel sorry for myself!" She bent over, burying her face in her lap.

"So do I, but I ain't gonna sit here and do it! If you don't wanna play, then I will!" Nella took the jacks from her pocket and placed them on the back of her hand. Mary raised her head from her knees, peeking out at her friend. Her cheeks were wet with tears.

Nella's hand swooped through the jacks and grabbed for the ball, but she missed it. It rolled down the steps, bouncing high and out into the schoolyard. She scrambled after it, then came running back with green eyes bright and a smile on her face. "I missed! Now it's your turn, Mary," she said, giggling. She shoved the jacks into her friend's hand.

"I said I don't want to play, Nella!" Mary yelled. She jumped up and took off around the school building in tears, leaving Nella staring after her in dismay.

"Nella."

Nella looked up to see Mrs. Holstan standing at the top of the steps. Descending, the teacher sat down beside her, tucking her skirt around her legs. A breeze sifted strands of her gray hair. "Nella, Mary doesn't mean to be unkind. It's so very hard for her to be happy with her mama gone. You'll have to be patient and give her time, be nice to her."

Nella nodded. "I will, Mrs. Holstan. She's my best friend."

"She sure is, Nella. A very good friend." Mrs. Holstan patted Nella on the arm and smiled. "And you are so good for her. And now, if you'll excuse me, I have to ring the bell. It's time for school to begin."

Chapter 44

Mrs. Holstan

Mrs. Holstan stood for a moment, watching Nella follow Mary around the school building. She recalled Mary coming back to school before Christmas and confessing that she had falsely accused her friend of taking the construction paper. The girls became even closer after that. Wherever you saw one, you saw the other, a whispery, giggling twosome.

The teacher rang the bell for class to begin, glad to see the two girls entering the classroom arm in arm. Nella would be good for Mary. The child knew what it felt like to lose a parent. And she was sweet and loving, so very full of life. She and Mary had such diverse personalities, one very outgoing, the other extremely shy, but this didn't seem to hinder their relationship.

Mrs. Holstan saw Leonard slip a note into Nella's hand as she passed his desk. She smiled, pretending not to notice the note passing from hand to hand, ending its journey in Mary's pocket. Love was a great healer. It looked like Mary would be receiving it in good supply.

Mrs. Holstan hoped Jewel and Billy were as blessed with good friends as Mary. Jewel was bussed into town now to the junior high school, but Billy was still one of her students. She had noticed him in the schoolyard with Marshall Crimmons and a few of the other boys shooting a game of marbles before school began. He seemed happy enough then, but now he sat staring out the window, thoughts painting blues all over his face. Mrs. Holstan sighed and sat down at her desk.

"All right, children." She tapped her ruler on her desk. "We'll begin with roll call. Sarah Atkinson?"

"Present."

Gerald Bosley?"

"Here."

"Sammy Tacket?"

Life goes on, carrying with it both burdens and blessings.

Chapter 45

Mad Dog!

Mary sat in the front porch swing beside her grandmother, enjoying warm gingerbread just out of the oven. A glass of cool milk, squeezed fresh from the cow that morning, sat on the porch rail beside her. "Jewel would be getting a pretty fine fella by marrying Russell," Grandma stated. "He's proved hisself to be a genuine Christian and a hard worker."

Mary, thirteen, showed promise of becoming a beautiful woman, awkward adolescence fading. Dark hair fell sleek and shining down her back, and her eyes glistened like polished mahogany. Work on the farm had given her tall figure a lithesome grace, accentuated by a small waist and long firm legs.

"I like Russell real well, Grandma. He's nice, and he treats Jewel good, but I sure hate to see them get married and Jewel leave home." Mary giggled. "Jewel says she's not interested in Russell, but she sure does fix herself up when she knows he's coming!"

"Jewel's got her heart set on a man with money who can take her away from the farm and give her a better life," Grandma said, "but I know from experience having a good man don't depend on money. Your granddad's been pert near penniless most of his years, but he's given me a good, happy life. Why, I couldn't ask for anything better. Then I've seen those that's married into plenty and they're miserable as a cow eatin' greenbriers."

Mary's moist eyes stared off into the distance. Grandma would never know what prompted Jewel's thirst for a better life. Days over the hot stove cooking and canning, nights after school standing over a hot iron or sitting at the sewing machine until her back ached to keep them all in clothes. Hours scrubbing the floors only to have them tracked up by Billy and Daddy when they came in from the barn or garden.

Daddy had grown more cantankerous as the months after Mama's death stretched into three long years. He grumbled when Jewel asked him to take off his shoes at the door. "I wipe my feet before I come in," he'd retort, "and I'll not be ordered around in my own house!"

Billy always followed his father's example, exhibiting a certain smugness in getting the best of his sister, resenting her air of authority that surfaced even more after Mama died. Mary knew Jewel, a born leader, reveled in her position as head of the house. She also understood that Jewel would gladly give up her position to have Mama back.

Mary tried to be as much help as she could to her overburdened sister, but she could never please her, no matter how hard she tried. Her best just wasn't good enough, and Jewel usually preferred doing the work inside the house herself. Mary compensated by helping outside all she could and just staying out of her sister's way.

"What's your daddy think of Russell courting his daughter?" Grandma Creel asked.

"He don't like it one bit, Grandma. He lets Russell come over every once in a while, but he gives him a hard time. I don't know why he doesn't like him. Russell's nice and polite and helps Daddy with the work. Jewel mostly gets to see him in church. They always sit together, holding hands and staring moon-eyed at one another." Mary giggled again.

"Well, Mary, I figger your daddy likes Russell well enough. He used to, didn't he, before the boy showed an interest in Jewel? Don't you think maybe he's just afraid of losing his daughter and her help? How will you'all ever get along without her?"

There! Grandma did it again! How did she always hit the nail on the head when it came to knowing what bothered her? If Jewel left, Mary would be in charge of the house, and she didn't know how she could ever fill her sister's shoes. And Grandma was probably right about her daddy. With all of his grumbling, he loved his youngun's and needed them. He'd really be lost without Jewel's help or her little ways of comforting him with special baked treats or tender

162

thoughtfulness. No matter how much he drank or how quarrelsome he became, Jewel always upheld him and encouraged Billy and Mary to give him respect.

"He's your Daddy!" she would reprimand in a firm voice, hands planted on her hips and fire in her eyes when Billy complained too loudly or Mary became too upset with her father's drinking. "He's your daddy and don't you ever forget it! Mama wouldn't like one bit you bellyaching about him. Daddy misses Mama and that's why he's so unhappy. So we've got to try to make up for her being gone."

Mary couldn't picture anyone missing Mama any more than she did, but she knew Daddy didn't have the comfort she had. When things got too hard, she'd escape to the barn loft and read Psalms until the pain eased a little. And Miss Jenkins was always ready to listen to her complaints and pray with her.

Nella was the best friend a girl could have and empathized with her. But the times Mary spent with Grandma Creel were the best comfort of all. She had come to love her like the mother she didn't have. Her grandmother always understood Mary and seemed to know just what bothered her. And Grandpop knew just how to make her feel better when she was down.

She recalled a time not too long after her mother died when she and her grandmother sat on the porch with fresh lemonade, discussing boys and romance, but it hadn't been Jewel's romance that was the topic at that time. Mary's heart had been broken when she'd returned to school at the beginning of the fourth grade to learn that Leonard and his family had moved away without so much as a goodbye.

"How could he?" she had snuffled into Grandma's apron. "He said he loved me!" Mary thought of all her hair ribbons. Had he thrown them away as he had their love?

"You can write," Grandma offered, stroking her hair with a loving hand. But the Freshour family left no indication of their destination. Mary never heard from Leonard again. Grandpop drove her into town that evening, where they sat together at the soda fountain in Leggit's Drug

Store, drinking tall, thick, frosty milkshakes that cooled the pain of a broken heart.

"Is your Daddy doing any better, Mary?" Grandma Creel's question pulled Mary back to the present. The sadness spilled over in her grandmother's gentle voice. Mary knew she wasn't the only one who sometimes needed comfort, but she had few comforting words for her grandmother.

"Some, Grandma," she answered quietly. "At least he's going to church off and on now." Mary turned to her grandmother. "But, Grandma, that's when he seems to drink the most! He almost always heads to the barn when we get home, and he's always nasty the next day."

Grandma Creel knew how hard Mary had prayed for her father in the years since Lindy had been gone, and how she never failed to request prayer for him at church. The child's faith was strong, but at times the burden threatened to overwhelm her, making her doubt that her daddy would ever find God.

"That's only natural, child. A good sign, really. It shows he's thinking, and thinking makes him want to run, to try and escape the Holy Spirit's conviction. Just keep praying, Mary. Don't give up on your daddy."

Grandma's words reminded Mary of her dream of Mama those three long years ago. She could recall it just like it was today. Mary, don't give up on your daddy, her mama had said. Help him. It depends on you. It was this dream that kept Mary praying for her father when she felt like there was no use. She couldn't give up. She just couldn't!

"I don't know whatever made your daddy turn to the bottle," Grandma said with a sigh. "Grandpop never drank a drop in his life. He's shamed by his son's drinking. So am I. But we'll just keep praying, Mary. That's all we can do. Just keep right on talking to the Good Lord and trusting Him."

Mary helped Grandma Creel gather the plates and cups and carry them to the kitchen. Then they headed for the garden to pick beans and strip ears of corn for supper.

Patches lay sleeping in the shade of the smokehouse. He jumped up when he heard the screendoor slam. He acted confused, like he didn't know them at first, then shook himself and lay back down with a groan.

"Poor old dog!" Grandma clucked. "He's been actin' awful weak lately, kind'a strange. Of course, old age is getting the best of him. He cain't hardly see nor hear now and seldom makes it to the woods and back with me anymore."

Grandma cackled. "'Course, I don't get there too much myself. Old age's done crept up on me, too, when I wasn't looking, and my joints don't bend or navigate like they should. And my eyes ain't like they once was. I've missed my mark on lots of game lately."

Mary felt a cold ripple of fear. She didn't want to lose Grandma Creel. She loved the old woman with a fierce love, was closer to her than anyone she knew. Yet time had to be running out for her grandparents.

Grandpop stood in the garden, shading his eyes from the sun's glare, watching their approach. The sunlight glinted off his white whiskers. Mary noticed he seemed smaller than he once was. Grandpop had always been a big man, tall and robust, but since his retirement from the lumberyard, he seemed to shrink a little each year. Rheumatism had twisted his hands and bent his back. He leaned on his hoe, resting between rows and wiping sweat from his brow.

"Well, Mary, I see you've put some life in old Patches," he said with a laugh. "That's the first time I've seen him venture out into the hot sun for days."

Mary looked back and saw Patches shambling toward them, shaggy head down and legs stiff. Pity for her old friend melted her heart. She started toward him, then noticed foam drooling from his mouth. His eyes were glazed and he growled deep in his throat.

"Grandpop, Patches must be sick," she called. Hurrying to the old dog, she was shocked to see his teeth bared and foam rolling from his mouth. She screamed as he lunged for her.

"Mary!" Grandpop yelled. "Get away from him! Run! Don't touch him! Ma-a-ry!" Grandpop hurried toward her as fast as his aged joints would allow. The dog staggered on toward Mary with madness in his eyes. His throat grumbled with growls unusual for him. Mary stood frozen in place, frightened at the change in the dog that had never in his life hurt or threatened her in any way.

"Mary! Mary!" Grandma Creel screamed. "Run, honey! Patches is gone mad!" She hurried behind Grandpop and grabbed Mary, pulling her away toward the house. Mary stumbled behind her grandmother to the front porch. They stood anxiously watching Grandpop strike at the crazed dog with his hoe. Patches went down and Mary screamed, but the old dog scrambled back to his feet, snarling and dodging the hoe, fighting to get to Grandpop.

"Stay here, Mary," Grandma demanded. She ran to the rock garden and grabbed up a rock. Mary couldn't stop screaming. She remembered Grandpop's gun and ran to the bedroom, jerking it from the rack. Frantic, she grabbed some shells from the drawer beneath the rack. They flew from her nervous clutch, rolling across the floor and under the bed. Mary dived after them, scrabbling in the darkness beneath the bedspread. She felt the coolness of metal against her fingers and grabbed. Scraping her back on the wooden bed rail, she backed from beneath the bed.

Rushing out the door, Mary tripped in her haste. Rolling down the steps, she lost her grip on the gun and shell. She could hear Patches growling and Grandma's shouts. She scampered, sobbing, through the grass on her hands and knees, searching for the shell. Patches yelped and all was quiet. Mary found the shell and jumped to her feet, racing toward her grandparents with the gun. "Grandpop!" she screamed. "I've got the gun!"

Grandpop and Grandma knelt over Patches, inert at the edge of the garden. The dog's legs convulsed, then were still. Saliva coated the animal's bared teeth and ran down his fur. Grandpop looked up at Mary, who stood gasping for breath, staring down at the dog in frightened awe.

"It's all right now, Mary," he whispered, face white and whiskers trembling. "Patches is dead."

"Oh, Grandpop! Poor Patches!" Mary cried. "I was so scared! What happened to him? He's never tried to bite anyone before."

"He was mad, Mary. Plumb mad! Hyderphoby!"

Mary had learned of hydrophobia in school, but she'd never seen a rabid animal before. She couldn't believe how it could change a dog. Patches had always been so gentle, so loving. "Poor old Patches!" she cried, falling down beside the still form, ready to hug her old friend.

"Don't touch him, Mary!" Grandpop warned, jerking her away. "Stay back!" Bewildered, Mary jumped to her feet.

"Just for safety's sake, honey," Grandma said. "Rabies is a dangerous thing. If you get that spit in your blood, you'd go mad just the same as poor old Patches."

Mary shuddered. "Grandpop!" she cried in alarm. "Did he bite you? Are you all right?"

"Fit as a fiddle, Mary," Grandpop chuckled a little hysterically. "Your Grandma might be gettin' old, but she ain't lost her aim. Thank God she ain't lost her aim! Now we'd best bury Patches and spread the warning that rabies is about before someone does get hurt."

Chapter 46

To the Rescue

"Mary, could you go to the garden and get me a cucumber and some tomatoes?" Jewel stood at the table cutting biscuits with a floured glass, placing them in a greased pan. Enticing smells filled the little kitchen. "And tell Billy and the others to come wash up for supper. These biscuits will be done in no time, and they're at their best pipin' hot."

Pink tinted Jewel's cheeks. Her eyes shone. Mary knew standing over the hot stove wasn't the only reason for her sister's radiant glow. She had confided in her the night before, after Russell left, that they intended today to ask Daddy for permission to marry.

Russell had offered to help paint the barn roof, showing up early that morning, but Jewel had been up long before him, washing her hair and brushing the black waves to a velvety sheen. She had ironed and worn her best dress, even though it was a workday. She baked two apple pies after breakfast. The dinner she fixed was more like Sunday fare, and a vase of fragrant and colorful wild flowers sat on the freshly pressed, red checkered cotton cloth that graced the old scratched and stained Formica table.

It felt good to see Jewel finally getting some enjoyment from life, Mary thought. Turning seventeen two years before, she had finished school, staying right on at the farm while most of her schoolmates found jobs in the city or married. Others — a fortunate few — attended college.

Bud still tried as much as possible to separate the couple, but knew better than to forbid them to see each other. After all, Jewel was of age and could leave anytime she decided. Jewel and Russell spent most of their time together in the Victory Church meetings. Russell would drive by to pick up Jewel and Mary and drop them off again when the service ended. Bud insisted on Mary accompanying them if he didn't go, and she was glad. She always welcomed the chance to be in church.

Russell and Jewel didn't seem to mind Mary's company and even invited Billy, but he usually refused unless he was certain Nella would be there. He was sweet on her, even though he had turned eighteen, and she was only fourteen. Mary thought they made a cute couple and hoped her best friend would someday, in an appropriate time, become her sister-in-law.

Jewel knew the reason Daddy had begun to attend church a little himself- to keep an eye on her and Russell, but at least he was going. Russell, well aware of Bud Creel's disapproval of him courting his daughter, remained polite and respectful, but persistent in the relationship.

"Your daddy likes me well enough," he told Jewel with a grin. "He's just afraid I'm going to steal you out from under his nose. We get along fine when we work together. It's when you come around that he gets cranky with me."

"Russell, You know I just can't leave home!" Jewel protested when Russell proposed to her. "Daddy depends on me to keep the house going."

"Jewel, you've kept house and cared for this family since your mother died," he reminded her. "Don't you think it's about time Mary did her share?"

"Russell, what are you thinking? She's only fourteen!" Jewel argued.

"And how old were you when your mother died, Jewel?" he asked softly. "Mary's not a child anymore!"

Jewel gave in to Russell's proposal, but she knew that even though he had won the argument, Mary would not be as capable as she was around the house. Mary echoed her sentiments when she learned of their plans. "Oh, Jewel, I'm so happy for you, but how will we ever get along without you?" She hugged Jewel's neck and kissed her cheek.

"Oh, you'll do fine, Mary. Just fine!" Jewel encouraged her with some trepidation. "Remember how we thought we'd never make it without Mama? Well, we have. We sure miss her, but we've managed, and you will, too. Besides, Russell

169

paid a down payment on Mrs. Crooney's house after she died, and he's making some improvements on it. We'll be living just a few miles down the road."

"If Daddy agrees," Mary reminded her. "Do you think he will?"

"If he doesn't, we'll just have to elope, Mary. I want Daddy's blessing, but I love Russell too much to let Daddy stop us. I'm just praying he'll come around to seeing things our way."

"Then I'll pray, too, Jewel. And we'd better pray for some help for me." She giggled. "Oh, Jewel, I don't want you to go either, but I can't expect you to stay here forever!"

On her way to the garden, Mary let the screen door bang behind her. Bud and Russell looked up from their paintbrushes. She motioned for them to take a break for supper, but Russell pointed to the small square of unpainted roof. He never liked to leave a job until it was finished. The wet paint of the barn roof shone a brilliant red in the hot glare of the summer sun. Strong fumes saturated the air.

Billy was busy scything weeds along the creek bank, dark hair plastered to his sweating brow and muscles rippling as he swung the heavy scythe. He looked more like Bud every day, except he had inherited Grandpop Creel's height. He worked evenings at the Cranshaw's grocery. Mr. Cranshaw had asked him to work Saturdays, too, but Bud insisted he needed him too much at the farm.

Billy would graduate the next spring. Then he planned to join the army. He had failed the ninth grade with Marshall moving ahead. Their forced separation seemed to shake Billy from his lassitude. He became more serious about his studies, asking Mary to help him. With her help, his grades improved considerably. Mary couldn't help but feel that her brother's new maturity was partly due to the influence of Nella's admiration for him.

Mary stood for a moment, watching her brother swing the scythe through tall weeds. She wondered what she and Daddy would do when both Billy and Jewel were gone. Billy worked hard, accomplishing much of the work on the farm. There was no way she and her father could complete all the chores, at least while Mary still attended school.

Bud's drinking was beginning to have an effect on his body. He wasn't nearly as strong as he used to be. Mary noticed, too, that lately his memory seemed to be failing, and he easily became confused. If only he would give up his grudge against God and accept Him into his life! She knew then that he'd lose his desire for the bottle.

Mary hurried on to the garden, picking a few cucumbers and tomatoes. She and Jewel would have plenty of work canning all the harvest before summer ended. The good rains, along with manure Russell and Daddy plowed into the soil, had produced a bumper crop this year. She was glad Jewel would still be around to help her with the canning.

Work! It seemed like that was all they did. What would Jewel ever do with her time in Mrs. Crooney's little house with all the modern conveniences? She would be awfully bored with all her free time. Or maybe she'd just be glad. Mary wished she could escape the work, too, but she really loved the farm and would never leave Daddy alone.

One thing, things were easier now than they had been when poor Mama was alive. Billy had saved his wages, and Russell had helped him lay a gas line to the house. He'd bought a gas cook stove and a pump to bring the water up the hill from the cistern. He'd even bought Mary and Jewel some clothes from time to time. Billy was a good brother and son, but Daddy kept after him all the time. Mary knew that's why Billy planned to join the army. He wanted to get as far away from the farm as possible. He'd leave as soon as he graduated to get out from under his father's rule.

Mary detoured down by the creek to tell Billy to come wash up for supper. She noticed that Russell was finishing up the last bit of the roof while Daddy descended the ladder. The red barn roof contrasted against the delft blue sky. Down by the creek bank, the aromatic scent of cut grass overrode the noxious smell of paint.

Suddenly Mary heard a low snarl behind her. Turning, she grew weak with fear. Her heart thumped against her ribs, and red juice ran down her hands from the tomatoes squashed in her grip.

"Billy!" she screamed. "Mad dog! Mad dog!" The crazed look in the stray's eyes and the drooling mouth reminded Mary of Patches a few weeks earlier. The dog thrashed wildly at the water as if battling an enemy, advancing toward Billy, with hackles raised. Emaciated and shaggy, the animal shook its head from side to side as if trying to shake off raging torment. Billy turned at Mary's scream and froze.

"Daddy!" Mary yelled. Bud stood at the foot of the ladder, looking confused. From his vantagepoint on the roof, Russell could see what was happening. He quickly descended the ladder, rushing past Bud and yelling for Jewel to bring the gun. Jewel appeared at the screendoor, color drained from her cheeks. She had heard Mary's screams and Russell's call for help, but couldn't make out his words. She thought her father had fallen from the roof, but when she saw him standing in the barnyard, relief washed over her. But what was the commotion all about? Where had Mary disappeared to?

"Jewel! The gun!" Russell yelled again, running toward the house. Mary threw her vegetables and ran toward Billy, but he motioned her back with one hand while raising the scythe between himself and the approaching dog with the other. He kept silent, afraid his voice would further antagonize the dog.

Jewel ran for the gun, wondering what awful thing was happening. She grabbed the box of shells and met Russell at the bottom of the porch steps. "Russell, what is it?" she cried. "What's wrong?"

"Mad dog, Jewel!" he panted. "He's after Billy!" Russell broke down the shotgun and plunged a shell into the barrel as he ran for the creek.

Bud at last saw the dog and ran after Russell. "Mary!" he yelled. "Get away! Get to the house and you and Jewel go inside and stay!"

But Mary could not move. She clamped her hand over her mouth, holding back screams. The dog lunged at Billy. She lost control. A shrill cry forced its way past her hand. Billy swung the scythe at the dog, but Mary's piercing cry had further maddened the animal, drawing its attention. It turned and staggered up the bank towards her, teeth bared, black eyes glittering with rage.

"Run, Mary! Run!" Billy yelled. He came after the dog, swinging the scythe. Jewel watched from the porch, trembling with fear. Russell took aim, but Billy and Mary were in the line of fire. Everything around Mary began to fade. She heard her own voice from far away, screaming and screaming. A swirling white haze pulled her down into unconsciousness. The last thing she saw before she fell was a blurred and frightening vision of the snarling dog leaping at her face.

Chapter 47

Saved!

Mary's consciousness returned with the touch of a cool cloth on her forehead. At first she couldn't remember what had happened and where she was. Feeling grass beneath her arms and legs, she opened her eyes. What was she doing lying on the ground? Jewel's anxious face swam above her, eyes streaming with tears. Mary's head began to clear. Suddenly she remembered. She began to scream again, scrambling to get up.

"It's all right, Mary." Jewel held her tightly. "The dog is dead. You're safe."

"Where's Billy?" Mary cried. "And Daddy and Russell? Is Billy all right?" Jewel bit her lip and looked away, fighting to control her emotions.

"Jewel!" Mary screamed. "Answer me! Where's Billy? What's happened to him? Where is everybody?"

"Mary, listen, honey." Jewel tried to calm her sister. "Billy will be just fine. Russell and Daddy have taken him to the hospital."

"To the hospital! What happened? Did the dog bite him?" Mary shook so hard her teeth chattered. She felt sick and dizzy. Her stomach heaved.

"Yes, Mary, the dog bit him." Jewel began crying again. Mary jumped up and ran for the toilet. Jewel raced after her. She heard Mary retching. Leaning against the toilet, she hugged herself, shivering in the heat of the summer afternoon. Mary finally came out, ghostly pale, lips beaded with sweat.

"Will — will he die, Jewel?" she whispered. "Do you think Billy will die?"

"No! No, Mary. Billy won't die. Now don't you even think such a thing!" But Jewel wasn't sure. She'd learned about rabies — hydrophobia — in school. After the sixth grade, she caught the bus and traveled to town to attend junior high and high school. Schools in town were better equipped than the little one-room country schoolhouse, with projectors and moving films. She faintly recalled a movie about hydrophobia in which several men held down another man who shook with convulsions.

The man's companions tried to force a drink of water through his clenched teeth. He turned wild, jerking from their grasp and sending the cup flying. Jewel could still see the man's glazed, bulging eyes and big drops of sweat that ran down his face as he thrashed and fought to free himself from the hands of his friends. Was there a cure? She couldn't remember. The film had seemed unimportant at the time, just scary and unbelievable.

Oh, God, she prayed, God, please help Billy!

Mary stood in deep thought, trying to recall what had happened before she fainted. She remembered Billy running behind the dog, swinging the scythe, and Russell aiming the gun. Had he fired it? She didn't remember hearing it go off. "Jewel, did Russell shoot the dog?" she asked.

"No, Mary, he couldn't. He was afraid he'd hit you or Billy, and Billy was afraid he'd hit you with the scythe if he swung it so close to you, so he just dropped it and lunged. He grabbed the dog by the hind legs just as it leaped for you. If you hadn't fainted and fell, it would probably have got your face. It turned on Billy and latched onto his jaw. Russell hit it in the back with the gun butt, and it let go and turned toward him. That's when he got a good hard lick in and hit the dog in the head and killed it."

"Where is the dog?" Mary asked, looking around as if she was afraid it would come back to stalk them.

"Daddy and Russell put it in the back of the pickup and took it with them so it could be tested to be sure it was mad. But it had to be."

Mary knew Jewel was right. The dog had acted the same as Grandma Creel's old dog, Patches, when he'd attacked Grandpop in the spring. Mary suddenly recalled something Grandma Creel said when Grandpop warned her not to touch the dead dog.

"But Jewel!" she cried. "Grandma Creel said if you got the dog's spit in your blood, you'd die! If the dog bit Billy, didn't its spit get mixed up in his blood? Billy will die, won't he?"

She began to cry hysterically, clutching her stomach and doubling over in pain. Floyd and Walter. She could barely remember them. And then Mama. Now Billy. Not Billy, too! She loved him so much! They were so close!

"Don't cry, Mary," Jewel begged. "I can't remember too well, but I think there's a shot or something they can give Billy to keep him from getting the rabies. Please, don't cry!" She rocked Mary in her arms. "Come on, let's go to the house and put the food away, unless you want something to eat."

"I'm not hungry, Jewel," Mary said. She didn't think she would ever be hungry again.

"Me neither, Mary. I hope someone comes pretty soon and tells us something about Billy. I'm so scared. Mary? Do you think we should pray?"

"I think I'd feel better if we did, Jewel. You go ahead and pray out loud and don't forget to pray for Daddy. I bet he's nearly scared out of his mind!"

If Mary could have seen her daddy, she would have known just how true her words were. Bud asked Russell to drive to the hospital while he sat with Billy hugged to his chest. Staring woodenly out the windshield as the truck rocked over the rutted road, he whispered, "Hold on, Floyd," trying to cushion his son from the jarring ride. "You're gonna be all right. Mama and I are gonna get you some help. Just hold on a little while longer."

Chapter 48

New Hope

"Now, Jewel, it would be for the best," Doc argued gently. Mary stood hugging herself, gripping her arms with tense fingers as she watched her sister's face. Russell sat beside Jewel, holding her hand in his. She wept softly, emphatically shaking her head at Doc's suggestion.

"Russell and I never even got to ask Daddy if we could get married." She spoke so softly she could hardly be heard. "We kept hopin' he'd get over his shock, especially when Billy didn't get the rabies, but he just kept gettin' worse. But Doctor Hillman, I don't want to send him away. He belongs here with us, with his family who loves him. He'll get better soon. I know he will."

Doc pulled a kitchen chair up before Jewel, straddling the seat backwards and leaning his arms over its back. "Bud's not getting any better, Jewel. You know that. And the home has cured a lot of folks. They've got a good, Bible-oriented treatment plan, and most people on the staff are Christians. I believe it'll give Bud a better chance to recover. At least he won't be able to get liquor, and you know drinking has affected his health and mind, too."

"Doc's probably right, Jewel," Russell said. "Bud keeps getting worse. Some time in The New Hope Rest Home might be good for him."

Doc got up and walked over to the window, patting Mary on the shoulder as he passed. He stood with his hands stuffed in his pants pockets, gazing out at the greening horizon. "I wasn't none too surprised at Bud's condition when you two brought Billy into the hospital last summer. He'd gone back to a time before any of his calamities happened. A buffer, I guess, against more grief."

Doc turned, stroking his mustache. "He broke my heart when he begged me to save his baby."

"I know what you mean," Russell said. "He kept asking me where Lindy was. I was at a loss for words."

Mary nodded. "When Russell brought Daddy back home and Jewel and I ran out to meet him, he jumped from the truck and grabbed me in a big hug. He told me not to worry none, that Floyd would be fine, that he wouldn't let him die." Mary's voice broke, and she turned her head.

"He thought she was Mama," Jewel finished for her. "Mary just put her arms around his waist and helped him to the house, both of us crying like two babies. We knew Billy would be okay, but now we had Daddy to worry about." She sighed. "I guess if you think it's best, I'll agree to him going, but I sure hate to see it. I thought when Mama went away . . ." Her voice broke, leaving her fears unspoken.

"Now, girls, your daddy will come back home," Doc assured them. "Don't you worry about that. He just needs help in letting go of his anger and grief. And you can visit him. New Hope's only thirty miles away."

In body he will be, Doc was careful not to add, but in mind he'd just as well be a million. Lord, I misdiagnosed the boys and promised these girls their mama would be back home in no time, too. Could you please help me keep my promise on this one? Bring Bud back sound in both mind and body, if it's not asking too much.

"Well, I'd best be goin', folks," he told the worried little group. "Russell, you help Billy take good care of these little ladies, you hear?" Doc wondered, as he went out the door, how many more times he would have to leave the little Creel farmhouse with such feelings of helpless doom.

Chapter 49

A Solution

"Isn't it nice how many people from the church are visiting Daddy, Jewel?" Mary asked. "Maybe if he sees how everyone's worried about him, he'll get well quicker and then go to church with us more often when he comes home."

Mary and Jewel waited on the porch stoop for Uncle Floyd and Aunt Corie. Today, Bud's brother-in-law and wife were taking their turn to visit Bud. Jewel and Mary had decided to let the work go and ride along with them.

"More quickly, Mary," Jewel corrected in her schoolmarm manner. "You'd best not let Miss Jenkins hear you using such poor English," She tempered her admonition with a smile. "Oh, Mary, I hope Daddy gets well soon, for all our sakes. Billy works so hard keeping the farm up without Daddy's help, and Russell insists on helping out, though he's got plenty enough to do already. And it's so hard to keep up with the chores with all the time taken up in visiting Daddy. But I just can't stay home if I get a chance to go."

"Me either," Mary agreed. She felt guilty, leaving Billy alone with all the work, but he insisted. She knew the visits to the home left him depressed and uncomfortable. She knew, too, even though Jewel didn't mention it, that her sister also hoped Daddy would be home for her wedding. "I don't know what we'll do when you and Russell get married, Jewel. There's so many things that will have to be let go."

Uncle Floyd's truck, sputtering up the hill, ended their conversation. When Bud first entered the sanitarium, these two big-hearted relatives had offered to give up their farm and move in with the Creel children to help out, but Billy and Jewel and Mary refused their generous offer. They couldn't ask that of them. Uncle Floyd and Aunt Corie had no life of their own until Mama talked Grandma Parsons into moving in with her. They just couldn't ask them to give up everything again.

But what will Billy and I do without Jewel and Russell? Mary wondered. Even though they had promised to help with the harvesting and planting, school wouldn't allow her and her brother to accomplish much from autumn through spring. She climbed into the truck bed beside Jewel, spreading out the quilt Aunt Corie handed them to sit on. I'll just have to trust God to help us, Mary decided. He knows our needs, and how much we love the farm.

Bittersweet memories of Mama and her two little brothers tugged at Mary's heart as she looked away toward the cemetery on the hill. How could they ever sell the place and abandon those bodies in the little graveyard? Yet Mary knew her mother and Floyd and Walter weren't really in their graves anymore. Just vacated houses for their souls lay there. They were at home with God in heaven. Still, she couldn't bear leaving them. It would be like saying a final goodbye to all the fond memories.

The deceased weren't the only reason Mary would hate to leave the farm. The work was hard, but she loved the sound of the rippling creek in the spring, and the way daisies pushed up through the green meadows, looking from a distance like patches of snow on the new growth.

She loved to sit on the porch in the fall, watching gentle wind swaying tall field grasses in a hypnotic rhythm while bright rays of the sun shimmered off the golden waves. She could imagine God reaching down with a tender, possessive touch, smoothing his hand across His creation.

Sometimes, in the early mornings, the fog lay thick, white and low in the valleys between peaks of the hills, appearing as if God gave his earth a bubblebath. At nights, she'd sometimes sit on the porch, the sound of crickets all around her, watching the full yellow moon circled by a soft golden haze. It reminded her of a rounded pat of butter melting into the heat of the warm summer sky.

Mary used to imagine angels sitting on one of the soft clouds, smacking lips over light, buttery pancakes drenched in fall maple syrup. Tree frogs and insects sang melodies in the quiet, dark night, lightening the burdens of her heart until it hummed a melody of peace along with them.

"Say, Mary – Jewel," Uncle Floyd interrupted Mary's reminiscing. He climbed from the truck cab. "Corie and I have been thinking." He leaned his massive weight against the pickup, crossing fleshy arms over the bed's side, the unbalanced burden tilting it sideways.

"We know Jewel's marryin' soon, and Billy'll be headin' out for the army. Mary cain't keep up this place herself, and you say you don't want to sell it. Have you thought about rentin'? Mary could come live with us."

Live with Aunt Corie? Mary tried hard to think of a plausible excuse to refuse Uncle Floyd's offer, but Jewel gave Mary a surreptitious wink and spoke before she could come up with anything.

"Why, that's a perfect idea, Uncle Floyd! Why didn't we think of that? But Mary needn't be a bother to you two. We'll have an extra bedroom in our new home. She can live with us! She'll be company for me while Russell's at work. Oh, Mary, say it's all right! I know Billy will agree, since he and Nella plan to make the farm their home after their marriage and help Daddy keep it up."

Mary smothered a relieved sigh. Aunt Corie, leaning out the window, waiting for their decision, brightened perceptibly.

Jewel's plan was perfect. Mary might not always get to live at the farm, but she could come back to visit. She and Nella had grown closer than ever as the years passed. She knew there would always be a welcome for her at the farm as long as Nella and Billy lived there.

. Mary had been thrilled to see the growing relationship between her best friend and her brother. Nella went forward one night during revival and accepted Christ as Lord of her life. Billy soon left his seat in the back of the church and knelt beside her. They had both come up crying and hugging each other and hadn't stopped hugging since.

Billy eventually bought Nella a small diamond engagement ring that she wore as proudly as if it were a full carat. He promised to marry her as soon as his hitch in the army ended. Nella's mother seemed glad for the delay. She loved Billy and approved of him, but felt that her daughter, even though mature for her age at fifteen, was much too young for marriage.

Marshall had been converted not long after the tent revival where Mary had knelt at the altar and opened up her heart to the Holy Spirit. The complete change in Billy's friend had been a great influence on him, but it was sweet, bubbly Nella who had won Billy over. When he witnessed her going forward during the altar call, it gave him the courage to loosen his death grip on the back of the seat in front of him and follow her example. He wasn't about to let Nella go anywhere he couldn't follow.

Mary was also glad for Billy and Nella's decision to keep the farm for Daddy's sake. She knew if her daddy — no! — *when* her daddy got well, his heart would be broken all over again if he couldn't return to the farm. With Mama gone, it was the love of his life, the only thing that gave him satisfaction.

Chapter 50

The Wedding

Mary adjusted the veil over her sister's black curls. Not even the full Chantilly lace could hide the beauty of Jewel's luxuriant hair falling around her shoulders in waves of glossy ebony. Her eyes were as shining as her hair as she studied her reflection in the mirror hanging on the wall in the basement of the new Victory Baptist Church.

The old church had been torn down and the new one built on the same site, with separate classrooms in the basement and a larger auditorium upstairs. A pastor's study had been incorporated into the upper level to one side of the choir loft.

The congregation had grown by leaps and bounds after the installation of Tom Hawkins as pastor. Pastor Crookshank had peacefully passed away in his sleep one night not long after Tom felt God calling him into the ministry. Tom humbly stepped into the pulpit to fill the late pastor's vacancy, after a season of prayer and a unanimous vote by the congregation.

When Tom relinquished his mail route to become full-time pastor, Marshall took over the job of mailman in his place. Many souls had been converted under Tom's ministry, among them Mr. Eckhart of the Eckhart Service Station, and the two ladies who observed Tom and Mr. Cranshaw on their knees on the oiled floor of the grocery many years before, praying for Bud Creel.

Mary, Nella, and Jewel, dressing for the wedding, now occupied the larger nursery room. Billy, Russell, and the pastor waited across the hall in the young adults' classroom. Mary had recently looked in on them to find Russell nervously pacing the floor.

Bud Creel, escorted to the church by two attendants from New Hope, now sat upstairs in a dark suit, graying hair combed and shoes shining. Grandma Creel sat on one side of her son, Floyd and Corie on the other. The confused man showed no evidence of knowing where he was or who sat with him. Grandpop waited in the vestibule, taking his son's place in escorting his granddaughter up the aisle.

Downstairs, preparations over, Mary stood back to admire her sister. "Jewel, you look so beautiful!" she cried.

"Oh, Mary, I'm so happy! I just wish Daddy could give me away. And Mama — I wonder if she knows how happy I am! Oh, I hope she does!"

"Well, Jewel, at least Daddy's here. We can be thankful for that."

"Girls, it's time to go," Nella interrupted. "Do I look all right, Mary?" she asked anxiously, touching the gold band in her hair that held a spray of violets. The lavender dress brightened her green eyes, emphasized a dewy complexion, and complimented her plump curves. The chiffon creation and the headband of violets were an exact copy of Mary's. Jewel had spent many hours stitching sheer delicate ruffles that trimmed the bodice of the dresses and flowed down to grace the hems below.

"You look beautiful, too, Nella. You'd better watch out or Billy will be applying for a marriage license before he joins the army," Mary teased.

Nella giggled. "That would suit me fine," she said, "but he'd probably have a hard time convincing Mama. She hates to lose me anyway. She's going to be lonesome in that house all by herself." The solemn thought subdued Nella.

Mary picked up the white bride's Bible and handed it to Jewel. The small bouquet of violets resting on it was Jewel's favorite flower. Each love knot on the trailing white ribbons carried a tiny gentian blossom by the stem.

Mary caught her own reflection in the mirror as they filed out the door. Her hair, as long as Jewel's, fell straight to her waist. She'd always envied her sister's soft curls. Her nose that had always been such an embarrassment to her when she was younger was still prominent, but more in proportion to her face now that she had outgrown adolescence.

The image looking back at her from the mirror was like looking at the portrait of her mother on the bedroom dresser at home. Attractive enough, she would never be pretty like Jewel or cute like Nella. Grandma told her once she had a graceful air that outshone good looks, but evidently the boys of Rushing Creek weren't interested in grace.

"Jewel," Mary whispered as she followed her up the stairs, "I'm going to miss you!"

"Why, Mary!" Jewel laughed. "You'll be staying with me as soon as Billy leaves for the army! Until then you can come and see me anytime you want."

Russell and Jewel had fixed up the Crooney place as pretty as a dollhouse. Mary couldn't wait to work in the yard full of flowers and the vegetable garden out back. Jewel had already told her she would be in charge of the yard, other than mowing, which would be left up to Russell. Jewel's domain was the inside. "I don't envy you the outside work at all," she told Mary.

"I'm glad you prefer it. I never could understand how you enjoy getting dirt under your fingernails and sweating in the hot sun with your back bent over a garden hoe. And all those sweat bees and grasshoppers! Ugh!"

Mary loved nothing more than the outdoors, but Jewel's yard would be a great change from the huge yard and garden on the farm. Many things were changing in their lives, some for the better, but not all. Daddy hadn't changed since he'd entered the asylum over a year ago. Jewel cried all night the day she and Russell visited him with Mary to tell him about the wedding. He had reached out and took Mary by the hand, pulling her close, his head against hers.

"Married?" he questioned with a faraway look in his dull eyes. "Lindy and me are gonna be married." Then he turned, looked in Mary's eyes, and smiled a crooked smile. "You are still gonna marry me, ain't you, Lindy? I don't have much to offer you but my heart. I hope that's enough."

Mary fell into his arms that day and cried like a baby. Jewel sat gripping the arms of her chair, struggling to hold back tears of disappointment and sorrow. Russell reached over and took her hand in his, trying to offer some comfort. Bud hadn't spoken since. He seemed to pull further away into the past, sitting silent and unresponsive each time they visited him from that day on.

Despair settled over Mary after each visit, but the memory of Mama sitting on the side of her bed, begging her not to give up on her father kept the rising hopelessness from completely drowning her faith that someday Daddy would come back to them. What was that Mama used to say when she was discouraged? Someday, Mary, our ship will come in.

And it will, Daddy, Mary promised, following Jewel up the stairs to the vestibule of the church where Grandpop Creel stood waiting, ready to escort Jewel up the aisle. Just as surely as your ship brought you back to us from the war, someday your ship will come in, and you'll be with us again. I know it!

On their way to the stairs, Nella had tapped a message on the men's dressing room door, letting them know it was time to make their way up the outside steps to the side door to take their places at the altar. The pianist sat at her instrument playing a repertoire of songs. The packed church had a few folding chairs set out on the sides of the center aisle.

When Nella appeared at the vestibule doorway, the pianist checked her watch. Time for "The Wedding March", but where were the men? She noticed the look of surprise on Nella's face, saw her turn and whisper something to Mary and Jewel behind her. Mary's head appeared around the doorjamb, looking toward the altar where the men should already be assembled. A whispered conversation worried back and forth between Mary and Grandpop.

The pianist flipped her music back to a previous song, improvising while time passed. She had heard of grooms backing out of a wedding before, but never the preacher and entire men's assemblage. There was nothing to do but to continue playing until given different instructions. People fidgeted and craned their necks toward the rear of the church. Mary disappeared back down the stairs, leaving Jewel and

Nella standing red-faced and uncomfortable at the doorway. The whispers buzzing over the church sounded like bees buzzing over clover.

Nella's earlier light tap on the downstairs door had made Russell's heart leap. Pastor Tom turned the knob to exit the room, but found the door stuck. Pulling harder, he was surprised to find the door unyielding. Perplexed, he let Billy try, and then Russell. The stubborn door refused to budge.

Billy, hearing the music begin upstairs, checked his watch. He heard a moment of silence before the pianist began repeating the list of prenuptial songs. By this time his sister and grandfather had to be ready to begin the wedding march down the aisle. Panicking, he yelled for help. Pastor Tom fell on his knees, jiggling the doorknob and peering through the keyhole of the jammed lock.

"It's locked!" he exclaimed. "I can see the key!"

"Locked!" Russell repeated, wringing his sweating hands. "Why in the world would it be locked?"

"I don't know," Tom replied, "unless someone made a mistake and thought we'd already left for upstairs. We've had some trouble lately with the children getting into supplies in the classrooms. We started locking the doors."

"But why leave the key in the door?" Billy asked. "The kids could just unlock it, couldn't they?"

"You're right, Billy," Tom said. "Is there a lesson sheet and a pencil or something here? Maybe I can push the key through."

Russell began sweating harder. No one had heard Billy's shout over the swelling of music upstairs. He began a frantic pounding on the door, not caring how much he disrupted the waiting crowd. He could picture Jewel standing in embarrassment at the foot of the aisle, wondering where he had disappeared to.

Pastor Tom stooped back down at the keyhole, poking at it with the pencil Billy handed him. The key turned and the door suddenly opened. The doorknob caught him hard in the eye.

"Oh, Pastor Tom!" Mary's head appeared around the door. "I'm sorry! But why in the world was the door locked?"

"Beats me!" Russell said, wiping his sweating forehead with a hanky. "I'm just glad you came to let us out."

Pastor Tom knelt on the floor, hands over his eye, rocking back and forth in pain. Mary knelt beside him, prying his fingers away to inspect the damage. "It's okay," he insisted, getting to his feet. "We'd better hurry."

Holding her dress high to avoid tripping, Mary flew up the stairs. Another whispered conversation passed between Grandpop and the waiting bride and attendants. The red-faced preacher appeared at the front side entrance and walked self-consciously to the altar, one red and swollen eye promising to be black and blue before morning. Billy and Russell followed behind, as mortified as Tom. Muffled giggles and suppressed gasps rippled through the auditorium.

Tom looked back over the amused and curious congregation. Many odd and sometimes funny things happened at weddings, but this one took precedence. He wondered if any rumors of a fight between the preacher and groom would circulate due to his wounded eye. Catching sight of Russell's brother, Marshall, he saw a wicked grin split the boy's face from ear to ear, his shoulders heaving in silent laughter.

So there's the culprit! Tom thought. He remembered Marshall opening the door a crack right before Nella's tap, remarking that the church was full. An avalanche of revengeful desire buried Tom's usual spirit of Christian forgiveness and indulgence toward Marshall's pranks. He hoped Marshall asked him to conduct his own wedding, if and when he found a girl who could endure his humor.

He also figured the boy had better be far out of reach when Russell and Billy discovered the identity of the culprit who held up the wedding, causing them so much anguish and humiliation. Even-tempered Jewel and sweet Mary might even find it hard to forgive Marshall this time.

Nella began her trip down the aisle, the incident forgotten for the moment. The crowd turned. The look on Billy's face wrote a story of romance. Then Russell's eyes, watching his bride's slow approach, told a sweeter story, taking Mary's breath away. She knew Jewel would be in good hands with this good Christian man. She couldn't help wondering if she would ever meet someone she could care for as Jewel and Billy cared for Russell and Nella. She wouldn't settle for just anyone. She desired and prayed for a husband who would give her happiness and share her Christian faith.

The eyes of one person in the audience trained on Mary's face. Involved so deeply in the proceedings, she never noticed. Marshall Crimmons, watching his best friend's sister as she studied the wedding pair with affection, for once abandoned any thought of foolishness.

Chapter 51

A Fleeting Memory

Kneeling at the altar, the newlyweds began their joint life with prayer. Mary added her own petition for her father. The sun, slipping down the evening sky, capping the horizon, shone through the church window. Parallel with the wedding party, the bright sunrays reflected a golden glow from the metallic bands adorning the bridesmaids' hair.

Sitting thoughtful and unmoving between his parents on the front row, Bud gazed intently at Mary. A sudden hint of recognition widened his eyes. As the wedding party rose from their knees, Bud kept his eyes on the reflection crowning his youngest daughter's head. Images swam in and out of his memory: a church altar — figures gathered around it — frogs charumping — songs and shouts of praise.

Mary! His little Mary! Why had he been so angry with her? Ashamed of his reaction, he rose to his feet to tell her how sorry he was. Before he could speak, everyone around him rose. People rushed down the aisle. His purpose escaped him. Why was he standing here? And where was he? Someone took him by the arm and led him out of the church behind a group of excited people.

Where was everybody rushing off to? Must be noon, he reasoned, eager for lunch. Led by the attendant into the reception hall and puzzled by the unfamiliarity of New Hope's Cafeteria, he slipped into his usual unresponsive state, refusing to eat and giving no sign of recognition when his family hugged and kissed him goodbye.

Ushered out the door and to the car for his return trip to the asylum, he wondered at the crowd that stood watching as they pulled away. Sadness settled over him, and he wept.

Chapter 52

Remembering

Four years had passed since Bud's admission to the New Hope Rest Home, years that for him came and went in unawareness of their passing, but for his family years of hoping and heartache. Now, on a balmy fall afternoon, he sat beneath the shade of a spreading maple on the grounds of the asylum. Warm winds ruffled his graying hair. Shifting of autumn-painted leaves over his head speckled the ground with spatters of darks and lights.

Bud watched the play of sun and shadow on the emerald lawn, intent on the ever-changing patterns. A young woman sat cross-legged on the grass before his bench, her face upturned, listening to a man sitting beside him. Oblivious to his visitor's identity, Bud from time to time lifted his eyes, engrossed in the changing patterns of the sun and shade on the lovely, young girl.

A golden beam of sunlight parted the branches of the maple, washing the girl's ebony hair in brilliance. A soft halo reflected from the jeweled band holding the thick hair back from her face. A faint memory stirred in Bud's mind. He tried to catch and hold it, but it came and went with the everchanging shadows. He struggled to concentrate, but the man's voice beside him droned on like a swarm of bees, insistent and distracting. In his frustration, he willed it to stop. He had to think.

What was it? What did the light about the girl's head remind him of? Rippling waters — a chorus of frogs and distant shouts — cool winds. And cars — and — and . . . .

Think! Water — and — and . . . .

That voice! Try again. Frogs. Distant shouts . . . .

The voice buzzed on, persistent and irritating. Bud felt as if his head would burst if the answer did not come. He reached out an impatient hand, gripping his visitor's arm in despair. The droning of the bees stopped. The man turned to him, asking, "What is it, Bud? Is something wrong?"

The voice seemed to be tied to his fleeting memory, but it eluded him. That voice and a smile. A smile that mocked his anger. Anger at what? He didn't know. He was tired. Too tired to think. The voice started up again. Irritation pushed its way up through Bud's chest and into his throat, choking him. He grabbed the man's arm again, shaking it in exasperation. Again the droning stopped. The girl had turned, watching him with anxious eyes.

"What is it, Daddy? What's the matter?"

As Mary's head turned in the dancing sunlight, the headband sparkled again, throwing off another radiant halo. Excited, Bud squeezed his visitor's arm, raising his other hand to point with a trembling finger at the suffused light crowning the girl's head. Pastor Tom Hawkins eyes followed the shaking finger.

Noticing the glow about Mary's head, he asked, "Is that it, Bud? Is that what you wanted me to see? Mary, the sun's making a halo of your headband." He laughed. "You look like an angel sitting there!"

Bud nodded his head eagerly. Angel! What? Almost. Angel? Halo?

"Reminds me, Mary," the voice said, droning again like persistent bees in Bud's ear and breaking his concentration, "of the night you were saved. I could have sworn when you stood up from that altar and turned your child's face toward heaven that a golden halo crowned your head. Of course, I know it was a trick of the lights, but it came just at the right time. The sight of it made my heart overflow."

The elusive thought receded into dark recesses of Bud's mind. The glimmering halo drew his attention again, mesmerizing him.

"I still remember the joy of that night and how my feet just wouldn't hold still," Tom continued. "I shouted and ran the aisles with your grandpa on my heels baying like a coon on the run." He wiped tears and chuckled.

Mary's warm eyes brightened. She had never forgotten the glory of that night. She had been — what? — nine at the time, but she could recall the wonder of her experience as if it had been only yesterday.

"It was a glorious time, Tom. Did I ever tell you about the vision I had that night? It was like the church roof just opened up and I saw Jesus carrying a lamb in His arms. I felt like I was that lamb and would be safe always. Then, after the service was over, and I ran to the truck to tell Daddy, he was angry. So very angry! I didn't understand then, but I do now. I was so hurt by his indifference, but it was like I walked in a protecting bubble of God's love, and the hurt couldn't reach as far down inside anymore. From that night on, things were so much easier."

Tom watched Mary's face as she talked. Eighteen now, she looked more like her mother every day. She had many of Lindy's mannerisms, and Tom knew her to be gentle and uncomplaining as Lindy had been. The girl had suffered more than most in her short life, but she had great faith that could move mountains. She had never stopped requesting prayer for her father's healing, both spiritual and physical.

"Daddy! What is it?" Mary asked in alarm. Tom turned and saw huge tears rolling down the cheeks of the man beside him. Bud didn't make a sound, but the tears fell hard and fast, the ashen face crumpled in anguish. Tom helped Mary lift her father to his feet. They supported him on either side as he shuffled past the curious visitors and gawking patients toward the hospital entrance. Silent, raking sobs came from deep within him, shaking his frail frame with spasms. Mary and Pastor Tom exchanged worried, puzzled looks as they gave Bud over to the attendant who rushed out to escort him to his room.

Mary's heart ached for her father. She didn't know what had caused his episode of grief, yet she couldn't help but feel a rise of hope in her heart. This was the most emotional response he had shown over the years of his convalescence and, even though she suffered with him, anything was better than watching him sitting so woodenly detached visit after visit.

Oh, God, she prayed, whatever this is, let it be a step on his way home. Please, Lord, let him come home to me — and to You.

Chapter 53

Great and Mighty Things

Pastor Tom and Mary excitedly discussed Bud's reaction on the way home from the asylum, tentatively agreeing that it might be a good sign. Tom didn't want to raise Mary's hopes too high, but he felt, as the doctor had said, that Bud had begun his journey back to sanity with this small touch with reality.

"The journey could be long, Mary," Tom warned. "Your father has gone a long way away from you and he might be a long time returning." He didn't want to mention that there was a possibility her father might not return at all.

"Don't expect too much too soon," he advised gently, reaching out to pat her hand.

Mary knew Tom was right, but she couldn't help feeling a rising joy. Her heart rang with a song of praise for this small beginning. Her apartment didn't seem nearly so bleak and lonely as Tom waved goodbye and drove away.

Mary had graduated that spring, assuming management of Cranshaw's Grocery. The owners had built a new house on the hill overlooking the store, and Mary moved into their old apartment to be nearer her job. She hated leaving her little room at Jewel's, most of all hated losing Jewel's company, but Russell and her sister, expecting their first child soon, badly needed the room.

Mary struck up an instant warm relationship with Mr. and Mrs. Cranshaw, traveling to church and back with them, except on Sunday mornings when she rode home with her grandparents to spend the afternoon. The store kept her busy through her days, days that would have been lonely without friendly customers and occasional wholesalers. She made a habit of spending every Saturday at the New Hope Rest Home with her father while Mr. Cranshaw attended the store.

With her frequent evenings spent with Jewel and Russell or with Nella, Mary didn't have much time for loneliness or depression. Her most depressing times were the Saturday nights after her return from visiting her father but, tonight, hope warmed her heart and lifted her usual despondency in the small apartment.

Mary lay awake a long time, reading her Bible and praying for her father. When she at last turned out the light, sleep would not come. Her practical mind kept telling her that her elation was foolish, but for every negative thought, her heart called up a positive scripture of hope.

The one that thrilled her most was one she happened on just before closing her Bible, from the third verse of Jeremiah 33: "Call unto me, and I will answer thee, and show thee great and mighty things, which thou knowest not."

Sunrays streaming through Mary's bedroom window the next morning woke her. She jumped up to check the clock. She had overslept and would have to hurry to be ready for her ride.

Mary's heart sang. She hummed as she scurried about the apartment. Hearing Cranshaw's car descending the driveway, she slipped on her shoes. Grabbing her Bible, she rushed down the steps, eager to share her seed of hope with her elderly friends.

"My sakes, Mary!" Mrs. Cranshaw exclaimed. "You're sure happy this morning!"

"I sure am, Mrs. Cranshaw," Mary replied, climbing into the back seat of the Rambler. "It's a beautiful day."

Mr. Cranshaw smiled at Mary's reflection in the rearview mirror. He liked to see Mary happy. She deserved a little happiness now and then. She'd had a hard life, but it never seemed to get her down. "How was your daddy yesterday, Mary?" he asked.

Mary perched on the edge of the seat, eager to answer his question. With her head between the couple, she told them of Bud's experience under the maple tree.

"And the doctor said it was a good sign," Mary explained. "They said not to get my hopes up too much, but it could mean Daddy's remembering a little. It was hard to see him cry like that and not know how to comfort him, but the doctor said that repressing his grief and not being willing to face it may be a part of what caused his breakdown."

"I'm right glad to hear such good news, Mary," Mr. Cranshaw said. Mrs. Cranshaw reached back and patted Mary's hand

"Yes, Mary," she agreed. "We'll just keep prayin'. We all know God does some great and mighty things."

Those words again! *Great and mighty things*!

Mary leaned back in her seat and hummed a happy little tune all the way to church. She could hardly wait for the time for prayer requests.

Chapter 54

Mary, Grandpop and Grandma Creel

After Sunday School, Mary helped her grandmother into the pickup, then climbed in beside her. Her grandparents would bring her back to church that night. After the service, the Cranshaws would give her a ride back home.

Whatever would I do without my family? Mary wondered. She had never learned to drive, but now that she was working and saving a little money, she had begun to entertain the idea.

I can't always depend on others to take me everywhere, she reasoned. Maybe I'll ask Russell to teach me to drive after Jewel has this baby. I wouldn't want to ask him to go off and leave Jewel alone now.

"A penny for your thoughts, Mary," Grandpop said with a smile.

"Oh, Grandpop, I was thinking about learning to drive. I just might buy me a little car some day."

"Uh-oh, Ma!" Grandpop teased. "We'll have to stay off the roads. Be too dangerous out there." He chuckled and rolled his eyes.

"Now, Dad!" Grandma shamed him with a smile. "Who put all these dents and scratches on this truck?"

"Well, you got me there. I'd blame it on you if you drove. Since you don't, I guess I'm guilty."

Mary giggled, delighted with their banter. It was going to be a good day. A wonderful day!

Mary followed her grandparents through the kitchen door, sniffing the aroma of homemade apple pies. Grandpop hung his hat on a wall peg, then went out for kindling for cooking the Sunday dinner. A freshly killed chicken waited in the refrigerator. Mary hummed her way to the cellar for jars of her grandmother's homecanned green beans and corn, and a bowl of the freshly dug potatoes.

Mary enjoyed her visits to the cellar where preserved garden bounty brightened wooden shelves, jar after jar of contrasting colors: purples, greens, yellows, and reds. Pale persimmon-colored squash, potatoes sorted by size in bushel baskets, and golden orange pumpkins lined the walls. Carrots, turnips and cabbages were buried in boxes of sand, freshness protected from the damp, musty air. Garlic, onions and dill hung from low rafters, exuding pungent scents.

Mary reached for a jar of beans. In the dim light, a dark, slim form slithered past her hand and onto the ceiling rafters. A shrill scream reverberated in the close cellar. The snake flicked its tongue at Mary, then slinked to safety. Mary's screams brought Grandma and Grandpop running.

"A snake! There!" she explained, pointing a trembling finger toward the cause of her fright. The snake plopped to the floor and raced for a crack in the mortar of the block wall.

"Aw, Mary!" Grandpop let out his breath with a whoosh of relief. "It's only a harmless black snake. It cain't hurt you."

"Lawrence Creel, you get that slimy varmint outta my cellar!" Grandma demanded. She stood with her hands on her hips, fury snapping in narrowed eyes. "I ain't havin' no snake breathin' down my neck ever time you're hungry!"

Guffawing, Grandpop reached out and grabbed the snake by the tail, just as its head disappeared into the hole. A volley of screams echoed off the ceiling, sending the startled snake slithering through the hole, but Grandpop kept a tight grip on its tail, Mary and Grandma's screams cheering him on, but it looked like there would be no winner in this bizarre tug of war.

"Git the axe, Mary. Hurry!" Grandpop shouted above the din. Mary clamped her mouth shut and ran toward the woodshed. She hated to see the snake chopped in two, but she knew she would never again get up enough nerve to go into the cellar if the creature got away. She returned with the axe to find Grandpop looking down in amazement at the tip of the snake's tail in his hand. Grandma stood beside him, cackling at his spoils of war.

"You're too late, Mary," he said. "I pulled the critter's tail right off. Now, there's one snake that was mighty determined to get away with his life!"

"Tail or no tail, no snake is sleepin' in my cellar!" Grandma declared. She demanded that Grandpa mix a batch of mortar and close off the entrance hole. "I ain't takin' one step outta this cellar until it's done!" she announced. Grandpop saw the gleam in her eyes and knew if he wanted any dinner, he'd better do as she said. He left the women in charge of patrol, mumbling to himself while heading to the storage shack and back with a bag of mortar and a bucket. Grandma stood with the axe head held firmly over the hole until his return.

"I ain't takin' no chances of that cold, evil creature gettin' back in here," she told Mary.

"That was a mighty fine meal, Ma," Grandpop complimented, rubbing his bulging stomach. "Well worth waitin' for." He leaned over and placed a kiss on the top of his wife's silvery head. "I'd grab a snake any day for a meal like that, wouldn't you, Mary?"

Mary shivered. "It was a wonderful meal, Grandpop, but I'm afraid I'd completely die of starvation before I'd pay for a meal in that way."

Tilting his chair on two legs, Grandpop bellowed, a hearty laugh that brought a smile to Mary's face. "Wimmen!" he said. "Finicky, I reckon!"

Suddenly his laughter died. His chair hit the floor with a thud. A spasm of pain paralyzed his face. Clutching at his chest, he gasped for breath.

"Grandpop!" Mary cried. "What's wrong?"

Grandma turned from the utility table where she stood slicing one of the apple pies into thick wedges. Her husband's flesh was gray. Sweat beaded his brow. She dropped the knife and ran toward him. Mary jumped up from her chair and ran to her grandfather's side. He waved them weakly away, shaking his head.

"Lawrence, are you all right?" Grandma cried, bending over him, her face crumpled in fear.

"I'll be all right," he gasped. He rubbed his chest and belched loudly. "Sorry," he apologized. "It's just gas. I feel better now."

"Lawrence, are you sure?" Grandma eyed him with consternation. He burped again.

"Sure, Ma. I'm fine," he assured her. "Just got too hungry chasin' snakes and patchin' up cellars and made a hog of myself."

Mary stood over him, relieved to see color returning to his face. She had been so frightened, sure her grandfather was having a heart attack. Her own heart beat erratically in her chest. She renewed her vow to learn to drive. What would they have done if her grandfather had been really sick, with no phone and no way to get him to the hospital?

"Grandma," she said, "I'm going to have you a phone put in right away. This week!"

"Now, Mary," Grandpop began, "you need your money . . . ."

"No buts about it, Grandpop!" she interrupted. "You scared me! You need a phone in case you do get bad sick."

"So I scared you, huh?" Grandpop teased. "Tit for tat!" He laughed heartily, good humor intact. "You nearly scared me outta my wits myself when you yelled like a banshee in that cellar."

Mary's tears started. Grandma hugged her tight.
Grandpop's face fell. "Well, now, Mary, I didn't mean ta make you cry," he apologized. "I was only teasin'."

"I know, Grandpop." Mary leaned over and put her arms around her grandfather's neck. "I'm only crying because I'm so relieved. I wouldn't want to lose you for the world!"

"Wimmen!" Grandpop muttered again, shaking his head in bewilderment. "I'll never understand 'em. Ma, bring me a whoppin' piece of that apple pie. The smell of it's drivin' me crazy!"

By the time church hour rolled around, the pie plate was empty and everyone's stomach full. Grandpop was right. The taste of that apple pie was payment enough for having a phone installed.

"The first thing Monday morning, I'm calling the phone company," Mary told her grandmother. Grandpop's bout of indigestion scared her more than the snake in the cellar. She didn't want to take any chances with his life.

Riding between her grandparents on the way back to church, Mary felt especially grateful for the old couple's comforting presence in her life. They had done their best to make up for the absence of her mother and father. She would miss them so much when they were gone.

Chapter 55

Grandpop Creel

A knock sounded on the door of Mary's apartment. She hurried to open it. "Billy!" she cried, hugging her brother. He looked so handsome in his khaki uniform, and for once his hair, a close-cropped cap of black, did not stubbornly refuse to obey. The scars from the rabid dog attack had faded from their angry red to a light pink.

Mary always experienced a surge of loving gratitude each time she saw the scars. They were to her a beautiful reminder of his sacrificial love, but they also made her feel sad and guilty, reminding her of her father's incapacitation, and that she was the reason for her bother's disfigurement.

"Mary, you look just like Mama standing there!" Billy exclaimed.

Nella stood beside Billy, beaming with pride, her arm linked possessively through his.

Mary stood back, welcoming her brother and his wife into her cozy apartment. "Jewel and Russell are on their way with Grandma Creel," she explained. The mention of their grandmother's name cast a solemn damper over the reunion.

"This brings back memories, Mary," Billy said. Cranshaw's old heating stove threw off a cheerful blaze. Mary's artistic touch had transformed the room into a peaceful blend of color and design.

Billy's remark transported Mary back to the long ago night when the elderly storekeeper had opened the door to a freezing wind, rescuing them from frozen feet and frostbitten faces.

"We stopped here to warm up and call a cab the night Daddy came home from the navy," Billy explained wistfully to Nella. "Do you think we'll ever get to welcome him home again, Mary?"

"I'm sure of it, Billy. I don't know how he can't get well with all the prayers being prayed in his behalf, all the people at the Victory Church and his family. I pray for him every day, and so does Jewel."

"And so do I, Mary, but you know how stubborn Daddy always was, especially when it came to spiritual things. He's got a will that's gonna be hard to crumble. I know that more than anyone!" He chuckled. "Remember the arguments we used to have? Seems like Daddy always took his anger out on me. It was only Jewel that kept me from leaving sooner than I did. She made me see what really bothered Daddy. He didn't hate me, she said. I just made him think of Floyd and Walter and kept his grief fresh."

Billy dropped his head, turning his cap around and around in nervous fingers. "Then I really put him over the edge by getting bit by that dog. That was a stupid trick."

"Billy Creel, you shush! It was not" Mary reprimanded him. "You saved my life. Besides, you can't blame yourself. It would have been me, if not you. And besides, I was the foolish one, screaming and not getting out of your way. But I do believe it was Daddy's fear of losing you that made him withdraw from life. He just couldn't cope with any more pain after the boys and Mama."

"How is he, Mary?" Billy asked. "Is he any better than he was the last time I was on leave?"

"I really think he is a little better, Billy. He's more responsive and even seems to recognize me at times."

"Maybe it was good that you put your father in the asylum," Nella remarked. "At least he's had some peace since he's been there and he's stopped drinking. It may be a long time in coming, but God might use this to bring Bud to Him. Look at all his years of drinking and hating God. It seems nothing anyone did or said pointed him in the right direction. He only became more bitter and angry."

"You may be right, Nella," Mary said thoughtfully. "I just know that in some way God is going to bring Daddy around. I just know it!"

A tap came at the door. Mary opened it to find Jewel and Russell standing there, Jewel's pregnancy more evident than ever. Mary hugged her sister, winking at Russell over her shoulder. "If this keeps up, I'll have to get arm extensions, Jewel. Where's Grandma Creel?"

"In the car, Mary. I told her we wouldn't be a minute. It's so hard for her to get out of the seat and up these stairs.

"Billy!" Jewel screamed in Mary's ear as she sighted her brother over her sister's shoulder. Billy gently hugged his older sister, then stood back and appraised her figure in exaggerated surprise.

"How much longer are you going to grow, Jewel?" he teased. "Hey, Russell," he quipped, "looks like you've got yourself a fat lady here!"

"Not for long!" Russell rejoined. "She should be slimming down anytime now. We've got her bags packed and ready to go."

"You're a fine one to talk, Billy!" Jewel said, hugging Nella. "You've gained a little weight yourself, haven't you? But you look good. Army food must agree with you more than my cooking."

"Now, Jewel," Billy scolded, "no one can cook as good as you. That's one thing I've missed as much as Nella. Your table spread." Nella jabbed him playfully in the ribs. "I just don't have to work so hard to earn my keep anymore." Billy's hearty laughter sounded good.

Russell checked his watch. "Well, gang, we'd better go. Grandma's waiting for us."

His reminder of why they were all together brought an abrupt end to their camaraderie. They all filed out the door and down the stairs in a solemn parade. Grandma's sweet, wrinkled face watched them through the rear window of the car, eyes hollow in the streetlamp's glow

Mary's heart went out to her grandmother. Why was it that death sometimes seemed to go hand in hand with new life? She remembered back to when Walter had been born, and they had found Grandma Parsons dead in her bed the next morning. Now they all eagerly waited for Jewel and Russell's first baby, due anytime, and Grandpop, dear, steady Grandpop, was gone, just missing his first great-grandchild. He had quietly slipped away in his sleep from heart failure, Grandma Creel just as quietly accepting his going.

"Now don't you carry on so, Mary," she'd consoled her distraught granddaughter, wiping her own tears away on a corner of her apron. "Death just cain't part me and your grandpop. Oh, it might take him away from me physically, but our spirits are still one. I ain't got too long before the Good Lord calls me, too, and until then He'll keep me just like He's done all these many years. Then I'll follow your grandpop into Glory."

Mary knew that, beneath her calm acceptance, her grandmother's heart lay broken, but the old woman had a firm belief that fretting never helped a matter. She would practice that belief until her living on earth was done.

The funeral home was full of neighbors and friends gathered for Lawrence Creel's wake. Grandpop Creel had been loved by everyone he met, and his life had at some time or other touched just about every person in the community. Mary felt as if she had been touched the most. Grandpop's stabling influence, his quiet, calm acceptance of all life's ills, had helped her over many an obstacle that seemed insurmountable.

"Mary," he had told her once, "prayer is the answer. It's like a lever. It'll help you lift loads that are impossible to lift alone."

And he had been right. Every tragedy, every problem big or small, had driven Mary to her knees, where she found God waiting. He had lifted her up, shouldered her burdens, and brought her safely through them all. Why Daddy had not seen the wisdom and simplicity of this way of life in his own father, Mary couldn't understand.

It seemed he stubbornly headed in the opposite direction of his father's influence, and the result had been a lifetime of guilt and bitterness until he could weather no more storms, but sought shelter in the deep, dark recesses of forgetfulness and anonymity. The shell that moved and breathed and ate and slept at the asylum was not her daddy. He had escaped himself, and she knew the only thing to bring him back to himself would be repentance toward God and freedom from guilt.

Chapter 56

The Funeral

Perfect silence settled over the church when Bud, flanked by Mary and Jewel, appeared at the double doors and shuffled up the aisle toward the casket. Grandma Creel held on to Billy's arm, erect and nodding from side to side in friendly acknowledgment of her husband's mourners. Russell, Nella, Corie, and Floyd brought up the rear. Life and death met at the coffin. Grandpop's inert body rested among a kaleidoscope of flowers, ribbons, and scents.

Bud seemed unaware of his whereabouts and oblivious to the crowd around him. Those who had never visited him during his stay at the asylum were shocked at his change in appearance. He looked shrunken and gray, much older than forty years. As he and his daughters approached the coffin, whispers buzzed around the church, the air tense with expectation.

Jewel's lips moved in silent prayer. Watching her father's face, Mary held her breath. His dull gaze traveled over the blanket of fragrant yellow roses and the satin-lined coffin lid, then down to Grandpop's granite face. He stood uncomprehending for a moment, then his cheek twitched almost imperceptibly. His eyes blinked and a tear fell, making a dark splotch on the white satin.

Raising his head, Bud studied his surroundings. His eyes came to rest on Mary. She watched closely for any sign of recognition, but he stared at her blankly. Fighting off the hands supporting him, he shuffled back down the aisle. Grandma Creel, sitting in the front pew by Billy, had up to now kept a tight rein on her emotions. She jumped up and ran after her son.

"Bud," she called softly. He turned, watching her approach. She threw her arms around him, sobbing on his shoulder. Bud stood stiffly with his hands at his side for a moment, then lifted his arms and placed them around his mother, ragged sobs tearing at his insides. Miss Jenkins sat nearby, a hanky clamped over her mouth as if to cut off her own sobs. Tears washed over her freckled face and swam in her apple-green eyes.

Grandma Creel led her son back up the aisle to where Mary and Jewel waited, clutching each others hands and lost in grief. Taking his father's trembling hand, Billy helped him into his seat. Mary and Jewel took their seats on the other side of their grandmother.

Bud sat flanked by his family, Billy holding his hand in loving support throughout the short service. Mary wondered if her father was at all aware of their identity. Her grief was double now, grief for her grandfather and her father, one whose body was dead, yet his spirit lived, the other whose body lived, yet his spirit was dead.

Chapter 57

Grandma Creel

The wedding vows Grandma and Grandpop Creel had taken before God and their complete unselfish love for each other had bound them so completely into one that Grandpop carried half of the one he left behind to heaven with Him. The other half drifted along day after day, yearning toward heaven with a deep homesickness and a desire for completeness. Mary worried for her grandmother's sanity. She felt as if Grandma Creel no longer lived in the body that continued daily chores.

Mary's visits to the farm left her feeling dissatisfied, with a yearning of her own for the days before Grandpop's passing. The arrival of Jewel's baby, a husky little Russell with Jewel's ebony hair and a striking resemblance to Grandpop's baby pictures, perked Grandma up like nothing else. Mary's visits with her on the farm were soon once again filled with joy. She took Jewel with her as often as possible, feeling that little Russell's presence fed Grandma's starving spirit.

Before long, even though Grandma's spirits revived, her health began to fail, eventually taking a toll. She could no longer live alone. Not finding any cause for her malady, doctors ordered rest. Mary bought a cot and set it up in the living room, giving up her own comfortable bed to her ailing grandmother. As the months passed, Mary worked days and hurried home in the evenings to enjoy Grandma's delicious suppers and delightful company.

But one evening she arrived home to find the stove unattended, her grandmother doubled over with abdominal pain. A frightening trip to St. Clair's emergency room and a battery of tests revealed bowl cancer, inoperable and terminal. Devastated, Mary felt as if heaven was filling with her loved ones, slowly emptying her heart and life.

"Mary, now don't you fret!" Grandma scolded. "You know I've lived a good long life. I've had mor'n my share of earthly days and I'm ready to go meet my Maker and your grandpop and mama and all the rest that's gone before me. The only regret I've got is not seein' your daddy home and well and things settled betwixt him and the Lord. But, Mary, it'll happen! Just keep up your prayers. Don't fail me, child, for I want to see my son walkin' through them pearly gates some day. And you, too! Why, heaven's gonna be so good when we're all together over there!"

Grandma's extended illness soon forced the sale of the farm to help cover her medical expenses. A buyer found, Mary and Jewel planned an auction to dispose of household items and farm implements. A few days before the sale, Mary decided to sort through the household belongings to decide what should and should not be sold.

As she drove up the hill to the farm, a deep sadness settled over her. Her life's journey had taken some sharp turns, and losing her grandparents and life, as she knew it on the farm, was one of the hardest to negotiate. She sat for a moment in the car, looking out at the deserted house and overgrown yard.

With a deep sigh, Mary reluctantly climbed from the car and climbed the steps of the back porch. Opening the kitchen door, she released memories that clamored at her heart. The familiar black iron cookstove sat cold and lonely in a corner.

Dust settled over its surface, a matter that would have caused Grandma much consternation. Rows of spices filled a rack on the wall of ivy-printed wallpaper. Mary felt almost as if she could sniff the aroma of her grandmother's delectable sauces and stews from the air. She walked past the clawfoot table, where she had enjoyed many a Sunday dinner, then into the spare bedroom, where she and Jewel and Mama had shared the high double bed every Christmas before her mother's passing.

Mary opened the tall walnut wardrobe. A pungent odor of mothballs escaped and a kaleidoscope of needlework greeted her. She lovingly fingered the quilts. So many intricate stitches, representing so much of her grandmother's life! These would not be sold.

Mary knew she couldn't bear to turn Grandma's handiwork over to some stranger. She and Jewel, Nella and Aunt Corie would choose between the quilts. She recognized the bits and pieces of shirts and skirts, dresses and aprons in the patches. Grandma had been a prolific seamstress. Many of her gifts on birthdays and Christmases had been creations of love.

The fond memories called Mary on into what Grandpop always referred to as "the main room", the central living room of the house. Mary recalled how she had sat in the rose-colored chair on that long ago Christmas day and watched her mother's exhausted, pale face as she napped to restore her waning energy.

A vivid picture of Walter crawling through the door with the pop-eyed frog dangling from his mouth caused her to laugh out loud, shattering the silence of the room. She could almost see shadows cast from the flames of the fireplace across tall ceilings that were beginning to grow cobwebs in every corner.

The old family Bible lay on the homemade blanket chest. Picking it up, Mary sat down on the sofa, leafing through wellworn pages, reading a scripture here and there. She noticed one boldly underlined and recognized it as her scripture of hope: *Call unto me and I will answer thee, and show thee great and mighty things which thou knowest not.* Grandma Creel, along with all of Mary's close acquaintances, knew very well her scripture of promise.

How much longer, Lord, will it be before you answer? Mary thought with longing. If only Grandma could live to witness the great and mighty working of God in her son's life!

Mary continued leafing through the Bible. Happening upon the section reserved for family records, she studied the small, neat handwriting. She found her own birth recorded, preceded by Jewel and Billy's and followed by Floyd's and Walter's. Then came the page titled "Deaths". Floyd and Walter's deaths were written there, and Mama's, then Grandpop's name scrawled beneath in a weaker penmanship.

Mary flipped the page over and read the bold black heading, "Important Events". Grandpop and Grandma's days of salvation were listed along with the day of the purchase of the farm, followed by other things important to the old couple's lives.

There was an entry for the day her father had gone off to war and another for the day of his return, but the one Mary lingered over the longest was the date of her spiritual birth. She had never thought to record it anywhere except in her heart, but here it was in Grandma Creel's neat handwriting: Mary Matilda Creel, Saved-May 20th, 1949.

Mary closed the Bible, reminding herself to take it when she left. She opened the front door with some effort, the dampness of the unheated house causing it to swell. She stepped onto the porch, the complaint of rusted screendoor hinges piercing the afternoon's calm. A wren winged away in frightened flight from a small nest in the eaves.

Mary sat in the swing in an overgrown cinnamon vine's cool shade, drawing peace from its shelter and the serenity of the deserted farm. The porch floor was in bad need of repair. Paint peeled. Swing chains screeched, metal against metal, as Mary swung slowly back and forth, looking out across the weedy yard and garden. Grandpop's tomato stakes, tied in a bundle, leaned, rotting into decay beneath the tool shed's overhang.

The flowerbeds still bravely produced some of Grandma's more enduring flowers: lavender Sweet Williams, pink and white Cleomes, and orange Tiger Lilies, peppered with black, towering above encroaching weeds. Mary hoped the new owners loved flowers as much as her grandmother, and would bring the beds back to life.

A gray squirrel chattered from the branch of a hickory tree, scampering across the limb. He sat, bushy tail quivering, surveying his territory. Mary recalled Patches, erratically rambling through rustling leaves on the floor of the woods, sniffing out animal scents. Grandma's cackling laughter rang down through the years. That'll teach ya ta bark at me! At the sound of Mary's involuntarily giggle, the squirrel darted around the tree out of sight.

Mary sat immersed in sweet memories until the deepening copper-red sunset melded into gray skies. Misty, windblown clouds stretched themselves like fingers of God warming themselves over scarlet flames, cast by the glow of the setting sun. Crickets in the dampening grass strummed songs of yesteryear to her aching heart. How hard it was to give up childhood memories to death and the relentless march of time.

Sighing, Mary stood, hating to leave this home that had been a safe haven for her down through the years, but she planned to visit Grandma in the hospital and didn't want to be late. She never knew which visit might be her last. She had gained permission to sit nights with her grandmother. She didn't want her to die among strangers. Understaffed, the hospital personnel welcomed her request. Jewel and Aunt Corie volunteered to help, alternating shifts by Grandma Creel's bedside while Nella babysat little Russell.

Mary returned to the living room, retrieving the Bible from the blanket chest, stroking the smooth leather cover. Strange, she thought, how inanimate objects outlast the lifetime of people so precious and close to your heart. Hugging the Bible to her chest, she knew it, too, would someday succumb to the ravages of time, but the message within was eternal and would never perish. And neither would memories of her grandparents. She would hold each one dear to her heart and never let them die.

Chapter 58

A Walk in the Garden

Mary read the familiar name typed on the chart hanging at the foot of her grandmother's hospital bed: Matilda Mae Creel. Matilda, she mused. How I used to hate that name!

Mary had always signed her name "Mary Creel", eliminating Matilda unless it was required. Then she squeezed it in, camouflaging it with the initial M with the hope that it wouldn't be noticed. But now that Grandma Creel lay near death, the name didn't seem so bad. In fact, it had a nice sound to it. She intended to display it more proudly in the future, giving it a full share of her pen.

A knock sounded at the door. Grandma Creel moaned and stirred restlessly in her sleep. The least sound seemed to disturb her now. Mary rose quickly from her chair, tiptoeing to open the door. Aunt Corie stood on the other side with Uncle Floyd behind her. Shoes on Aunt Corie's feet always looked odd to Mary. Another strange feature was a faded purple felt hat framing her pinched face. Straggling wisps of hair, streaked with gray, escaped from a wound braid beneath the crumpled brim.

"How is she, Mary?" Aunt Corie's raspy whisper seemed louder than normal speech as she stepped into the room. The years had found her skinnier than ever, and Floyd a little heavier.

"About the same," Mary replied. "She's in and out. The nurse says drugs are the cause of that. She's in so much pain when she's the least bit conscious."

Aunt Corie gave Mary's hand a quick self-conscious squeeze, then tiptoed over to the bedside of the dying woman. Uncle Floyd hugged Mary and kissed her cheek. His hair was snow white. Time had pulled his jowls down until they disappeared into his chest. He squeezed his large frame into the protesting Naugahyde chair with some effort. He hadn't spoken a word since their arrival.

Uncle Floyd had never been much for words. He conveyed his feelings pretty well without them, but Mary knew he had been more conversational at one time. She figured her Aunt Corie's finding fault with everything he said had, in the span of their lifetime, formed his habit of silence.

Aunt Corie had mellowed somewhat over the years, shedding reticence and becoming less irascible. Life with her had been give and take, and Floyd had freely given until her crabby spirit absorbed some of his easygoing nature. Her tongue had lost much of its edge, and smiles seemed more at home on her wrinkled face. Over time, developing a better understanding of her aunt, Mary realized she was a good woman, even if peevishness shadowed her goodness.

Grandma Creel groaned, drawing her legs up beneath the sheets. Her face twisted in agony. "Lindy! Lindy!" she called in a hoarse whisper.

Mary rushed to her grandmother's side. Since the old woman had become so ill and was so heavily sedated, her confused mind had taken her back in time. She often called Mary by her mother's name. At first Mary corrected her, but after a while, she gave up, accepting her mistaken identity.

"What is it, Grandma?" she whispered, bending over the frail form on the bed.

"Lindy?" the hoarse voice was strained, the faded gray eyes staring and wild.

"Yes, Grandma. I'm right here."

Mary gently smoothed the sparse, silvery hair back from her grandmother's clammy brow. "Do you need something, Grandma?" Mary had to lean close to understand the hoarse rasping from the throat of the woman thrashing about on the narrow bed.

"How much longer will it be, Lindy? When's it ever gonna be over?"

"What's that, Grandma?" Mary thought her grandmother spoke of her approaching death. Soon, she thought in pity. For your sake, I hope it's very soon.

"The baby!" Grandma clutched her swollen abdomen where the cancer ate into her bowels. She moaned again. "Ain't that baby ever gonna come? It's been forever, and I cain't stand it much longer!"

"Oh, Grandma!" Mary cried. She lay her head against the leathery cheek of this woman she loved with all her heart. "It won't be long now. Not long at all."

Aunt Corie came over to the bed and began to massage the swollen stomach. Grandma Creel shrank from her touch, crying out shrilly. Mary gently pulled her aunt's hands away.

"I'm sorry, Aunt Corie," she spoke kindly, "but Grandma hurts to be touched."

Aunt Corie's face was spastic. "I--I-didn't know." she stammered. "I only meant to help."

"I know you did, Aunt Corie. I wish we could help her, but there's really nothing we can do but pray."

Floyd shoved himself up from his chair.

"Mary," he said, "we came so's you could go home and rest. Come on and I'll take you home. I'll come back for Corie in the mornin'."

"I can't leave Grandma, Floyd. I just can't! She's not doing too well and the doctor said it could be anytime. I couldn't rest if I did go home."

"But, Mary," Corie persisted, "I know you're wore out. You've got to rest or you'll be ailin', yerself. We'll let you know if she gits worse."

"I'll rest when Grandma's rest comes," Mary replied, adamant. "But, Aunt Corie, I would appreciate you staying with me. I can nap some in the lounge chair, and I'd feel better if someone were here to listen for Grandma."

"Sure, Mary, I'll be glad to stay the night. That's why I come. Floyd, you can go on home if you want. Jewel's comin' in the mornin'. Mary can bring me home then, cain't you, Mary?"

"Of course, Aunt Corie, I'd be glad to."

Floyd pulled some bills from his wallet. "In case you and Mary want or need somethin'," he said, pecking his wife's cheek. "I'll see ya tomorra, Mary. You see that you git some rest. You look right peaked."

"I will, Uncle Floyd." Mary kissed him. "See you in the morning."

Carrying on a whispered conversation with her aunt for a few moments after Floyd left, Mary soon yawned and excused herself, stretching out in the lounge chair, completely exhausted.

It seemed to Mary that all she did lately was visit hospitals. Little Russell had come not too long before her grandmother's admission. Since then Mary had traveled back and forth between St. Clair and New Hope for weeks. She slept lightly, her body geared to awaken at the least sound from her grandmother. Aunt Corie sat on the other side of the room, awake and alert to the patient's needs.

Sometime in the early hours of morning, Mary abruptly awoke. The dark pitch of night was fading into gray dawn. Muffled sounds of the stirring town made it difficult to determine if she had heard a low voice in the room or if she had imagined it.

She could see, by the illumination of a streetlight slicing through Venetian shades and falling across Corie in soft, buttery bars, that her aunt had given in to the quietness of the night. Her head reclining against the chair back, she snored lightly through her open mouth. It hadn't been Aunt Corie Mary had heard speaking, unless she talked in her sleep. She tried to ease from the lounge, but the creaking of the imitation leather brought her aunt quickly awake.

"I thought I heard Grandma talking," Mary explained.

The thin form of the woman lay motionless on the bed, the usually drawn-up legs relaxed. A pleasant smile replaced the grimace of pain. The pale eyes stared at the ceiling. For a second Mary thought her grandmother was gone. Her heart flew up into her throat. Then she noticed the slight rise and fall of the sheet. Grandma Creel looked more relaxed than she had in days.

"Grandma?" Mary whispered. "Did you call for something?"

"What? Oh, no, honey." Grandma Creel's head turned toward Mary, eyes filled with peace. Her voice was jubilant. "It was the Lord and me, walkin' in the garden. I was tellin' Him how pretty the flowers are this time of year."

Mary looked over at Aunt Corie. Her aunt's wrinkled face crinkled in tears. The sun broke out across snow-covered buildings of the town, rays finding their way through the shade slats and caressing Grandma in a soft blanket of light. The old woman's eyes closed and she slept.

Chapter 59

The Way of All Flesh

The door to Grandma Creel's hospital room slid quietly open. Jewel tiptoed in. "How is she?" she whispered.

Mary turned, tears in her eyes. "Oh, Jewel! You came a minute too late." She and Aunt Corie interrupted each other, explaining Grandma Creel's experience. "I thought sure she was gone, Jewel," Mary said. "I'm afraid it won't be much longer. For her sake, I hope it's soon."

"Mary, you look worn out," Jewel sympathized. "You, too, Aunt Corie. You both get out of here and get some rest. Nella's mom offered to keep little Russell today, so Nella will be over after a while to sit with me. Floyd's outside waiting for you."

"I'll go home and try to sleep a while," Mary said, "but I'm coming back this afternoon. I don't believe Grandma will make it through another night." She bent over her grandmother, kissing her lightly on the cheek. Then she slipped out the door with Aunt Corie. Uncle Floyd stood waiting outside the door.

Mary's sleep was troubled. After tossing and turning for a while, she finally gave up in early afternoon and headed back to the hospital. Jewel called about Little Russell to learn he was crying.

"Take Jewel on home, Nella," Mary insisted. "I'll be fine by myself until you get back."

After Jewel and Nella left, Mary drew her chair up to Grandma's bedside. Her grandmother's condition seemed to have worsened since morning. Mary knew each breath might be her last. She smoothed straying white wisps from the wrinkled brow. The unnatural coldness of her grandmother's flesh felt like the touch of death, skin, stretched over the skeletal form, colorless and dry as parchment.

Lips that used to wear a sweet smile gaped wide, revealing toothless, shriveled gums. Her long, luxuriant hair had become thin and brittle, tangling easily until an exasperated nurse came in one day with scissors and gathered it all up in one hand, with a single cut shearing it from her patient's head.

Grandma Creel's hair had always been her pride and joy, hanging to her ankles when she let down her wound braids. Like Mama's hair, it had never been cut until the day the nurse decided caring for it was too much trouble. She had asked Mary's permission to remedy the problem.

"What does it matter, anyway?" Mary overheard the nurse whisper to her fellow workers outside the door. "The old woman's been in a coma for days. She'll never know."

Tears welled up in Mary's eyes. She knew the nurse was right, but cutting Grandma Creel's hair had been another step toward saying goodbye.

As the hours wore on, the only evidence of life in the frail body was intermittent moaning and frightening seizures. Mary's vigil of the night before took its toll in the quiet room. She dozed off in spite of efforts to stay awake.

Something woke Mary. She leaned carefully over her grandmother's bed. Had she heard Grandma Creel call her name, or was it only a wistful dream that interrupted her light doze? She detected no movement, but felt her grandmother's warm breath on her cheek.

Mary sat through the afternoon, trying to recognize her grandmother in this stranger who lay as still as death. Little remained of the woman she had known and cherished. Her grandmother's plumpness had melted away, and the eyes that once radiated happiness were sunken and the eyelids transparent. Her teeth were out, and ragged breathing drawn through an open mouth left her tongue parched and her lips cracked and dry.

Mary gently smoothed a drop of cream across them. Grandma started at her touch, moaning lightly."Grandma," Mary whispered, "can you hear me?" There was no response. Mary leaned down and whispered softly in her ear, "I love you, Grandma."

The doctors had told Mary that they had no idea if their patient was aware of anything. Since she had lapsed into a coma, they determined she was either in a deep sleep from exhaustion, her worn-out body refusing to cope with life, or she had suffered a massive stroke. With all the modern technology, how could they not know?

Mary sighed. What difference did it make? They were only marking time with the feeding tubes and the daily weigh-ins until Grandma's spirit finally gave up its tenacious hold on the frail, earthly dwelling.

Mary became angry each time they brought in the huge scales. Like a pair of giant ice tongs, they lifted her grandmother's fragile body, the nurse nonchalantly recording her weight. What purpose did it serve, except to cause Grandma Creel's spasmodic seizures to begin again and do more harm to her body already bruised and riddled with angry bedsores?

Deep down, Mary realized the hospital staff, concerned, caring people, were doing all they could, but it hurt to see her grandmother suffer. If Grandma could speak, she would shame her for her thoughts. Her grandmother, dying as sweetly as she had lived, had never had a harsh word for any of her caretakers.

Mary's mind went back to the first chaotic days when her mother had died. Everything had changed so, nothing like happy days before tuberculosis had stolen Mama's health and robbed her of life. Grandma and Grandpop Creel had been her salvation. Emotional wounds were healed in the cozy kitchen of their home.

She recalled sitting as a small child on a stool and watching her grandmother fry the yellow garden squashes to a crisp, delicious tenderness, piling them high on a platter to accompany the squirrel simmering in a pot on the back plate of the old iron cookstove. A gentle smile played across Mary's lips as she remembered what Grandpop had said that day when he came home from work.

You never know what kind of supper you'll come home to with a woman like mine. Mary's smile faded. Grandma should have been paralyzed with grief the awful day Grandpop died, the way her husband's love for her encircled her life, but her strength came from God, whose love encircled her soul.

Life without Grandpop had never been the same, but with the passing of time, Grandma soon became the same cheerful, kind person Mary adored. The day came when they sat in the radiant sunshine in the old wicker porch swing eating buttery ears of corn and drinking sweet, cool lemonade. She and Grandma had laughed together like a couple of giggly, teenage girls. Life was once again warm and good — until Grandma's cancer struck.

A sudden harsh intake of breath from the bed broke Mary's reverie. She panicked at the sight of Grandma struggling for air, her head thrown back in an arc, face blue from deprived oxygen.

"Grandma!" Mary screamed. Forgetting the call button by the bedside, she raced from the room, yelling for a nurse. By the time she and the nurse returned, Grandma was gone, her face peaceful and serene.

Climbing on the bed, Mary gathered the tiny woman in her arms, stroking her hair and gently rocking her back and forth like Mama used to do her sick babies when they were fretful with fever. Finally the nurse coaxed her to come away. She led Mary to the waiting room, leaving her there in the care of one of the St. Clair volunteers.

"Your grandmother is better off, dear," the volunteer consoled Mary. "Now she won't have to suffer anymore."

"I know," Mary whispered. " But I'm going to miss her so much." The tears she shed were not only for her grandmother, but for her dead mother, and most of all, for her father who sat day after day in the asylum, his mind clouded with the past.

Chapter 60

Harbor Lights

After calling Jewel on the hospital pay phone in the hall, Mary gathered her purse and sweater and headed for the entrance doors. A nurse called her name. Holding out Grandma Creel's Bible, she came hurrying down the hall toward her. "I thought you might like to take this with you," she offered.

Thanking her, Mary took the Bible and stepped out into the gently falling spring rain, the pleasant perfume of pink roses along the walk reminding her of nature's resurrection. She knew that someday she would see Grandma Creel again, along with Grandpop and Mama and all the others who had gone on. And maybe — just maybe — she could find her daddy soon in the mentally disoriented man at the asylum.

Climbing into her car, Mary pulled from the parking lot and into the flow of traffic. A taxi passed. A small boy looking out the back window waved at Mary, his friendly face pressed against the glass. The cab sped ahead, weaving in and out of traffic.

The scene took Mary back to the freezing wintry night nearly twenty years earlier and the trip in the taxi to the train station to welcome her father home from the war. She recalled how she had thought of her mother's favorite saying in their poverty: *Someday our ship will come in.*

And it had. Not a proverbial ship of wealth, but the one carrying her father over the vast ocean and home from his stay in the United States Navy. It seemed to Mary, as a child, that from the time he had gone away until his ship pulled back into the harbor had been a long, long time.

"And I've waited a long time for Daddy's ship to come in once more," she whispered. "Oh, please, God, let it happen soon. Please let Daddy get well and come home. I need him so much."

Call unto me and I will answer thee, and show thee great and mighty things which thou knowest not. Mary's scripture of hope seemed to be a palpable, living thing in the car. She felt a loving Presence. She could hardly see to drive for hot, flooding tears. Relaxing her head against the headrest, she let memories of Mama and her grandparents, and years gone by, slip in and out of her mind as the miles to the asylum diminished beneath the wheels of her car.

Mary soon pulled up to New Hope's entrance and parked. A guard left the guardhouse and admitted her through the gates. The air had warmed. Her father, wearing a thick sweater, sat on the stone bench beneath the massive maple. The sun, shimmering through limbs of the magnificent tree, dappled his impassive face. He seemed swallowed up by his surroundings, desolate and forsaken.

Mary's grief returned. She ran to her father, kneeling before him. Dropping her grandmother's Bible in his lap, she took his soft, lax hands in her own. She couldn't help but remember how callused and strong they had once been from the hard work on his beloved farm. "Daddy?" she spoke gently, looking up into his blank eyes. "Daddy, Grandma Creel is gone."

Mary's voice broke. She buried her face in her father's lap. Her tears soaked his cotton hospital robe. Seemingly oblivious to Mary, Bud sat for a while unmoved. Then her grief seemed to touch something deep inside him. Gradually his bland eyes took on an expression of awareness. His trembling hands pulled from hers and lifted slowly to smooth the black hair from her forehead.

At her father's touch, Mary's crying abruptly stopped. She looked up in astonishment, breathless, searching her father's dark eyes for some sign of recognition. She saw his lips part.

"Mary!" he crooned in a voice rusty from disuse. "My little Mary!" Bud took Mary's face in his hands, gently touching his lips to her forehead. "Don't cry, baby," he soothed. "Everything's gonna be all right. The doctor said Billy's gonna make it."

Tears welled up once more in Mary's eyes, tears of mingled grief and happiness. Her father had lost four years, still living in the past, but at least he knew her and had begun to accept reality. He was on his way home at last.

Bud picked up his mother's Bible from his lap, studied it for a moment, and then hugged it to his chest. His blue eyes misted. "Mary, I've been such a fool," he said. "Do you think God can ever forgive me?"

"Oh, Daddy!" Mary sobbed. She jumped up and hugged her father. Joy flowed through her, assuaging grief. Her ship had been tossed on the stormy seas of life, sometimes almost swamped with mountainous waves of despair and doubt, but she had clung to her mother's advice to not give up on her father.

The scripture she had held on to, promising great and mighty things, had finally come to pass. God had been her captain, and with her obedience to his leading and trust in His promises, He had faithfully steered her into a safe harbor. Mama's prophecy had been fulfilled at last.

Now she and her father could ride the waves together until they docked into the final port. She knew for a certainty Mama would be there, standing on heaven's shore, welcoming them home with open arms. And not only Mama, but Floyd and Walter, Grandma and Grandpa Parsons, and Grandpop and Grandma Creel, along with many others who had weathered life's storms.

"We're comin', Mama!" Mary whispered, enfolded in her father's embrace. She wept and laughed at the same time. "Daddy's on board at last and we're on our way home!"

Chapter 61

Cloud of Witnesses

With her father's arms around her, Mary turned and walked, triumphant and smiling, toward two orderlies rushing out to meet them. She wondered if they could sense the presence of all those who walked with her and her father. Grandma had been right, as always. Death may physically separate loved ones, but spiritual unity could never be broken. Only Satan could cause that complete separation, if we allowed him. Mary could almost hear her Grandma Creel cackling, There, Satan, that'll teach ya!

Evil spirits that had imprisoned Bud Creel lay bruised and conquered from the victorious assault of prayer. Grandma Creel's spiritual aim had been good, and she had taught Mary well.

The orderlies approached Mary and her father, amazed at what they saw. The look of peace and awareness on Bud Creel's usually blank and furrowed face was a miracle in itself, but what really held their attention and almost caused them to stop and stare was the beauty of the young woman's triumphant face as she hurried toward them.

Her eyes shone with a luminescence in their black depths. Her cheeks were pink and glowing. But most amazing of all, around her head of shining, raven-black hair shimmered a translucent halo of soft, golden light. The glow seemed to dispel around the daughter and father, surrounding them in an ethereal cloud, pulsating with hazy shapes and shadows.

If the orderlies hadn't known Mary from her years of visitation at the New Hope Rest Home, they would have thought Bud Creel was escorted and protected by one of God's heavenly angels. "Just a trick of the sunlight!" one spoke to the other.

"Yeah!" breathed his companion with a sudden sigh of relief. "Sure! That's it. A trick of the sunlight!"

They hurried forward to help Mary escort her father inside. In their excitement at his beginning recovery, neither of them looked to see if the halo vanished as they stepped into the shade of the building's enclosure.

Nancy and her granddaughter, Teagan, pose for a photo
at The Rapture House Bible Book Store, Ripley, WV

OTHER BOOKS BY NANCY

Sips of Nectar
Copyright © 1991, Out of Print

Just for Kids
Copyright © 1999 by Lillenas Publishing

DOWN LIFE'S PATH with Mom and Dad

Printed by INFINITY PUBLISHING.COM